LADY OF PROVIDENCE

THE UNCONVENTIONAL LADIES

BOOK THREE

ELLIE ST. CLAIR

CONTENTS

Facebook: Ellie St. Clair

Cover by AJF Designs

Do you love historical romance? Receive access to a free ebook, as well as exclusive content such as giveaways, contests, freebies and advance notice of pre-orders through my mailing list!

Sign up here!

The Unconventional Ladies
Lady of Mystery
Lady of Fortune
Lady of Providence
Lady of Charade

The Unconventional Ladies Box Set

For a full list of all of Ellie's books, please see
www.elliestclair.com/books.

PROLOGUE

LONDON, 1810

*T*he scent of fresh parchment and long-forgotten leather-bound bank ledgers wafted through the office, which was lined with mahogany shelves of endless records. Elizabeth sank into one of the plush leather chairs, which enveloped her as comfortably as an embrace from her grandfather. She returned the smile he bestowed upon her from across his solid wood desk as she picked up the glass of amber liquid that had arrived during the last hour, which they had spent reviewing the bank's latest profit and loss statements.

"You learn quickly, Lizbeth," he said, and Elizabeth's heart warmed, for her grandfather never provided a compliment that he didn't feel was deserved.

"Thank you, Grandpapa," she said, lifting her glass to him before they each took a sip of the brandy, which he always insisted upon, though Elizabeth could admit she rather enjoyed the taste. "But I must say it is easy to learn when the subject is as interesting as this."

He chuckled. "Not all feel the way you do, unfortunately. Why, your cousins..." he sighed and shook his head, and Elizabeth smiled ruefully, knowing his opinions on most of her cousins.

"They are all either more conceited than one could ever imagine or such fools I could hardly stand the time in their company. Not only that, all but you have turned down the invitation to spend time here with me learning the trade."

"It is their loss," Elizabeth said, arching an eyebrow, "For I can think of no better day than one spent with you. Thank you for sharing your knowledge — despite the fact that it is solely for my own enjoyment and I am taking you from far more important business."

"Well," her grandfather said gruffly without meeting her eyes. She knew that her words had touched him, but he would never, ever admit it, as he maintained his hardened exterior despite the softness she knew lay deep within. "Nothing is more important than my time with you, Lizbeth. I am only pleased that you understand the business as well as you do. It is not unheard of for women to be involved with banks, you know. I can tell you of more than a few who have done an excellent job as a partner, though most are within the countryside. Now tell me, what do you think of what we have just reviewed? Does anything concern you?"

Elizabeth paused for a moment, contemplating his question as she looked around her at the comfortable room that was the very essence of her grandfather — and rightly so, for he had been the senior partner of the bank for the past fifty years, since his own twentieth birthday. She wasn't sure whether he had ever spent more than a day away from the building in all of those years. The solid brick mortar that was the home of Clarke & Co. was as strong as the business her grandfather had built over the past many decades. The small bank he had inherited in his youth had become one of the most reputable and best known in London.

Elizabeth loved nothing more than following him through the long corridors, watching him greet each of the many people working in the building by name, whether they be the most junior of clerks, or the most senior of partners next to himself. He always told her that a small gesture such as an inquiry regarding a man's family meant more than anyone likely realized.

She returned her thoughts to the subject at hand — the ledgers he had asked her to review.

"It seems as though there is some strange anomaly — a pattern if you will," she said. "It's so small it is hardly noticeable, and yet the ledgers are out ever so slightly by the same amount from the same area far too often."

Her grandfather, Thomas Clarke, nodded at her in approval. "Very good," he said. "And how would you next investigate what is occurring?"

"I would ask to see the more finely detailed ledgers of those particular accounts, to determine what is common about them. Is it the same staff who are working on them? Are the accounts related?"

"What if you find that one clerk in particular is at fault?"

"He should be removed from the bank."

"And what if said clerk is working not only for himself but along with one of the partners?"

"Then the partner should also be released of his responsibility," she said without hesitation. "Why, is this what has occurred?"

"I believe so," her grandfather said with a sigh. "You know, Lizbeth, I have always been so careful as to who I named partner, for it is much easier to welcome a new partner than to remove a current one. And yet... it seems I have made a mistake."

He looked so disappointed with himself that Elizabeth leaned forward across the desk and placed a hand upon his.

"It is not your fault," she said. "People often hide their true characters. As you well know from your experiences with the people of the *ton* — no one is who they profess themselves to be."

He shook his head, his gray hair still rather full, emphasizing the stately look he had always upheld. The only real acknowledgment to his age and the years spent analyzing books was the spectacles he now wore low near the tip of his nose in order to read the words scrawled amongst the bank ledgers.

"I shall never understand why your mother was so determined to find a way to make herself one of them," he said with a sigh. "But, fortunately for her, your father, the Viscount Shannon, was enamored with her beauty and, with a little help from the significant dowry I provided her, she was able to receive everything she ever wanted in life. Everything that was, apparently, only attainable with a title. Unfortunately, she now thinks herself above the rest of us, but somehow her daughter turned out to be the most magnificent woman — next to your grandmother — that I have ever met."

Elizabeth's cheeks reddened. She was aware of how lucky she was to have her grandfather in her life, particularly because her own father hardly noticed that she existed. He was far too busy at his clubs and with games of chance, which she never understood. She preferred what was a sure thing.

"She must, deep down, appreciate all you have done for her. And I am forever grateful to what you have provided me throughout my life."

Thomas snorted.

"I am well aware you are, Lizbeth, but as to your mother — it is kind of you to attempt to placate an old man, but I am well aware of the truth. Now, as to this matter at hand. I currently have the power to choose which partners remain and which we hire on," he explained. "It is both a privilege and a curse."

"I can understand why you would feel such a way," Elizabeth said. "What will you do?"

"I will discuss with the partner what I believe has occurred, and remove him if I must. If I do so, once I have proof of his actions, I will be sure to provide a full explanation to the other partners, of course," her grandfather said, leaning back in his chair. "It's important, Elizabeth, to be able to trust all of the partners of the company. This bank has been founded on integrity, loyalty, respectability, and honor, and if that were ever to change, I fear what repercussions there might be."

"Well, then, we are fortunate that you are at the helm to guide the ship," Elizabeth said with a smile, but her grandfather wore a serious expression.

"I will not always be here, Lizbeth, so I must ensure that my legacy remains intact."

"Oh, do not say such a thing," Elizabeth said, her eyelids fluttering down to conceal just how much his words affected her. While she knew both her grandparents were getting older, of course, she hardly wanted to think of what life would be like without them, for they had always provided her with the warmth and understanding she had never felt from her parents.

"It's the truth," he said with a shrug. "I wish I could hire someone like you on as a clerk to work your way up through the company, but of course, that would never do. As my own son died far too young, and his son is an incompetent disaster... I must, therefore, impart all of my knowledge to someone who will listen. Your brother is affable enough, but I couldn't hold his attention for an hour if I tried. I need someone I can trust." He paused before continuing, and she wondered to whom he was referring. She wished it could be her, but alas, she was a woman, and therefore, it could never be. "My apologies for the morbidity of such discussion. Now, when it comes to the staff and their salaries, one must pay them highly enough to retain loyalty and to ensure they are well looked after and able to care for their families. It's important to seek out talent and to reward those who go above and beyond. Does this make sense?"

"It does," Elizabeth said with a nod. "Though I must ask — why is it so important to oversee all of this yourself? Do you ever think that you might like to spend more time at home with Grandmother, to begin to leave this work to someone else? Mother says that there are perfectly capable people working within the company, and while I am very aware that none of them could come close to providing the same scrutiny and care that you do within this bank, could some of them not be of more help to you?"

Elizabeth's grandfather steepled his fingers under his chin and rested his elbows on the desk before him, careful not to smudge the fresh ink within a ledger.

"You have already touched upon the answer," he said. "No one else cares for a business as truly as the person who is most invested. I do not take the responsibility of senior partner lightly, for no one else built this business, or can trace it back generations to the time when our family forged gold. My very blood is within this bank. If I want to ensure it is running at the best of its capacity, I must do so myself, and make certain all is as it should be."

Elizabeth listened carefully to his words, nodding as she

agreed with him, then finished the glass of brandy on the table in front of her.

"I should likely be going now, Grandpapa," she said "Mother would not be pleased if I were to be at home a minute past the allotted time for gathering in the parlor. Heaven only knows who she has invited to dine with us today."

Elizabeth began to rise, but her grandfather held up a hand to stop her. It seemed he had one last question of her.

"I have heard that you have become particularly friendly with a certain Lord Gabriel Lockridge, son of the Duke of Clarence," he said, a twinkle in his eye. "But as this information comes to me via your mother, I thought that I best ask you myself as there is no guarantee that anything she tells me is accurate."

Elizabeth was sure that her cheeks were now a flaming red, but she kept holding her head high. This was her grandfather, a man who knew her nearly better than anyone, save perhaps his wife, her grandmother.

"He and I have become rather close, it is true," she said, unable to meet his stare despite her attempts to appear unaffected. "I know it seems a rather unlikely match — myself and a man who will one day be one of the most powerful in England. His family and my father's, however, have been friends for many years, and we have come to know one another well."

"I am assuming it is not the fact that he will be a duke that draws you to him?" her grandfather asked with an eyebrow raised.

"Not at all!" exclaimed Elizabeth. "In fact, I find that to be more of a detriment. Can you imagine the pressures society must place on a duchess? But he is rather charming, and most importantly, he is quite intelligent, and I find that he most often sees the good in people, though he has a roundabout way of showing it. But I do believe, were we to find ourselves in a serious courtship, that life with him would be most... interesting."

"Life is what you make of it, Lizbeth," her grandfather said sagely. "I believe I will have a conversation with the young man, to learn more about him. You must know, however, Lizbeth, that more than anything I wish for you to be happy, and loved. But I also hope that you are able to live your own passions, outside of the role a man may bring you."

"Of course, Grandpapa."

"Do you promise me that? You will never put a man's desire for his life above your own?"

Elizabeth started. "I'm not sure that any man would be pleased with such a sentiment."

"Just promise me, Lizbeth."

"Very well," she said, her eyes wide. "I promise."

CHAPTER 1

*G*abriel Lockridge, Duke of Clarence, possessor of no fewer than five estates and manors, a seat in the House of Lords, guaranteed entrance into every social event he could possibly wish to join, and a man with unlimited wealth to spend as he pleased, was bored.

He sat in White's Gentlemen's Club, staring out the window at the rain falling from the sky, drenching the passersby who hurried from one destination to the next on this dismal, dreary day. Idly, he had one ear tuned into the conversations around him, but if anything, the inane gossip that drifted toward his ears only frustrated him. Idiots, all of them. Ever since his closest friend, Jeffrey Worthington, Marquess of Berkley, had married, Gabriel had been sorely lacking acquaintances whom he could stand for more than five minutes.

"Fancy a game of whist, Your Grace?" one newly-minted, eager marquess requested, but Gabriel waved him away, though he managed a tight-lipped smile. He was being rude, he knew, but it was difficult to summon much enthusiasm. Why he had even come here tonight, he had no idea, but he supposed it was better than sitting at home and staring across his study at the portrait of his father, frowning dourly back at him.

"Clarence," he heard from behind him, and when he turned, Gabriel was relieved to see a face he actually welcomed. Mr. David Redmond, second son of the Earl of Brentford. While below Gabriel on the social ladder, he was actually somewhat entertaining, despite his reputation as a veritable rake — although perhaps that was one reason why Gabriel so enjoyed his company. Redmond knew how to tell a story, and while some may be slightly embellished, most were rather amusing.

"May I join you?"

Gabriel waved once more, but this time it was to the chair across from him in an invitation for Redmond to sit down.

Redmond took a seat, running a hand through his hair which was so light a brown it was nearly blond, much unlike Gabriel's own dark locks, which he always ensured were perfectly coiffed.

Redmond settled back into the folds of the forest green leather chair, lighting a cheroot as he fixed his gaze on Gabriel, though his expression soon turned serious, his eyes narrowing and his brows settling low overtop them.

"Something the matter, Clarence?" he asked. "You do not typically look so somber. Calculating, yes, but somber? Never so."

Gabriel sighed, taking another sip of his drink.

"I am bored, Redmond," he said and tipped his head back to look up at the ornate ceiling and the intricate chandelier hanging from the middle of it.

"Bored?" Redmond nearly snorted. "Whatever do you have to be bored about?"

Gabriel shrugged. "This life. One party after another, one woman after another — none who are any challenge. While I do not dally with married woman, it seems as though I could have nearly any I choose. The people who frequent said gatherings are the same, night after night, telling repeated stories, bragging about their acquaintances, most of whom are standing across the room. What's the point of it all?"

Redmond stared at him incredulously. "Are you serious?" He asked. "You could have anything you'd like, Clarence. Bored at a party? Go to a gaming hell! Bored with one woman? Find another! Bored with riding? Take up a fencing match! I hardly see what you have to complain about it."

"And that is the biggest issue of them all," Gabriel said with a nod of his head.

"Besides," Redmond continued, "I had been expecting you to return from Newmarket a few months ago with a fiancée on your arm after I heard all the gossip that came flying back to London on the wings of little birdies. But no, the great Duke of Clarence seems to have been bested by a jockey!"

"I was never bested," Gabriel said indignantly. "My intent was never to actually court nor wed the Lady Julia."

"Then whyever would you pursue her?"

"Call it a puzzle, if you will, Redmond," Gabriel responded. "One to which I already knew the solution, yet my help was required in order to reach the conclusion."

Redmond shook his head.

"You speak in riddles, Clarence, but so be it. And how is Parliament these days?"

"A bore. Grown men squabbling because they feel as though they should when the answer is plain and simple, mattering not whether one is a Tory or a Whig, but whether one has common sense — which none of them do."

Redmond steepled his fingers together and rested his chin upon them.

"Your estates?"

"I stay abreast of the business within each of them, certainly," Clarence agreed, "But I have trusted, loyal stewards in place who seem to do a brilliant job in overseeing them."

He stared out the window, his gaze landing upon a small lad hustling down the road, his cap pulled low over his face in an attempt to shield himself from the rain falling in earnest. His clothing was rather tattered, and clearly, he had not a great deal in this world. In fact, he very likely found himself here on James Street in order to pick a pocket or two, but there were none to be found as most made themselves scarce in such weather.

He looked back at Redmond, shaking his head. "This is a ridiculous conversation regarding the plights of one of the richest men in the land, whose bank account holds more funds than most would ever see in their entire lifetime."

Redmond seemed slightly confused for a moment, but then he tilted his head ever so slightly as he studied Gabriel.

"I've heard you are a partner of a bank — is there any truth to that?"

"Yes, if you can believe it — Clarke's. Although I'm not altogether sure that I want to hold such a position. It is rather unusual, for a duke. I was named a few years ago, when ... circumstances seemed to point to me becoming even closer to the family. Then everything changed, except for the partnership. I didn't take an active role, so Clarke seems pleased to keep me on board, and I appease him by voting with him when necessary."

"You are not interested in the affairs of the bank?"

"Of course not," he responded incredulously. "And like

everything else in my life, I do not see that changing anytime soon."

* * *

One week later

ELIZABETH SAT STIFFLY on the edge of her bed, gazing at herself in the mirror above her vanity. Black, she decided, did not suit her. It made her skin so white she looked practically translucent, which would have been fine did it not make the few freckles upon her nose become much more prominent. She resembled a witch of sorts, with her hair red enough to seem not quite proper, despite the fact that it was pulled back into a smart chignon, without a wisp of curl escaping it.

Elizabeth pulled herself out of her thoughts, berating herself for her vanity as she looked down at her hands in her lap, clenched so tightly together that they were nearly white.

Her grandfather was dead. The man who had meant so much to her, who had shown her what it was to be responsible, loyal, trustworthy, and honest, was gone, leaving a hole in her heart. It was one that certainly would not be filled by her parents, she thought grimly as she stood and forced herself out the door, gripping the banister of their townhouse staircase as she descended the steps to the cold, austere drawing room, where her parents awaited her.

"Elizabeth Moreland, wherever have you been?" her mother questioned her. "Your father and I have been waiting for nearly an hour now. We must be at the reading of the will in good time in order to hear everything and to make sure that no one does anything unsavory in order to receive their portion of Father's riches. Though the partnership will likely go to your cousin Henry, of course. Oh, if only Terrence had shown more promise, or if you had been a son, Elizabeth, then you might have had the opportunity as my father was always so taken with you."

"I am so sorry, Mother, to have disappointed you," Elizabeth said dryly.

"That's all right, my dear," her mother sniffed, and Elizabeth wanted to roll her eyes, but now was not the time to cause any type of rift between them. "Now, we must go!"

"Are you excited, Mother?" Elizabeth asked, horrified at the thought, but unfortunately, it seemed to be true, as her mother turned her narrow, pinched face toward her with eyes gleaming in anticipation.

"Of course not," was her mother's denial, though Elizabeth knew far better. As she followed her parents into the carriage, she despaired for what would become of Clarke & Co. were it improperly managed by someone like Henry. She could hardly think on it, though she doubted her grandfather would leave it in Henry's hands, knowing as she did just what Thomas had thought of her cousin.

But it was a difficult thought to ignore when they entered the drawing room of her grandmother's home. Elizabeth greeted her younger brother, Terrence, who pinched her cheek in a show of affection. Elizabeth loved her brother immensely, as he was the charming sort with a heart of gold, but he also spread his love for others — particularly women — perhaps a bit too far. He had left their home long before in order to take his own rooms at a boarding house, for he told Elizabeth he could no longer take the disapproving stares from his parents regarding the hours he kept nor the questions on where he visited.

Elizabeth greeted her grandmother with a heartfelt embrace — tasteful enough, yet also conveying all she wished to say, for she couldn't tell her exactly what she was feeling at the moment in front of all of these people, family or not.

They were vultures, the lot of them, she decided. When was the last time any of them had ever considered one action that benefited someone besides themselves?

Her mother had two siblings — an older brother, deceased a few years now, who had children of his own, including Henry, and an older sister, the mother of three daughters and a son.

The drawing room had likely never been so full as it was in this moment with all of them gathered. A dapper looking solicitor, his black hair slicked back neatly over his head, sat in front of the lot of them upon a chair with a back as straight as his own.

He raised his spectacles to his eyes and cleared his throat in an attempt to capture their attention but was promptly and decidedly ignored.

He frowned in consternation and attempted one more time with a loud "harumph." Elizabeth felt sorry for him — it mustn't be a pleasant aspect of his job, meeting with grieving families, though besides herself and her grandmother, most of the room did not look particularly unhappy — uneasy, if anything.

Which partially made sense. Thomas Clarke had loved Elizabeth with all of his heart and ensured she knew it; however, he also thought most of his family to be "idiots, the lot of them," and he did not keep silent in his opinions.

Elizabeth sat next to her grandmother on the small settee, grasping her cold hand within hers. Justine Clarke looked straight ahead of her at the man in the chair, saying nothing more to Elizabeth, though she squeezed her hand tightly in thanks for her support as she clearly wanted nothing more than for this entire process to be over.

The solicitor stood and rapped his knuckles on the small

writing table that sat beside him until he finally gained the attention of the crowd in front of him. He sighed in such relief that Elizabeth would have laughed had it been under other circumstances, and then sat back down in the wooden chair that had been brought in from another room within the house — likely storage, for Elizabeth's grandmother was proud of her home and always ensured it was within the latest fashion.

This room itself, the drawing room, was a long room on the south side of the house. Sash windows lining the room emitted plenty of daylight, while the white crown molding accented the pale yellow walls, which were lined with beautiful portraits of the family as well as landscapes of the English countryside. The Clarke family had never actually owned a home outside of London since they had moved to the city a couple of generations ago, but Justine had come from a small country town and she enjoyed reminders of home upon her walls.

Today, the furniture had been rearranged to suit the occasion so they were all looking up at the solicitor like church-goers in front of the pastor. But the funeral itself would come later. This was an entirely different matter.

"Thank you all for your attendance," the solicitor said in a pinched voice. "Please allow me to express my sincere condolences to all of you. I am Mr. Smith, and it has been my pleasure to serve as solicitor to Mr. Clarke over the past few years, as it was for my father for decades prior. Thomas Clarke was a man who prepared for everything in life, and his death was no exception. I have in my hands the will he prepared a few years ago. While my father oversaw the drafting of the will, I was in the room as well and can attest to the fact that he was of sound mind and countenance."

"Get on with it," muttered Henry from two seats over, and Elizabeth leaned around Terrence to glare at him.

"Very well," Mr. Smith said, though he was clearly not at all pleased. After introductory remarks, he began to list the names of the various family members within the room, pronouncing annuities for each of them, none of them insignificant — Thomas Clarke had been a very wealthy man.

"'For the remainder of her life, my estate, besides the annuities previously listed, will be left to my loving wife, Justine,'" he read, and Elizabeth's grandmother barely contained a slight sob. "My home in London, the senior partnership of Clarke & Co., and, upon my wife's own departure from this earth to join me, my entire estate, will be left to my granddaughter, Lady Elizabeth Moreland.'"

CHAPTER 2

*G*asps resounded around the room as the solicitor read the last line, a smile covering his face as he had clearly been looking forward to the reaction of the family before him — the family who had not exactly ingratiated themselves to him as they had practically ignored him until the time came to read the contents of the will. Every face in the room was turned toward Elizabeth, who was as shocked as the rest of them. Justine, having obviously been aware of what was within the will, squeezed Elizabeth's hand and bestowed upon her a watery smile. Terrence's eyes were wide, but he grinned at Elizabeth when she turned to him and he ever so slightly nodded his head in support, while a murmur began somewhere within the room, growing louder with each passing moment.

Elizabeth could do nothing but sit in stupefied silence. *She* was the senior partner of London's most renowned bank? She had always thought her grandfather was passing on knowledge for her own enjoyment, but she had never considered... this.

"You cannot be serious!" Henry finally called out, and Mr.

Smith waved his hands in the air in a gesture telling them all to quiet down.

"Mr. Clarke did leave an explanation if you would like me to read it."

"I should bloody well hope so!" Henry raged.

"Please note that these are his own words and not my own," the solicitor said, looking up at all of the angry faces before him with a faint look of warning before returning his eyes to the page.

"'I am well aware that most of my family will not be pleased with my decision, as they all have some preconceived notion of their own worth. However, it matters not that Lady Elizabeth is a woman. She is the only family member who ever displayed any interest in the workings of the bank. She is the only family member who spent any time with me at all. And she is also the only family member with a head on her shoulders who is intelligent enough to take on such a role.'"

"Well, I never!" Henry's mother, Elizabeth's Aunt Betsy, exclaimed.

Mr. Smith paused a moment, looking slightly ill, before continuing. "The rest of you are greedy, selfish, or incapable of any responsibility — some are all of the above. Take your pick. That is all."

The gasps that were emitted then were more than simply horrified, but outraged. Elizabeth's jaw must have been nearly on her chest, for a soft, white-gloved finger was soon gently closing it, the arm it was attached to then returning to snake back over Elizabeth's shoulder.

"Gather yourself together, daughter," Elizabeth's mother whispered in her ear, causing Elizabeth to jump in surprise. She hadn't even realized her mother was behind her as she had been so caught up in Smith's words but moments ago.

Elizabeth could feel her mother's fingers upon the back of

her chair as Lady Moreland stood and gracefully crossed the room to stand next to the solicitor, a smile covering her face as she looked between the man and the rest of her family before her.

"Thank you, Mr. Smith, for attending to us this morning in order to impart our father's wishes with us," she said. "It has been most... interesting, I believe we can all agree. I am sure it will take some time for us all to overcome his passing, as well as digest just how... generous he has been to some of us. All of us."

She cleared her throat.

"Thank you again. Should we have any questions, we know where we may find you."

How did her mother turn everything she said into a threat? Elizabeth wondered, but then the solicitor was nodding at the rest of them. He approached her, asked if they could meet again in the near future in order to ensure all was in order, and Elizabeth managed a weak smile in return before turning around to find that the rest of her family was still staring at her.

"But she is a *woman!*" It was Elizabeth's cousin Frederick now voicing his displeasure. His mother was Thomas' other daughter. "How in the world is a woman supposed to take on such a position? Is it even legal?"

"It is," the solicitor said from behind her, chiming into the conversation, though his contribution was met with glares. It didn't seem to overly bother him. "There is additional information within the will in which I did not suppose you would be interested at this moment, but Mr. Clarke was meticulously detailed as regards Lady Elizabeth's inheritance. I was going to speak with her about this in a separate meeting, but perhaps it is best you are all aware. The will reads that 'the bulk of the estate will go to Elizabeth, for her sole and disparate use, independent of any debts or contracts of her present or future husband."'

One of the ladies — one of her cousins, though which, Elizabeth had no idea for they all were so alike — laughed from across the room and Elizabeth rolled her eyes. She was well aware that none of them believed she would ever be married, and perhaps they were right. She just wished it was due to choice and not the fact that she remained a cold, practical woman who had no time to simper behind a fan at any gentleman who may be so inclined to look her way. That was likely to change, she thought with a rueful smile, as she was now an heiress and there would be many who would be more than interested in assuming such a fortune, despite however meticulously her grandfather had been in his wording of the will.

Her cousin Henry clearly misinterpreted her slight smile as he stalked toward her.

"'Did you know?" Henry hissed.

"Of course not!" Elizabeth exclaimed, gathering herself together. This was no time to allow anyone to be aware that she was at all affected by what they might think. She heard her Aunt Betsy snort but steeled her spine to the responses that she was sure were coming. Henry would be the worst, she was well aware, and he didn't disappoint as he now stood in front of her, a finger in her face.

"That partnership should be mine," he said in a low voice, though Elizabeth saw that her grandmother could hear his words and did not look particularly pleased with them.

"And why would you feel that way?" Elizabeth asked, coolly raising an eyebrow.

"I am the eldest male grandchild of all the family. I do not have a father who is a lord and can pass down his title and all that is entailed."

"I will neither receive such a thing, you do realize," she

replied, reflecting on the fact of how right her grandfather was when he came to Henry — her cousin was a childish idiot.

"Obviously," he came up with in response. "And so why would you ever think that you should inherit so great a responsibility as a bank, where it is not only your own livelihood at stake but that of every client who banks with you?"

"I can certainly handle it much better than you ever could," she retorted.

"Oh?" he challenged her. "And what are you going to do? Walk around asking who would like tea every morning? Embroider the clerks' coverings for the walls?"

She could have slapped him in the face — her friend Phoebe certainly would have — but Elizabeth took a deep breath and counted backward from ten within her head in order to maintain her calm.

"I'll tell you what *I* would do," he said, narrowing his eyes, and clearly he had put some thought into this, apparently having been under the impression for some time that he would be the one in the seat behind Thomas' desk.

"Do I even want to know?"

He ignored her and continued.

"Major changes are needed at Clarke & Co.," he said with much assurance. "The partnership needs new blood. It can no longer be composed of Grandfather's contemporaries and favorites. I know of many people who would make terrific partners, and I will be sure to share those names with you — for the time being. I suppose you will be in tomorrow? I certainly would be. Now, as for salaries. They are far, far too high. Why, these people are clerks, not partners, and they need to be paid as such. And Grandfather's donations, oh, those definitely must be abolished. Why should we pay for someone else's dinner when those people could work themselves?"

"That is an interesting question coming from a man who would propose to cut wages of employees — some who have large families to feed. How, then, would you suggest that people keep from requiring donations of those who have more than they need?"

"You're going to run that place into the ground," Henry snarled, and Elizabeth stiffened her spine as she began to retort in an altogether polite, proper, yet no-nonsense manner. Before she could open her mouth, however, a soft hand touched her arm and gently tugged her back.

"Henry, dear, I am ashamed of you," their grandmother said with a stern gaze. Justine Clarke was nearly eighty, and yet she retained the inner strength that she had always held, which Elizabeth well admired. Justine was a tall woman, nearly as tall as Elizabeth, and was proud of the hold she retained upon her youth.

"Grandmother?" he asked with some consternation.

"Your grandfather did as he saw best. All that you are proposing to Elizabeth would undermine the very principles upon which he built this bank, and for you to suggest that she might do anything other than what she feels is right is ridiculous. When was the last time you attended a church service, child? For your grandfather was there, sitting in the front pew every Sunday, and when God told him to provide for those in need, he certainly did so — through the bank as well as through his own personal means. You would do well to learn from such lessons. Apologize to your cousin. For she doesn't deserve your idiotic words."

Henry fixed his astonished gaze to his grandmother, before turning it to Elizabeth and finally to his own mother, who had come to join them after obviously hearing such a commotion from their corner of the room.

"Henry," she said politely. "Perhaps do as your grandmother says, and then we might have a word just the two of us?"

Elizabeth had no strong feelings regarding her Aunt Betsy. She had always meekly followed along with her husband, and once he was gone, she had always done what she had always felt was in Henry's best interests.

"Apologies, Elizabeth," he muttered, and then led his mother away from them.

Justine turned to Elizabeth and brought her cool hands to Elizabeth's cheeks. She wore no gloves, having never considered herself requiring dress much more intricate than that in which she had been raised.

"Thomas knew what he was doing, darling," she said, her eyes flicking over Elizabeth's face. "You are the only one he trusted, and I know you are entirely capable. You can do this."

Elizabeth nodded, but in reality, she wasn't so sure.

CHAPTER 3

*E*xactly one week after the reading of her beloved grandfather's will, Elizabeth was sitting at her vanity once more, contemplating the night's upcoming events.

Attending her grandfather's funeral was not a practical idea. It was certainly not a proper one — for a woman, that is. And it was, with all certainty, nothing that the Lady Elizabeth Moreland of even two weeks ago would have even contemplated.

But she was now more than Lady Elizabeth Moreland. She was Elizabeth Moreland, granddaughter of Thomas Clarke, and now the senior partner of Clarke & Co., the largest bank in England. She walked with a target on her back, and yet she was well aware that if she didn't attend an event such as this, it would only provide her cousins — particularly Henry — with more credence as to why all should be taken from her. How they would do it, she had no idea, but they had certainly vowed to do so.

After the nightmare that was the reading of the will, Elizabeth had remained stunned during the meal, in which most of her family simply stared at her, most with loathing. Her mother was all smiles, of course, though the moment they had entered the carriage, all she could speak of was how wonderfully wealthy they would soon become, and when did Elizabeth think she could begin to earn income?

Elizabeth told her mother that unfortunately, she had no idea, but that once an acceptable period of time had passed — perhaps, she asked politely, after her grandfather's funeral had taken place? — she would visit the bank and ask all the questions required.

"But—" her mother had begun to say, but Elizabeth quelled her question with a look that requested her mother's silence — for the moment, at least. Her father, a man of fewer words than her mother (although most people were), looked rather smug as he sat with his arms crossed, finally providing the only advice that seemed to permeate his thoughts.

"Hire the people you can trust, then take yourself out of there. Keep your share, of course, and collect the funds from it. By all means, do not involve yourself in any operations, Elizabeth. That would only cause utter scandal."

That very night, Elizabeth began to itemize her possessions in order to determine what was, in actuality, hers and what was her parents'. She had thought about it long and hard and had decided that she couldn't ignore what her grandfather had given her, which was the responsibility and the position that he knew she would love with her very soul. In order to move forward, she needed the freedom to come and go as she pleased, to not have to be greeted by her parents and their multitude of questions every time she walked down the stairs.

Such as at this moment. Elizabeth had waited until her

father had left, and she hoped to avoid her mother, who certainly wouldn't be attending the parade to the church nor the service itself — no, it wouldn't be at all proper for an English lady to do so, which was certainly how Elizabeth's mother presented herself, despite the fact that she had been raised in the home of Thomas and Justine Clarke, who had come from modest beginnings.

Well, Elizabeth may be a lady, but tonight she was going to be true to her grandfather and what he would expect from her. As he had often told her, he cared little for the nobility and their rules, nor did he believe in what was always referred to as a lady's sensitivities. So now, as his successor and the senior partner of Clarke & Co., Elizabeth was going to the funeral, whether her mother liked it or not.

Elizabeth looked out the door of chambers and tiptoed down the steps, cringing as the black crinoline rustled with each step she took. Drat this damn material, she thought as she rounded the stairs, pulling her cloak tighter around her. Her mother would be sitting in the drawing room at the front of the house, and Elizabeth only had to get past the door to the outdoors, where she could go around to the mews and have a carriage prepared.

"Elizabeth Moreland, where do you think you are going?"

Elizabeth had been so close — only footsteps away from the door — when her mother appeared in the entrance of the drawing room. The woman could have been a Bow Street Runner, the way she knew anything and everything that was happening not only in her house but amongst all of her acquaintances. It was part of the reason that Elizabeth had to leave as soon as possible, in order to see to her own affairs.

"I am going to Grandpapa's funeral, Mother," she said, holding her head high, and her mother, who looked so like her with her auburn hair pulled back, her sharp, pointed nose, and somewhat hollowed cheekbones, stared at her incredulously.

"You cannot be serious! Elizabeth, what are you thinking? What if someone were to see you?"

"That is the point," Elizabeth said calmly. She and her mother may look alike, but their countenances were entirely different. While they both kept hold of their emotions when out in public, at home her mother was known to frequently cry out in rage or despair. She loved the attention. "Grandpapa would have wanted me to go," she said more gently now, before changing to a tack she was sure her mother would understand. "Besides that, if I do not go, it is only one more opportunity for the rest of them to convene against me, for them to find a reason to declare me incapable of the position, or Grandpapa's will invalid."

Elizabeth's mother tilted her head and sighed. "You do, unfortunately, make a valid point. However, your father will be there, as will Terrence. That will be good enough."

"No, it will not," Elizabeth said in even tones. "Neither Father nor Terrence is the senior partner of Clarke & Co. And more importantly, Father did not know Grandpapa as I did and Terrence was always rather... busy. I wish to pay my respects to Grandpapa, Mother. I loved him, very much."

Her mother sighed and waved a hand in the air.

"You spent far too much time with him in that dratted bank," she said. "You should have been furthering your education instead."

"If you are referring to needlepoint and watercolors, then I am afraid I would have failed either way," Elizabeth with a chuckle to which her mother seemed to take exception. "Besides, Mother," she continued, "I do not need your permission."

"If nothing else, those parades can be dangerous!" Her

mother exclaimed, and Elizabeth softened somewhat at the fact that her mother was, in part, concerned for her safety and not just her reputation.

"I'll take an extra groom. Goodnight, Mother."

And with that, she was out the door, off to find her carriage and a groom with broad shoulders.

* * *

IT WAS the first time Elizabeth had ever ridden within a funeral possession. It was quite dreary, really, everyone in black as they rode through the dark streets of London, with few lanterns to guide their way.

Two men of the Moreland household rode atop the carriage in order to see to her protection. Her mother was right in that it was one of the reasons women did not attend funerals — the processions, held at night with the nobility upon their horses and within their carriages — were often seen as easy targets, all clustered together in the dim light as they traversed between the home of the deceased and the church. Why they didn't simply move the procession to earlier in the day, Elizabeth had no idea. Perhaps because it was all planned by men, she thought with a wry laugh.

The Clarkes had lived in Knightsbridge for the past twenty years and the church wasn't far, but more people lined the street alongside Elizabeth than she could have imagined. Her grandfather had been a well-known man, and it was somewhat heartening to see them all here paying their respects.

She thought she recognized some of the houses they passed as she peered through the carriage windows, but soon they were replaced by the inky hole of what, during the day, would be the green of Hyde Park.

Her grandfather had loved the park when he had a moment outside of the bank, Elizabeth thought with a smile. She began to review the many memories they shared, nearly all fond. Her reveries, however, were interrupted as the carriage came to a jarring halt. Elizabeth soon heard shouts from her driver and groom, who apparently had been caught unawares as the door banged open, startling her as she jumped half a foot in the air.

"What have we here?"

The voice was raspy and guttural, coming from a mouth hidden behind a black beard. The man was rather large — not typical for a thief, that was for certain, but he hoisted himself up as he began to make his way into the small space with Elizabeth.

"Get out!" she cried as his stench filled her nostrils, but when he looked up at her and grinned, showcasing a few gaps where teeth had used to be, she swallowed hard. He was dressed in a mixture of items, some torn and ragged, others quite fine, which seemed to prove that this was not the first attempt at stealing from people such as Elizabeth.

She looked about her for anything she could use against him — anything at all, but found nothing, until she felt rather than saw the metal grip of the umbrella she held in her hand. Just as the man attempted to launch himself fully into the carriage, Elizabeth raised her arm behind her and then swung with all her might, the pointy tip of the umbrella crashing into the man's nose.

His hands come up to catch the sudden gush of blood but then the door was empty of him as quickly as he appeared — which had actually been a graceful entry for a man his size.

Whatever was she to do? It seemed the procession had continued on without them, and she had no idea where the man had gone. Elizabeth doubted he had been alone, however, for the carriage had stopped nearly immediately as he entered. Even if she could fight off whoever else threatened, she had no idea what state the driver and groom were in, and they would be left alone in the middle of the London darkness.

Both doors of the carriage now opened, and Elizabeth was chagrined to see a man attempt to enter from the other side. She could perhaps take one with her umbrella, but two? Well, she had to try. A random thought entered her mind that her mother had, unfortunately, been right, but Elizabeth pushed it away, for there were currently far more important considerations.

As she shouted for help, Elizabeth swung out wildly from one side to the next, attempting to find tender spaces such as the nose and groin, but they were too fast, working together as one pinned her arms back and the other began groping her fingers, her wrists, likely for jewels of any sort, as he held a hand over her mouth to keep her from calling out once more. They could take what they wanted — Elizabeth didn't care, as long as she came away unscathed — but her pride forced her to fight on despite the hopelessness of her current situation. She bit the man's hand, and she heard him curse before he raised his hand back. Elizabeth flinched as she waited for the slap in the face that was to come, but when she felt nothing but the night air against her cheek, she opened her eyes to see what had convinced the man to hold his anger in check.

He was gone. Instead, another figure filled the doorway, one that was very tall, very broad and very… familiar. He let out a bit of a growl as he entered the carriage on nearly a leap. Elizabeth ducked her head as he went barreling behind her, knocking over the man who had held her arms.

She turned in astonishment to thank the man and determine his identity. For as much as she hated to admit that she couldn't have fought her foe alone, she would never have extricated herself from such a situation without him.

Elizabeth turned and opened her mouth, but no words came out as she could only stare at him in shock.

For standing in the doorway of the carriage, his silhouette illuminated by the light of the moon and the streetlamp behind him, was Gabriel Lockridge, the Duke of Clarence.

CHAPTER 4

"*W*hat are you doing here?"

Gabriel narrowed his eyes at her words as he stared at Elizabeth, who, despite the aura of certainty and proprietary that always surrounded her, now looked rather vulnerable and alone.

Her hair was disheveled, hanging in tendrils around her pretty, oval face. Her eyes — those violet eyes unlike any he had ever seen before that had always drawn him in, drowning him in their depths — stared back at him, wide in her shock, which she was very clearly attempting to hide from him. She began to tug at her clothing — a hideous dress of black material — in order to make sure all was properly arranged.

"Is that any way to thank a man who just rescued you from such ruffians?" He asked, leaning out and quickly calling to his driver to carry on without him before he re-entered the carriage and slammed the door behind him with such force she jumped as she settled herself back on the seat and folded her hands primly in her lap.

"I had the matter under control, though I thank you very much for your assistance," she said with a sniff, and Gabriel reached down to see what weapon she had been brandishing against the men who had entered her carriage. When he lifted what he had thought was a piece of metal, he could only stare in astonishment.

"An umbrella? You were going to fight off three attackers with an umbrella?"

"For your information, I had already defeated one with it and I'm sure the next two were close to follow had I more time."

"As stubborn as ever," he muttered under his breath as he sat across from her and pulled on his gloves, which he had retrieved from the floor following his brief skirmish. He ran a hand over his own hair to ensure all was in place — it was — before fixing his gaze upon her.

"Pardon me?" she said, one eyebrow arched, and he was aware that she very clearly knew what he had said, but was attempting to provoke him further.

"Oh, I'm just telling myself how fortunate it was that I was in the carriage next to you when I heard you cry out. I was also congratulating myself on a job well done, as quite obviously you were not going to do so."

She shot a glare toward him, one he sensed even in the dim light.

"You are as conceited as ever," she said with disdain.

"I only speak the truth."

"As you see it."

"When one is a duke in England, he may typically decide what is the truth."

"And that, *Your Grace*, is precisely the problem."

They sat in silence for a moment, until Elizabeth suddenly jumped out of her reverie.

"My goodness! The driver and the groom — I have to go check on them to see if they are all right."

"Allow me," Gabriel said, though of course, Elizabeth didn't listen. No, she stood and tried to brush past him, but he blocked her with his body.

"Stay here, Elizabeth. It's bad enough you are out on the streets at all tonight, but to be out of the carriage would be more than foolish."

He could tell she wasn't pleased with his words but, at the very least, she listened, though she crossed her arms and looked rather perturbed as he let himself out the carriage door. In truth, he did care about her safety, but he was also rather concerned about what might be awaiting outside.

Fortunately, the driver was brushing himself off, and while the groom was rubbing at a bump on his head, they both seemed to be in fair enough condition.

"Just a few scratches, Your Grace," they told him after he shared his identity and what had occurred, and Gabriel nodded, confirmed they were able to continue the short drive to the church, and returned to Elizabeth, who was tapping her foot impatiently.

"Now tell me. Just what do you think you are doing out here alone?" he asked, and she sighed as though answering his question was a hardship.

"That is a rather idiotic question, especially coming from a man I know to be far more intelligent," she said with an indignant look toward him. "I am attending my grandfather's funeral, of course, just as you are."

"If we are speaking of intelligence, then I must ask, Elizabeth, if you had not expected that something such as this might occur?"

"I thought of it," she responded. "That is why I brought Glouster."

"The groom?"

"Yes."

"A lot of good that did for you."

"How would it have been different if I were a man within this carriage? If I were my brother? What protection would he or you have that I do not?"

"I have a dagger in my boot, for one."

"You do not."

"I do — would you like to see?"

"Not particularly."

"A woman is far more likely to wear jewels, to have riches available for the taking," he continued in what he felt was a fine argument.

"I am wearing no jewelry but a pair of ear bobs. I am in mourning."

"They do not know that, Elizabeth. Where are your parents?"

"My mother is at home, wearing her disapproving face, while my father is likely somewhere ahead in the procession."

He raised an eyebrow. "Dismissing propriety, then, are we Elizabeth?"

"While I typically find that it is far better to do what is expected, to live one's life within the rules of society, there is also, at times, the occasion to break with convention and do what is necessary."

"Such as your friends, who have found themselves in rather... interesting situations lately," he said, being very aware of the recent actions of two of her closest companions. "Perhaps the results of their experiences have convinced you that propriety is not always best."

"They have been lucky," she said primly. "I still believe it cannot be so for everyone."

"That's a rather gloomy way to look at it."

"Yes, well, experience has taught me so."

Silence stretched between them for a moment, and he marveled at the fact that despite she had recently been attacked, she hadn't lost any composure, nor her headstrong attitude.

"Elizabeth—"

"I do not believe you have leave to call me by my given name, *Your Grace*."

"Oh, you gave me leave to do so in the past." As he remembered just exactly what that past had included, a rush of heat flooded his body. A rush he hadn't felt in some time, was he being honest. On that night, which remained burned in his memory, Elizabeth had been nothing like the cold, proper woman she was today. Oh, no — Gabriel knew a side of her that no one else did, a side that was hot, wild, and passionate.

"That was the past — a mistake," she said, and he could tell she was no longer looking at him, but at a corner of the carriage. "What are you doing in here, anyway? It certainly isn't at all proper for us to be alone together like this."

"What do you think I will do?" he asked, crossing his arms and leaning back into the squabs as he grinned, "Take your innocence?"

He could tell it wasn't the response she had been expecting, but she straightened as her gaze returned to him.

"It's a little late for that, do you not think?"

Gabriel said nothing, as he could hear the pain in her voice. No longer was she teasing and taunting him — she was speaking from her heart, and he was well aware that he had done it a disservice five years ago. He had regretted his actions for longer than she knew. Not all that had occurred between them, but the part that had made her feel as though she wasn't worthy of the love of one man.

"Elizabeth... I know I acted more than dishonorably all

those years ago, and I do offer you my sincerest apologies, as I should have done long ago. Oh, I know I said I was sorry, but over time, I have come to understand just how wrong my actions were."

"We both became carried away that night, when we… when we… made love."

Made love. What a way to describe it — not how he typically thought of the act, but it certainly had been different with Elizabeth.

"I am aware of that," he said softly. "We were young and full of romantic thoughts, were we not? I would have married you, Elizabeth. I told you I would."

She snorted. "I had no desire to be married to a man who would take a string of mistresses. In fact, I am glad that I found you in the arms of Lady Pomfret. For had I not, then I likely *would* have married you and lived a disastrously unhappy life. In fact, I should thank her one of these days."

Gabriel swallowed hard, saying nothing. He did not enjoy being wrong. In fact, he was proud of the fact that he hardly ever was. But in this, she was altogether correct. He had been a fool, and youth was no excuse.

"I'm sorry," he said quietly, but she didn't respond, apparently done with their conversation. In truth, he had no wish to speak of it any longer either, but she did deserve his apology.

He could still clearly remember nearly every moment of the night they had come together. She had just had her come out, while he was a couple of years older. He had been attending events long enough to know that women were eager for the attention of a future duke, though young enough that he did not yet understand what repercussions could come from flirtations — or more — with unwed young women of the *ton*. Elizabeth had caught his eye the moment she walked into Lord Holderness' ballroom that evening.

She stood out, for she was tall for a woman, but it was more than that. She carried herself with a confidence most women lacked, so self-assured, so composed. She was beautiful in a classic sense, though not particularly striking, not like the woman with midnight black hair who accompanied her, nor the little blonde pixie nymph beside her. But she was graceful and elegant — something about her captivated him. Then she had turned and when those violet eyes had met his, the room could have been held up at gunpoint and he wouldn't have been able to look away. It took a moment for him to realize she was the daughter of the Viscount Shannon — a girl he had known in her youth, for their countryside summer homes had been quite close to one another. But gone was the awkward, bookish little girl. In her place was a woman — one he wanted to get to know better, beyond the few teasing words they had exchanged when they were but children. That night they had danced, spoken easy words to one another, and then a walk in the gardens had turned into so much more when they had found a cushioned bench within a gazebo.

He could still remember the way the moon and stars had illuminated her fine cheekbones. Gabriel hadn't meant to take things as far as they did. But when she had asked, it hadn't been within him to say no. He had meant to do right by her — had courted her properly afterward, and had nearly proposed, despite the fact he wasn't ready to wed — but then she found out that he had allowed his eye to wander. He had been such an idiot.

"It may have been both of our decisions, but I should have known better, and I should have done right — truly right by you," he said softly now as he stared out the window, realizing they were nearing the church. "Elizabeth… I'm also very sorry about your grandfather. He was a good man, one I was pleased to come to know over the

39

years through my dealings with your family and with the bank."

"Thank you," she said quietly, though to which apology she was referring, he wasn't entirely sure.

CHAPTER 5

Thankfully the remainder of the evening had been uneventful. Elizabeth hadn't been surprised to see that the church was filled with people paying their respects to her grandfather. He had been a well-liked, respected man, and his clients ranged from the wealthy and powerful to those whose sums may have been small, but to them, they were fortunes nonetheless. Elizabeth recognized many of those who sat at the front of the church in their finery, while others near the back may have been less well-dressed, but perhaps more sincere in their grief. Thomas had treated them all equally.

Elizabeth had received many wide-eyed stares as she made her way through the church, choosing a seat near the front, where she held her head high. Appearances were important now, she reminded herself. While many of these men may question her choice to attend, it was paramount that she appear strong and capable — which she was. Her mother would have been proud, for Elizabeth showed no emotion, despite the fact her heart was breaking as she listened to the vicar reading words of the gospel over her grandfather's body.

She had seen Terrence enter the church, late as always, and find a seat on the other side next to her father, who she had tried, as well as she could, to avoid.

Gabriel — she shouldn't think of him as such, but she really couldn't help it — had sat next to her during the service, but he quickly learned it was best to not offer any words or touch of support, as when he lifted a hand as though to place it over hers in a gesture of comfort, she sent him a glare that had him returning the hand to his own lap rather hastily. Afterward, he had insisted he would escort her home, but her father had approached them, his expression thunderous at Elizabeth's appearance, and took her arm to lead her into his own carriage, dismissing Glouster and the other driver. Elizabeth had time to offer Gabriel only a quick thanks before she and her father were out of the church and heading toward home.

"What were you thinking?" he hissed as they took a seat, and Elizabeth stared back at him in equal measure.

"I realize that it is not at all done for a woman of the *ton* to attend a funeral, Father," she said matter-of-factly. "But you must understand that I am now the senior partner of Clarke & Co. If I were a man, it would be unheard of for me *not* to attend the funeral, as Grandpapa's successor. I mustn't show any sign of weakness, or these men will feed upon it."

"I don't know what Thomas was thinking, naming you his heir," her father muttered, crossing his arms over his chest, a frown covering his face.

"Then we are fortunate he did not ask for your opinion," she retorted, and her father now uncrossed his arms and leaned forward in the seat toward her.

"Well, I never... Elizabeth, whatever has gotten into you? We did not raise you to be so insolent."

She sighed but refused to apologize. "I am grieving, Father. I am also coming to terms with the responsibility that has been placed upon me and the fact that I have few who are willing to support me in it. While I know Mother doesn't entirely approve, at the very least she is happy about it all, as she sees financial gain for herself."

"She knows nothing of the business," he said with a bit of a snort. Elizabeth's parents tolerated one another, but she couldn't say with all certainty that she had ever seen a moment of happiness between them. "You may make money — if you are lucky and clients don't go running at the first mention of a woman taking on the role of senior partner. But that means nothing for us unless you are inclined to share. Somehow I doubt it."

"Well, with that type of attitude toward me, your assumption sounds reasonable."

Elizabeth trembled slightly inside, as she had never before spoken to her father in such a way, but when he only shook his head, clearly dismissing her words, she decided she had enough of this conversation. She was exhausted, from the attack in the carriage, her verbal sparring with the Duke, the requirement to hide her emotions throughout the service, and now the lack of support of any kind from her father.

"It's late," she said. "Perhaps we should take this up another day."

"That we will," he said, tapping his finger on his other arm. "That we will."

* * *

THE VERY NEXT DAY, to be precise. While Elizabeth felt like doing nothing but lying in bed for the day, the bank would be open, and if she wasn't present to begin to guide the ship in the direction she wanted to go — or encourage that they stay the course, as it may be — then she was well aware that it could end up lost at sea.

And so she summoned her maid to help her dress in black, left the reprieve of her beautiful violet-and-cream chamber and made her way downstairs, hoping she could breakfast alone.

She was disappointed.

"Elizabeth," her mother said as Elizabeth sat down, pouring coffee for herself. She enjoyed tea during the day, but first thing in the morning, coffee seemed to help her to focus. Particularly when she was sitting down with her parents.

"Your father and I have been discussing this... situation. I know we have mentioned it before, but we think it would be best if you forget this nonsense of involving yourself in the bank. There are many others who are capable of managing without you, and you can simply collect the income as necessary."

Elizabeth carefully folded her napkin in her lap before looking up and meeting her mother's gaze.

"Thank you for your concern, Mother. I do appreciate it. However, I have thought this through, and Grandpapa clearly named me his successor for a reason. He trusted no one else, and that includes those within the bank."

"Oh for goodness sake, Elizabeth, have some sense!" Her father suddenly burst out, as his fork clattered to the plate and he raised his hands in the air to emphasize his words. "You are a lady. One who should be focused on finding a husband. What are you going to do, live here, with us, for the rest of your life? Become a spinster? Why, you are practically there already! You have no time to be loitering around the bank, and it will certainly do nothing to further your chances of having a gentleman think anything proper of you."

Elizabeth refused to respond to his emotion, instead taking a careful bite of her toast, chewing thoughtfully as her father spewed his thoughts from across the table and her mother eyed her narrowly.

"You are correct about one thing, Father," Elizabeth said after she swallowed, clearly surprising Lord Moreland, which delighted her, though she would never allow him to see as such. "I cannot live here for the rest of my life. That would not work — not at all. It is fortunate, then, that Grandpapa has seen to my future for me."

"Whatever are you talking about, Elizabeth?" her mother asked. "Do stop speaking in riddles."

"The bank partnership allows me the ability to earn funds to provide for myself. He also gave me a house where I am free to reside."

"You do realize your grandmother still lives there?" her mother asked.

"I do," said Elizabeth. "And I am sure she would welcome my company. Of course I shall have to ask her. Perhaps I will call on her later today after I see to business at the bank."

"You are going to the bank?" Her mother's eyes nearly came out of her head.

"Yes. It is open today, is it not?" Elizabeth asked matter-of-factly.

"But… your grandfather died not long ago. You are in mourning. Elizabeth—"

"If Terrence had been named senior partner, would you suggest that he go into the bank today, or remain at home to mourn?"

Elizabeth's query was met with silence.

"This is important, Mother," she said. "Now, I must be off. I hope the two of you have a wonderful day."

As she rose and left the table, feeling the stares at her back, Elizabeth allowed herself the smallest smile of victory.

* * *

ELIZABETH PAUSED for a moment at the front door of the bank, resting her hand on the warm red brick that arched around the entryway. She closed her eyes, knowing it was silly, but found some comfort in the fact that while her grandfather may be gone, this building was a standing reminder of all that he had built, all that he had worked so hard for. And it was up to her to ensure that his legacy remained.

"Good morning, Lady Elizabeth," Anderson, the wizened doorman said as he opened the door for her. He was practically part of the building itself, he had been here so long, and was expected by all who entered.

"Good morning, Anderson," she returned, fixing a smile on her face. It was people like him who made this bank a success. He may not have anything to do with the partners nor the accounts, but he made people feel as though this was home for them and their hard-earned savings.

As Elizabeth walked through the front lobby and up the stairs to her grandfather's office — her office now — she felt the eyes turn toward her in interest and in question, but she turned her head to greet each person with a smile, a nod, and a greeting with a name if she knew it. All were men, which she knew she would have to become used to in this business.

Most actually seemed somewhat pleased to see her. Though she supposed with her grandfather at the helm, he had chosen quality people to work with — and she herself had been among the employees long enough to come to know them well, and for them to know her in turn.

The thought buoyed her spirits as she walked down the long green carpet of the third-floor corridor to the office at the end. If *they* believed in her and her capability, then why could she not do this?

Her optimism deflated, however, when she walked into the office and found that it was not empty. No, Henry sat in one of the leather chairs of the small seating area, flipping the pages of what looked to be a ledger on the small table in front of him.

"What do you think you are doing?" she asked, allowing the door to shut behind her as she walked through the office, fighting back the tears that threatened at the familiar scents which so reminded her of her grandfather.

"Ah, cousin, how lovely to see you," Henry said, lifting his head from the book and smiling up at her, though of course, his smile was insincere, his thin lips forcibly stretched. His black hair was slicked back as always, and reminding her of a rat. One that was currently slinking around her office, and she had to deal with as quickly as possible.

"Next time you would like to see me, Henry, I would ask that you please make an appointment. I will be reviewing my schedule today, so by tomorrow I should know when I have time to see you."

He narrowed his eyes at her words but stood, clasping his hands behind his back as he began leisurely walking toward her, stopping when he reached the desk as Elizabeth seated herself on the other side. The tabletop was full of papers of all sorts that had been left here over the past couple of weeks, and Elizabeth was eager to begin to review what was now her work. She just needed Henry to leave.

"Elizabeth," he said with what she assumed was supposed to be a winning smile on his face, but she simply looked up at him in wait.

"Yes?"

"You and I both know that this will not work out well. Grandfather was generous in giving this all to you, but perhaps you could keep the house and the funds bestowed upon you, while I'd best look after the business?"

"Why would you suggest that to be in anyone's best interest? Grandpapa was always of sound mind and judgment. He built this business beyond what anyone could have imagined, and I believe he decided as he did for a reason."

Henry shifted from his heels to his toes, rocking back and forth.

"Yes, but those were in his younger years. It is almost as though he allowed emotion to get the best of him. Come, Elizabeth, I know you hold great sentiment toward him, but is this what you really want? To spend your days in an old bank, reviewing ledgers when you could be out having picnics and parties and calling upon your friends? Besides, as I'm sure your mother would have pointed out by now, do you not want to find a husband? That will be difficult while you are working at a bank all day."

"Thank you for your concern, Henry, but I think we are just fine as it is," she said with a tight smile. "Now, I do apologize but you must excuse me. I have a great deal of paperwork to get through."

"Elizabeth," he said now in a more threatening tone as he placed his hands upon the desk, and Elizabeth looked from the backs of his hands to his face with a pointed stare. "The partners will never agree to this. To be led by a woman. Enjoy your time here, but just you wait until the next meeting when I'm sure they will all have something to say about this."

"I'm sure they will," she said, forcing a polite smile upon her face. "And I am positive it will be words of welcome. Now, Henry, it is time for you to leave."

She stood, rounded the desk, and walked to the door, holding it open for him. He glared at her but picked up his hat and briefcase and stalked toward her. He purposefully allowed his shoulder to hit hers as he passed, but Elizabeth refused to even flinch. Just when he was beyond the door, he turned back to look at her.

"This isn't over," he hissed. "And you are going to regret forcing me out like this."

"Oh, that reminds me," she said as though he were a friend who had just left a quick meeting over tea, "please never again enter this office uninvited and read confidential information, or I will have to ask our employees to prevent you from entering this building ever again. Farewell, cousin, have a lovely day!"

And at that, she shut the door in his face, brushed her hands together, and then went to work.

CHAPTER 6

*G*abriel had just finished reading the day's papers when his butler appeared at the door to advise him he had a caller.

"A caller?" He asked, confused. "It is hardly eleven o'clock in the morning."

"Should I tell him to return later this afternoon?" his butler asked, clearly as disapproving as Gabriel himself. Gabriel was about to tell him yes, please do so, but then curiosity got the better of him. Which proved that he really did have too much time on his hands these days.

"Show him in," he said, before adding, "Who is it, anyway?"

"Mr. Henry Clarke," said the butler before turning on his heel to collect the man, and Gabriel rather wished the butler hadn't been so hasty in his retreat. Gabriel was, unfortunately, well aware of Henry Clarke. Elizabeth's cousin, and a man that he had met on a few occasions, none of which Gabriel remembered with much fondness. The man was like a rat, looking to ferret out the best morsels of everything for himself, not caring about the means in which he found them or what he left behind.

Gabriel remembered the way he had always spoken of Elizabeth and recalled Thomas' disgust with his own grandson.

And then— here he was.

"Ah, Your Grace," Clarke said, entering and bowing deeply, to which Gabriel waved a hand to force him up. He did not rise himself, but bid Clarke take a seat in the chair across from him. Gabriel had settled himself in the corner of his deep brown leather chesterfield, from where he could look out of the window across the room. He wasn't sure why, but he enjoyed the view of the gardens and the mews beyond his London townhome, which was large by most standards, as one of the most opulent in Mayfair. He hoped Clarke was suitably impressed, despite the fact he had provided the man with the most uncomfortable chair in the room, a wooden straight back chair where Gabriel's mother liked to sit as her back had always bothered her.

Gabriel wasted no time on idle chatter with the man.

"What brings you here at such an hour, Clarke?" he asked, picking up a cheroot and lighting it, inhaling without offering Clarke one, despite the fact the man gazed at it rather longingly.

"I, ah— a matter of business, I suppose you could say."

"Very well. Continue."

"As you know, my grandfather, Thomas Clarke, recently passed."

"I am aware," Gabriel said dryly. "I was at his funeral."

"Of course," said Clarke as he smoothed his hands down his jacket. "He was, as you know, the senior partner of Clarke & Co."

"Of course I know this." Gabriel took another puff as he crossed one leg over the other.

"Right. Well, then I assume you know the terms of his will?"

That gave Gabriel pause.

"Actually, I am not entirely familiar with the details."

"Oh!" Clarke said, looking pleased that he had information Gabriel did not, despite the fact that as the man's grandson he would have actually been present at the reading of the will. "Well, my grandfather clearly allowed emotion to overtake him at the end of his life, for, outside of a few small stipends, he left all of his assets, funds, home, and senior partnership to one person."

Surely the man had more sense than to have left it all to Clarke.

But then the man's eyes narrowed, hatred filling his face, and Gabriel's faith in Thomas Clarke was restored.

"He left it to my cousin — Elizabeth."

As much as this bit of information shocked Gabriel, he took a deep inhale of the cheroot in an attempt to hide his thoughts. Elizabeth? She had not mentioned a word of this the other night. But then, she likely wouldn't have said anything unless she had been directly asked about it.

"That is... interesting," he finally managed.

Clarke snorted. "Yes, well, it's ridiculous. She cannot seriously think she is going to run such a business, can she? It is not done, not at all."

"Actually," Gabriel said, cocking his head as he thought of it, "I believe it has been done before in some of England's other banks. Some women choose to take a more active role than others, but she wouldn't be the first to do so."

"I do not care if there is precedence or not. I am fighting this!" Clarke said, rising in his anger, and Gabriel watched him, amused at how worked up he had become. "My grandfather had no right to do this. No right at all! Something must be done about it all. First, I must contest the will.

However, I am aware that may not necessarily work, so I do have one other thought as to how I could set this all to rights. Which is why I am here."

Gabriel simply raised an eyebrow in question.

"You are a partner of the bank," Clarke continued.

"Not a very active one."

"The past no longer matters. It's the future. You could take a greater role — actually be present for meetings, have others agree to vote with you on matters. The most major issue being, of course, Elizabeth's role. You must not only poison the other partners against her, but we must find reasons as to why she is ineffectual in her role as senior partner. If she has no confidence from any others, she will surely step down, will she not?"

Gabriel was astounded at the vehemence in the man's tone. Thomas Clarke had been an astute man, one whom Gabriel had always looked upon with fondness. His decision to choose Elizabeth over this Clarke was one which Gabriel applauded. Not that he would actually tell Clarke any of this.

"Very well, Clarke," he said, waving his cheroot in the air, the smoke framing his face. "I will help you."

"You will?" Clarke looked astonished. Clearly, he hadn't been expecting Gabriel to agree so easily. "I know you and my cousin had… dealings in the past, and I was not sure if that would mean you would be loyal to her, or if it would prejudice you against her, help you decide that this was a terrible decision."

"Oh, it's not that so much as the fact that I agree with you, old chap — women should not be running such things, now should they?"

Actually, Gabriel had come to realize, especially lately, women were capable of much more than most gave them credit for.

"They certainly should not," said Clarke, a smug grin

covering his face.

"Very good," Gabriel responded, suddenly needing this man out of his drawing room, his home, and his life. "I will attend the next partners' meeting and see what I can determine. Until then, farewell."

"Farewell, Your Grace!" Clarke said, as though they were suddenly the closest of friends. "And thank you very much!"

Gabriel began to laugh once Clarke was out the door and out of earshot. That was far too easy. Gabriel, of course, had no desire nor any intention of actually helping Clarke with his request. But by agreeing, Gabriel would placate the man and hopefully distract him from actually attempting to remove Elizabeth from her position. For the truth was, Gabriel thought she would be rather competent in such a role, and if Thomas Clarke believed in her, then Gabriel would as well. She didn't need jealous, insecure men such as her cousin Henry to be coming after her with a knife in hand.

For now, he considered that a threat to Elizabeth was a threat to the bank as well.

Knowing Thomas Clarke as he did, Gabriel didn't think there was any chance of the will *not* being upheld. It was sure to have been created in only the most straightforward and legal of circumstances. Thomas' faculties were fully intact right until the end. The physicians believed it had been his heart that had failed him — certainly not his mind.

And then there was the fact that Gabriel had only recently been lamenting of his boredom. Well, perhaps now the perfect solution awaited him. He could involve himself in protecting Elizabeth while becoming an *active* partner in the bank.

Not only would it provide him with something to do, but he could do that something very close to Lady Elizabeth, who after so many years still intrigued him. He was interested in seeing her in action, in determining just how well she took on the role. Not only that, but she would need some support in the room when she faced the partners. From what he could remember, they were all stand-up gentlemen, but did their trust in Thomas Clarke reach further than their distrust in a woman?

That, they would find out soon enough.

* * *

ELIZABETH WAS surprised when there was a slight knock on the door and one of the footmen arrived with a new piece of paper. So far this morning she had successfully managed to sort the correspondence on the desk into four neat piles — those no longer requiring a response, those she must consult others about, those to respond to, and those she had no idea to what they referred but would require further investigation on her part. Next on her well-organized list was to begin preparing for the partners' meeting that she must schedule nearly immediately. She was sure they would all have questions that must be addressed, and it was imperative to gain their confidence.

"My lady," the footman greeted her, slightly out of breath from having traipsed up the stairs.

"Do come in," she said, waving him in.

"Correspondence for you, my lady," he said, holding out a few sealed envelopes.

"You do not have to call me 'my lady,'" Elizabeth responded, looking up for a moment. "Miss Elizabeth or Miss Moreland will do."

"Lady Elizabeth?" he said with question in his voice, and she laughed slightly. She didn't want them to see her as a member of the nobility, but rather as part of her grandfather's family. But she supposed each was a piece of her identity and she must embrace both roles. People accepted those who were true to themselves. "Very well. Lady Elizabeth it is."

She took the note from him, feeling her brow furrow as she read it. She had immediately recognized the rich, heavy scrawl which was that of Gabriel Lockridge. He had penned the odd love note to her when they had been courting. In fact, he was rather proficient in poetry, though his poems had become tainted once she realized she was likely not the only lady to read his words of love. Not that any of it mattered anymore.

Gabriel was requesting a meeting in order to discuss his finances. That was odd. He was a partner himself, and she was certainly not the one with whom to discuss finely detailed matters as he would have an account manager. Which, she realized, he would be well aware.

So clearly he wanted a meeting between the two of them for another matter entirely — likely he was curious about her new role at the bank. She was surprised he hadn't said anything to her of it the night of her grandfather's funeral. One thing about Gabriel, he seemed to know all that was happening, about those within the *ton* and beyond.

Elizabeth longed to say no, for she had no desire to even see Gabriel again, let alone speak to him. But to refuse a duke — even one who she had more than good reason to ignore — was not done by the senior partner of a bank, nor by a lady. Elizabeth found paper within a drawer, sitting next to her grandfather's seal. She picked up a piece of paper and dipped the quill into the ink sitting at the edge of the desk, and, in her elegant handwriting which had been long practiced with her governesses over the years, she wrote a note of acceptance as well as a suggested time for tomorrow.

She might as well meet him sooner rather than later, and determine just what, exactly, he might have to say to her.

CHAPTER 7

When Gabriel walked into the office which had forever been that of Thomas Clarke, he was struck by the familiar. Somehow he had expected it to feel altogether different, but no — the same bookshelves full of ledgers lined the room. The furniture had not been touched, the small sitting area looked as comfortable as ever, and the large mahogany desk stood as reassuringly steady and sturdy as it had always been.

Except there, behind the desk, sat a figure that, while as familiar as any of the inanimate objects in this room, was far from the stately gray-haired gentleman he was much more accustomed to seeing in the tall leather chair.

"Elizabeth," he greeted her with a smile as she rose from the desk and rounded it, pointing to the small cluster of chairs that surrounded the circular table in the sitting area of the office. He reached out to take one of her hands to lift it to his lips, but she deftly skirted him and sat instead.

"Your Grace," she said, her lips lifting into her steady, practiced smile and he quirked an eyebrow at her formality. So this was how it was going to be, then, was it?

She folded her hands in her lap demurely, though Gabriel couldn't help but notice the slight twitching of her pinkie finger. It was the one sign of her nervousness — one he didn't think she even realized.

"Lovely to see you again," he said, knowing it would spark her anger, cause her to emote something other than this coolness he so hated.

"You say that as though our meeting today is a coincidence," she said, her violet eyes boring into him. "We both know very well, however, that is not the case."

He laughed then, chuckling at the fact that if there was one woman he may never outwit in a war of words, it was this one.

"Very true, Elizabeth. However, most women would giggle and agree with me."

She looked at him reproachfully. "You also know very well that I am not most women, and while I would not want to be rude, I also will not play the part of a fool."

"I do not believe anyone has ever accused you of such — certainly not I."

"What can I do for you today, Your Grace?"

"I do wish you would call me Gabriel."

"I will not."

He sighed. "Very well. First of all, I have come to congratulate you on your new position."

"I have not won a prize. My grandfather died."

Gabriel felt chastened. He had certainly not meant his words to convey such a flippancy for Thomas Clarke's passing.

"Of course not," he acknowledged. "But you must be pleased with this new responsibility."

"Yes," she said, though her pinkie finger began to twitch again. Ah, so she wasn't as self-assured in this new role as one might think.

"Many would not believe it a proper position for a woman."

Elizabeth bristled at his words.

"It is not a position, as you keep calling it. I am not an employee who is to be paid for my time. I am a partner — the senior partner — and as you well know, that is something else entirely."

"That it is," he said, leaning back in his chair and crossing one leg over the other. "I will not argue with you on that point. However, I do not change my statement in that you must find some are not particularly… pleased with this turn of events."

Elizabeth tilted her head down to look into her lap momentarily before returning her gaze to him, and he lost himself in her exquisite features, seeing the slightest of freckles dusting her nose. She had always thought them to be horrid — he had rather enjoyed them.

"To be honest, I have not had a chance to speak to most people who might think otherwise. I have spent most of my time so far here in this office, reviewing correspondence and the like. In due time I must review some of it with the appropriate staff, but first I will determine the roles within the company."

"Ah, that is why you are going through the ledgers, are you?"

She glanced down at the table, seeing the book placed between them.

"Not exactly," was all she said, and Gabriel could tell there was more to this story.

"Then what were you doing with this book?"

"*I* was not doing anything. Nor is it any of your concern," she responded.

"And your parents, what do they think of this?"

Elizabeth emitted a wry laugh. "My mother is a proponent of it, so long as it provides her with wealth and prosperity. My father is not altogether pleased. He believes it will mean that I will spend the rest of my life in his home. I have assured him that is not the case."

"Oh?" Gabriel sat up straighter at that. Had Elizabeth found a man? It would make sense. She was certainly long past the age to take a husband, and now that she was an heiress, well, there might be a few more men at her door, though he hoped she would be perceptive enough to see which ones were sincere. But why did the thought of her marrying someone else cause such a twinge deep within his gut? He'd had his chance, and in the end, it hadn't been right. He still cared for her, but in the protective way of a man who was looking out for a woman alone.

"Yes," she said matter of factly. "My grandfather also left me his home, though of course my grandmother still resides there. I spoke with her yesterday and she would be more than happy for me to actually take up residence with her."

"You're leaving the home of your parents?"

This was not an action he expected of Lady Elizabeth Moreland. Perhaps more had changed with her inheritance of the partnership than he had thought.

"Yes," she said with a nod. "My parents are not in support of my involvement with the bank. They feel as though I should keep the partnership, but not actually take an active role. I do not think, however, this bank would be as successful as it is without my grandfather's involvement in various activities. He taught me and taught me well. I just didn't know that all his lessons were with a purpose."

Her voice somewhat trailed off as she spoke and looked away from him out the window, her thoughts clearly elsewhere. He said nothing, allowing her the moment until she ever so slightly jumped, came back to herself, and turned toward him.

"My apologies."

"It's all right," he said with a wave of his hand. "Is there any chance that one of your family members might contest the will?"

"Of course," she said, shaking her head ever so slightly at him as though he were an idiot. "I expected it the moment the solicitor said the words. Henry has already begun proceedings and I have applied for probate through a proctor. Interrogations of witnesses are to begin next week."

Well. Clarke had moved much more quickly and stealthily than Gabriel had given him credit for.

"It will be fine," she said without any worry on her face. "My grandfather was a meticulous man."

"Have you thought at all, perhaps, as to whether your parents, Clarke, or any of your other family members might be correct?"

"Pardon me?" Her gaze hardened as she stared at him.

"I just mean that, perhaps, it would be much easier for you were you to rely on the people who have sound knowledge of the bank — such as the clerks and the account managers — and allow them to meet with clients. Conceivably even some of the other partners would be interested in doing so. What could you do that no one else couldn't? I don't foresee any issues for a woman to attend meetings, so perhaps you could still take on that role, but otherwise, you surely have better things to do with your time, do you not?"

His smile was one that he knew would be slightly patronizing, as he had meant it to be. She simply stared at him.

"You cannot be serious."

"Whatever do you mean?"

"You know very well that I would not have any better things to do with my time. What is it you would suggest?" she asked, her voice becoming ever so slightly more heated as she spoke. "Watercolors? Weaving? Pouring tea? Have you been sent here by my parents, by any chance?"

"I do not follow orders from anyone," he said, his words clipped. "And I certainly do not appreciate your tone."

"My tone?" she repeated, raising an eyebrow. "Oh, do forgive me, Your Grace, if I have at all *offended* you. Heaven knows I would never endeavor to do so. It would be the height of rudeness."

Her words were tinged with sarcasm, and he remembered how she had always used it to hide her true emotion.

"I ask only with your best interests in mind," he said, ensuring his own voice remained steady and true. "Your grandfather may have allowed you to follow him around this office, I know that well enough. But how much did you actually retain, not knowing that you might someday require this information? I mean no offense, Elizabeth. I am well aware that you are as intelligent as a man — perhaps more so. However, you cannot argue with the fact that you did not receive the same type of education as most men do. Not because you didn't want to, but you were not afforded the opportunity — 'tis no fault of your own."

"I had an excellent governess for most of my youth, and the rest of my education was the first-hand experience taught to me by my grandfather and what I learned myself through books available to me. You question how much I retained? All of it, Your Grace. I can review profit and loss statements. I can understand a bank ledger. I can assess salaries. I can review and decide on partnerships. I have no issue with any of that. And no, it would not be a better task for someone else. My grandfather knew what he was doing, and he chose me for a reason."

"That all may be so," he said, smiling ever so slightly at the vehemence in her voice. "But can you run a partners' meeting?"

She kept her chin high in the air and didn't lower her eyes, but she said nothing for a moment, and he was aware that he had finally found the nexus of her nerves.

"Of course I can."

"Do you believe they will listen to a woman?"

"They will have no choice. I am the senior partner."

"True," he said with a slow nod. "But it will be difficult to gain any traction if none of them have any faith in you."

"Is this why you came?" she challenged him now, "To question me and my competence?"

"Not at all," he said. "I came because I wanted to discuss with you my accounts, as well as potential investments."

"Should you not speak with your account manager regarding such matters?"

"I am a partner in the bank as well," he said, raising an eyebrow at her. "I do not wish for my affairs to be discussed by just anyone. But since you are suggesting I speak with someone else, it makes me question your competence. Are you able to provide me the information and counsel I seek?"

"Of course," she said smartly, reaching out a hand and snapping up the pile of papers he had placed on the table between them. "Just as I am able to run a simple partners' meeting, no matter how I am challenged. And yes, Gabriel, I will be prepared."

He had rattled her. She hadn't even realized she had reverted to using his given name. Inwardly, he smiled, having achieved his objective. She was upset now, riled up, and he was glad of it. She needed that spunk, that winning attitude, if she were going to face down a table full of partners who would, despite their allegiance to Thomas Clarke, in all like-lihood question her abilities and her competence. It was why he had come today, to see if she was ready, and she had been — almost. She had just needed that final push.

One thing that he couldn't break? That frosty, cool exterior. It seemed the fiery, passionate side of her had disappeared. Elizabeth had no desire to be a woman to show emotion, to provide any type of warmth, any love. It was partially what had pushed him away from her all those years ago. She had been passionate, loving one night, and then the next day it was as though nothing had ever happened. He wanted to know fire, heat, desire, and as far as he could tell, Elizabeth Moreland had only felt them one night in her entire life. Whether she ever would again? That was certainly none of his affair.

"Very well," was all he said. "Then let's see to these accounts, shall we?"

CHAPTER 8

*E*lizabeth called the partners' meeting for later that week. In the meantime, she was kept busy as she was true to her word and moved her residence to her grandmother's home. Her mother and father said nothing further about it, though she did feel the wrath of their disapproving stares.

"Mother, Father," she said on her last dinner in their townhouse, an occasion for which her brother had joined them. "I do not want there to be any ill feeling between us. But the truth of the matter is that I do not know when or if I will ever marry, and as Father has noted, I cannot live in your home forever, waiting for a day that may never come. Grandpapa generously gifted me his home, and by moving there neither you nor Terrence has to worry about me."

"I was never worried about you, Elizabeth," Terrence said, winking at her. He had a similar look to her, though his face was slightly fuller where she knew her own was pinched. Perhaps it was just because she had always been far more uptight than he. She wasn't sure why, but it seemed that all of the responsibility and practicality that Terrence lacked, Eliz-

ELLIE ST. CLAIR

abeth felt she had to make it up for it. They had the same tall, lanky build, though Terrence's smile came much easier.

"You'll make some bloke happy one day, I'm sure," he continued, ever the optimist.

"I am *not* so sure following her current decisions," her father opinioned, staring at them both down his disapproving nose. "As for you Terrence, running all over London doing Lord only knows what with who, I do not even want to imagine. It is certainly not the way to win yourself a bride."

"I'm young, Father!" Terrence said, practically laughing at Lord Moreland, which certainly didn't help matters. "I'll settle down in time, not to worry."

"I believe that is enough of this conversation at the dinner table," Elizabeth's mother said. "You can save it for a gentleman's discussion following dinner."

"Oh, Mother, it's not as though Elizabeth doesn't—"

"It is not Elizabeth's ears I am worried about," she said as her glance slid over to her daughter, clearly saying that she didn't think much of Elizabeth's own morals anymore. "But my own."

Terrence only snorted at that, while Elizabeth ignored it. One more meal, and then she would no longer have to worry about her parents' disapproval — or, at least, the constant reminder of it, for she was sure their disapproval would follow her no matter where she resided.

Besides, she didn't have *time* to worry about it any longer. Tomorrow was her first partners' meeting, and more than anything, she had to be well prepared for it.

She tried not to think of the fact that Gabriel might be there. Why it mattered, she wasn't sure. Perhaps it was because she knew he was not a man she could outwit. It bothered her that he would think her not capable to take on the position of senior partner. If he, a man who knew her well and was aware of her abilities, did not believe in her, then who would?

Her grandfather had, she reminded herself. Now, she just needed to show the rest of them what he had seen in her. If only she knew exactly what that had been. Her grandfather had certainly recognized her interest in the bank, which was why she had thought he had always been so ready to reward that interest with all of the instruction he had provided. Elizabeth reflected on all the tests he had put before her, all of the times he had asked for her opinion on a situation. She had enjoyed it, had appreciated the opportunity to feel useful, and for her opinions to be respected by a man such as him. But she had also always thought it was for her own benefit. Never had it crossed her mind that Thomas might be preparing her to step into the role — why he had never said a word of it to her, she would likely never know.

* * *

As GABRIEL DRESSED THAT MORNING, he actually found himself looking forward to an event on his schedule for the first time in many days. In fact, the last time he had anticipated anything so much, it had been his meeting with Elizabeth. Why that was, he had no idea. Perhaps the fact that, unlike most aspects of his life, it provided a situation he could entirely control — which was something that had become rather thrilling, and how sad was that?

"What do you think, Baxter?" he asked, turning from one side to the other in front of the floor-length mirror. Gabriel had always been quite aware that one was always taken much more seriously if he looked the part expected of him.

"You look quite exceptional, Your Grace, very much so," his valet said as he tied Gabriel's cravat, ensuring that it was immaculate. Gabriel eyed himself critically, wondering for a moment if the striped pattern on his waistcoat was *too* slimming, but then decided that it was just fine and he was being ridiculous. It was a bloody bank meeting, not a ball with the Prince Regent in attendance.

He arrived at the bank with some time to spare, as he always did, pleased that most recognized him when he entered.

"Good day, Your Grace," Anderson said, nodding his head as Gabriel walked by. Ah, Anderson. He was as much a part of this bank as the brick walls himself. Gabriel walked into the front foyer, gazing up at the stone vaulted ceiling above him, upon which stood the sculpted guardians of the bank who looked down from their dome at all below them.

Clerks lined the long counters throughout the room, some assisting their clients while others scribbled in ledger books, awaiting the next arrival. He passed them all, looking about him with new eyes at the Cararra marble walls around him, which were inlaid with engravings of the Clarke family crest as well as the alchemical symbol for gold, a nod to the origins of the bank. All of this, Thomas Clarke had built. And all of it was now under Elizabeth's watchful eye.

Gabriel took the large marble stairs that spiraled up and around the corner as he sought out the room where they would meet. It was large enough to fit a table for eight partners and, at times, the senior manager or a clerk, but it was also rather intimate, with dark shelves lining the room and portraits of Clarke descendants hanging on free space.

Gabriel was pleased to find that he was the first to arrive although, of course, Elizabeth was already present, seated at the head of the table with a couple of tidy stacks of paper and a pen in front of her.

"Prepared as usual?" he asked as he entered the room, though he didn't yet sit, but leaned against the doorjamb to watch her.

She jumped slightly when he spoke, as he had clearly taken her off guard.

"Of course," she said easily, hiding her momentary relapse of the wall of protectiveness with which she surrounded herself. "And you are early."

"Though it seems I could never be quite as early as you," he said, entering now, walking around the table to the chairs that were across from her, at what would become the back of the room. He always preferred to remain behind everyone else, so that he may observe the behavior of the rest of them before he came to his own opinions — or, at the very least, made them known.

She said nothing but simply returned to reviewing the paper in front of her. As silently as he could, he rounded the table so that he could peer over her shoulder.

"I see you've made an agenda."

While she had jumped rather high before, Elizabeth nearly flew from her seat now — her head came up, crashing into Gabriel's face. His eyes were instantly blinded by tears and a sudden shock of pain, and then he felt the filling of his nose the moment before it began to drip blood.

"My goodness!" Elizabeth said, coming to her feet completely now as she looked around desperately for something with which to help him. "I'm sorry, Gabriel, but you startled me. I had no idea you were there—"

He waved away her words as he held his nose in one hand, rifling through his pockets in search of his handkerchief with the other. Seeing what he was doing, she reached into his pocket for him, finding a beautifully starched white linen and holding it to his face, where it was instantly stained.

It was at that moment that the first partner arrived, stopping in the doorway with a stunned look on his face as he took in the scene in front of him.

69

"My word," said Mr. Cartwright, a longtime acquaintance of the Clarke family. "Is everything all right, Lady Elizabeth?"

"Fine, fine," she said, holding pressure on Gabriel's nose until he finally succeeded in swatting her hand away, noting as he did so that a fine bead of perspiration had broken out on her forehead. "I might just step away for a moment to find some assistance. If you'll excuse me, gentlemen."

She was out the door in a swish of black silk before either of them could say anything. Gabriel gingerly nodded at Cartwright as he felt the liquid beginning to lessen. It wasn't long before Elizabeth sailed back into the room, her practiced smile fixed on her face, though Gabriel could tell she was slightly agitated. Clearly, this wasn't how she had anticipated her first meeting to begin. She was accompanied by a footman, who quickly cleaned up any remaining mess. Unfortunately, no one could do anything to help Gabriel himself. His immaculate cravat was now stained with drops of red blood, though thankfully he had worn a black jacket over his waistcoat which hid any blemish. Gabriel sighed. This was undoubtedly not the impression he had hoped to make, and Baxter certainly would not be pleased with him.

"Thank you, Giles," Gabriel heard Elizabeth say to the footman as he took his seat at the back of the room. The remainder of the partners soon began to filter in and he greeted them as they arrived, most of them well known to him. They all looked at him with slight confusion, and he was well aware why — he wasn't sure anyone had ever seen him quite so disheveled, in addition to the fact that he rarely attended partners' meetings unless there was a matter upon which he needed to vote.

"Welcome, everyone," Elizabeth said, standing at the head of the table as she looked around the room, meeting the gaze of each of the six men. "Thank you for coming on rather short notice. Upon the passing of my grandfather, I thought it pertinent that we meet as soon as possible to ensure the continuity of the management of the bank. Unfortunately, Mr. Mortimer is unable to join us today due to his ill health."

One of the other gentlemen seated around the table leaned forward with a finger in the air.

"Ah, excuse me, Lady Elizabeth, but I must ask. Are you planning on actively working within your role as the senior partner?"

She looked at him for a moment as though she were confused.

"Well, yes, Mr. Lang. That is why I am here, leading this meeting."

"And how would you know what to do?"

He bestowed upon her a kindly grin, one that Gabriel was sure he meant to use in order to soften his words, but it didn't seem to make a difference to Elizabeth.

"Unlike my grandfather, Mr. Lang, who had to discover for himself how to both build and manage a bank, I had the opportunity to learn directly from his experience. I cannot tell you how many hours I have spent within the walls of this building. I believe he named me his successor in order to ensure that the legacy of this bank remains consistent, and I intend to uphold the trust he bestowed within me."

Her words were matter-of-fact, strong, and yet still respectful. Gabriel admired her manner — though, he always had.

"But, Lady Elizabeth," said another man, a young baronet, "Do you not have other commitments to which you must attend?"

"Do you mean accepting callers in my drawing room, Sir Gray?"

The man looked slightly chastened. "I would be referring to various social events that a woman such as yourself would be expected to attend."

"I can assure you, Sir Gray, that nothing is currently more important to me than this bank."

Which was exactly why many men would shy away from Elizabeth. Gabriel was sure that once she had committed herself to something such as this, it would remain her top priority. Where would a husband fit into that?

Not his business, he reminded himself. Though this meeting, this bank, certainly was.

The meeting continued on in this way for a time — partners politely questioning Elizabeth and her upcoming commitment to the role, how she would handle various aspects of the business. She answered it all with polite grace.

"Now," she said finally, "I do not want to take too much of your day today, but there is one last matter which we must discuss. I previously mentioned Mr. Mortimer's illness. Unfortunately, his health is failing, and he has decided that he is going to give up his share in the bank. As much as we will miss him and his wisdom, I'm sure we all understand his decision. He has not yet named a successor, but I anticipate him doing so very soon. If not, he will forfeit his shares, and we will determine whether the remainder of the partners will absorb them, or if we will choose to name another in his place. In the meantime—"

Her words stopped suddenly as the door swung open, emitting a familiar figure, who stood looking at them with a smug smile on his face.

Henry Clarke.

CHAPTER 9

"Cousin," he said, entering the room and taking one of the free seats at the table before looking around at the rest of the partners. "Gentlemen."

"Henry," Elizabeth said with a tight smile, for the benefit of the rest of them assembled around the room. In actuality, she would prefer to fling herself across the table and bodily push her cousin from the room. "While it is always a pleasure, I must ask you to wait outside until our meeting is concluded. This is for partners only."

"Ah, yes, I am well aware of the fact," he said with a self-satisfied grin. "Meet your newest partner."

Elizabeth narrowed her eyes as he slid a piece of paper across the table.

"You will find there, Cousin, that John Mortimer has signed his share over to me, Henry Clarke. I must tell you just how pleased I am to be here. Now, what have I missed?"

Elizabeth read the short note three times. It was as he said, though she wondered at the note's legitimacy. She was also unsure of how advanced Mr. Mortimer's illness had progressed, and whether he had the full capacity to make such a decision. Knowing Henry, she had a feeling that perhaps the man had been coerced. It sickened her, but there was nothing she could do about it at this moment.

"I do not believe we can accept this as fact, Henry, until we have heard from Mr. Mortimer himself. This is a document, but not a legal document. We require that or his very presence to provide us with this information. Is that not right, Mr. Bates?"

She looked to the bank's manager, who sat on the outskirts of the room as an observer, and he nodded.

"Come, Elizabeth, that is not very charitable of you, seeing how sick Mr. Mortimer is," Henry said, tilting his head as though he were the benevolent, gracious one when clearly he had taken full advantage of Mr. Mortimer's illness. In fact, Elizabeth was aware that poor Mr. Mortimer was suffering a malady of the brain, one that had left him devoid of most memories, be they more current or in the distant past. His family, however, was not particularly inclined to share such information, and Elizabeth would never betray their confidence. How she was to prove Henry's manipulation, she had no idea, but she certainly couldn't do it while entertaining this table of partners.

"I suggest we conclude for today," Elizabeth finally said. "Also, please remember," she shot a pointed gaze at Henry, "That as senior partner, I maintain final approval on the naming of all new partners."

She could tell some of the partners were slightly uneasy at this information, as they shifted in their chairs, for they were aware that she not only held the power to name partners but remove them as well. Regardless of their discomfort, however, she knew she must not relent.

"Now, it was wonderful to see you all. I wish you good day, and look forward to working with you in the future."

And with that they were soon gone, filtering slowly out of

the room, with but a couple of exceptions — Henry, and Gabriel. Elizabeth sighed. Two men she no longer had any desire to verbally parry with. She was tired and wished to retreat to her office — alone — before going home for some well-deserved rest.

"I do hope you are not threatening me, dear Cousin," Henry said as he rose from the table, leaning forward against it with his fists on its surface. "You should be welcoming me to the bank — it is a family affair, is it not?"

"Grandpapa had every opportunity to name you a part-ner, or to leave the bank to you, Henry, and he chose not to," she said, rising as well so that she was nearly as tall as he was. "What do you suppose that says about his faith in you?"

"So you played the part of the perfect little princess every time you saw him," Henry responded with a sneer. "You played it well, and look what you have for yourself. But it won't last. This is a man's world, Elizabeth, and not one where you belong."

She opened her mouth to retort, but another voice interrupted.

"Upon her conduct throughout this meeting, I would say that she belongs very well indeed," came Gabriel's deep, smooth voice from the corner of the room. In the last few moments, Elizabeth had almost forgotten that he was there, so silent he had been while Henry had taken all of her focus. Gabriel had likely been the one partner who had not ques-tioned her throughout the meeting. She had watched him, as much as she tried not to. He had sat back, his fingers steepled under his chin, his blue eyes shrewd as he listened to her as well as others around the table.

"Ah, the Duke of Clarence," Henry said, turning to look at him. "What an interesting statement, coming from you."

The way he looked at Gabriel, Elizabeth felt there was something unspoken behind his words, though she had no idea what that could be. "I do remember a time when you would have been her savior. Though not only Elizabeth's but plenty of other women's as well, am I not correct?"

Gabriel's eyes hardened, and Elizabeth couldn't stop the memories from rushing into her own mind.

"That's enough, Clarke."

But Gabriel's words of warning certainly weren't enough to stop Henry, a man who had no respect for the nobility — nor most people in particular, if Elizabeth thought on it.

"In fact," Henry continued conspiratorially, "I would be interested to learn more about what happened with the lovely Lady Julia — Elizabeth's good friend, of course. You pursued her in Newmarket, did you not? It was quite the scandal when she chose a groom over the Duke of Clarence."

"I believe Eddie Francis is actually a jockey, Clarke," was all Gabriel said, but Elizabeth noted that his entire body had turned rather stiff, as though he were holding himself back. Henry was goading him on purpose, of course, and while Elizabeth wanted to shove Henry's words aside, she had to admit that some of them were getting through to her. For as much as Henry was being an idiot, he had reminded her of all Gabriel had done to attempt to court Julia, one of her closest of friends, but a few months ago with Elizabeth looking on. Elizabeth had thought it was all some game to him, but why he might care any longer about what she may think or feel, she had no idea.

"Julia is very happy," Elizabeth said simply. "And that is all that matters. Now, Henry, it is time for you to leave, or I will have some of the footmen come and escort you out."

"No need, I have another engagement," he said, making his way to the door. "But rest assured, Cousin, this is not the last time you will see me within the walls of this bank."

With one last sly smile and an exaggerated bow, he was out the door, pulling it closed behind him.

Elizabeth all but collapsed in a chair, exhaustion filtering out of her, when suddenly she remembered Gabriel was still there.

"Enjoy the show?" she asked.

"It was no show," he said, and she looked up to see that his eyes were bright and clear, with no hint of any game on his face. "I was serious in what I said. You did well today."

"Thank you for your approval," she said, unable to help the sarcasm in her tone. She was annoyed by the reminder of Newmarket, and she couldn't rid the thought from her mind.

"You're upset about Lady Julia," Gabriel said, as perceptive as ever.

"Not at all," she said, attempting nonchalance. "There is nothing to be upset about, is there?"

"I am happy to explain the situation," he offered, but she shook her head, not wanting to hear any more.

"There is nothing to explain," she said. "In all honesty I am simply tired and have been longing to go home since halfway through that meeting — or shall I say, interrogation."

"You responded well," he complimented her once more, and she narrowed her eyes, wondering what his current angle was — for Gabriel always had an angle, in everything he did. "What?" he asked at her look. "You did. I am only telling the truth."

He looked so handsome, standing there in the late afternoon sunlight that filtered in through the window, his typically immaculate hair ever so slightly mussed, by she herself when she had attempted to stem the flow of blood from his nose, that she nearly forgot everything in the past and approached him as a woman would a man she had a deep connection with.

His cravat was slightly crooked now, and hesitantly, she couldn't help herself from stepping up and ever so slightly straightening it. He caught her fingers in his warm, strong hands, clutching them to his chest as he looked down at her and her breath caught in her throat.

His lips were a breath away from her forehead as he tilted his head down toward her, and she could practically feel his pulse where his hands touched hers. Not wanting to stain them with ink, she had removed her gloves in order to take notes during the meeting, and now she was, at this moment, glad she had done so, for the feel of his bare skin upon hers was exquisite.

She closed her eyes as a flood of feeling coursed through her — the attraction that had instantly bound her to him, that she'd had to fight even when she hated him so; and the way he made her feel, as though she were the only woman in the world that mattered, that he would always be there to make everything right.

His prominent, patrician nose brushed against hers, and then under a will of its own, her head tilted up and her lips met his. The first taste was soft, hesitant, a reminder of who they were and all that had been before, and then once they found one another again, their lips fused together, locked on one another as though it was where they were always supposed to be.

Elizabeth hated him for weakening her like this, for making her forget all resolve and submit to him once more, but in the same breath, this was all she had been longing for since they had parted ways five years ago, despite her denial even to herself. He was the one man who had matched her perfectly, was the reason that no one else she had met since him had ever seemed to suffice.

Gabriel's right hand left hers, coming around to the back of her head, cupping it as he held her against him in such a possessive manner.

Which caused another image to suddenly fill her head. One of Gabriel and another woman — a widow his elder by ten years, if Elizabeth recalled correctly. She had happened upon them at a ball one evening, when he was holding Lady Pomfret in the very same way he held her now.

It was more than enough to cause her to bring her hands up against his chest and push away from him as she stepped back out of his arms' reach, listening to the sound of her own harsh breath coming hard and fast.

"Elizabeth," he said, his voice just over a whisper, and it seemed as though the kiss had affected him nearly as much as it had her. Or perhaps it was an act, some game he was playing. He had always liked to manipulate, hadn't he? Was this all to do with the bank, some sort of play for power?

"That was a mistake," she said, willing her voice to be firm, to not betray the turmoil of emotion within her chest.

"I don't think so," he said, his smoky voice swirling about her, tempting her to come deeper into its depths.

"I know so," she said resolutely, straightening as she willed her mind to take control of her emotions once more. "I see no reason why you and I cannot be friendly acquaintances, colleagues in this bank. Anything more than that will never be — not again."

His stoic countenance faltered for but a moment, and Elizabeth wondered at what she saw there within his eyes as he stared at her — was it regret? Disappointment? But no. The Duke of Clarence never regretted a thing.

"Elizabeth, I am sorry you were hurt—"

"Hurt?" Elizabeth choked out. "Gabriel, we were to be *married*. And you— you betrayed me."

She took in a deep, shaky breath as she forced herself to calm down, to conceal her emotions. Allowing him to realize just how much he had hurt her would do nothing but leave her even more vulnerable in front of him. She was far better off to keep all of their interactions to business, which was why she would never allow them to be alone like this again.

"I know," he said softly. "And I am very sorry for that."

"Those are but words, Gabriel."

He nodded. "If I could change the past, I would. But alas... I cannot. The man I was five years ago, however, is not the man I am today. Can you not see that, Elizabeth? Realize that I am here for you?"

"Those are pretty words, Gabriel, but mean nothing."

"Then look beyond words," he said, stepping back toward her. "Tell me that you didn't feel something when I held you in my arms, when my lips touched yours. Tell me and I will go and never speak of it again."

Elizabeth did all she could to force her racing heart to slow as she looked up at him.

"I— I," She couldn't say it. She had to, needed to, and yet... the words refused to roll off her tongue. Damn it all. The worst part about it? He knew.

"Goodbye, Gabriel. I will see you at the next meeting. My apologies about your nose."

CHAPTER 10

*E*lizabeth, ever the perfect hostess, poured tea for the three women who sat in a circle around the service in the middle of her grandparents' drawing room. Which was also hers now, she realized, though it was all still rather incredulous.

"Besides everything that has happened, how are you feeling?" Sarah asked, her brown eyes soft as she gazed upon Elizabeth, as perceptive as ever to Elizabeth's emotions.

Elizabeth paused for a moment before she poured the third cup, looking up at her friend. She had been so busy and so concerned with taking on all of the responsibility awaiting her that it had been some time since she had stopped and considered how it was all affecting her. In fact, she preferred it that way. She hated to dwell on her emotions, to allow grief to creep in. It only left her feeling drained and desolate.

"I miss my grandfather, that is for certain," she said slowly, putting down the teapot for a moment. "Though it has helped both me and my grandmother for us to be together in this time, I believe. And yet somehow, being here, in his home, in his office at the bank, has allowed me to feel as though he is still with me, if that makes sense at all."

She hastily blinked away the tears that suddenly threatened as her friends nodded in understanding.

"It's good to give yourself time to react to tragedy," Sarah said encouragingly, but Elizabeth shook her head, dismissing her words. To allow the emotion in now, at this moment, would only cause her to lose all control, and that, even in front of her closest friends, she would never do.

Julia, her tiny frame already becoming slightly round with the child she had just discovered she was expecting, laid a hand upon Elizabeth's. "You know if there is anything we can do, we are more than happy to help. I know that sounds trite, but it is the truth."

Elizabeth smiled at her. "I appreciate that, I do. But you have much to worry about yourself."

Julia waved a hand. "All is well with us. Lots of travel, to be sure, but the timing could not have been better, for the racing season will be over by the time this babe is to be born."

"I can hardly wait to see how you fare," said Phoebe with a sigh, already having one at home herself. "I do hope yours sleeps."

They smiled the shared smile of understanding between two mothers before returning to the matter at hand. Elizabeth rather wished they would continue speaking about children, for she didn't have much interest in continuing their previous conversation.

"How is everything at the bank?" Phoebe asked, coming to the business side of Elizabeth's life which was, of course, unsurprising as she was involved in business herself, secretly running *The Women's Weekly*, a publication for women.

"It all seems well so far," Elizabeth said slowly. "We have not had any clients leave — yet, although I have heard some rumblings that there are a few who are not exactly content with a woman at the helm of the financial institution holding all of their wealth. My plan is to try to meet with as many people as I can, to allow them to see that I am knowledgeable and competent, that there is nothing to fear."

"Which is wise," said Phoebe with a nod.

"I hope so, though it means a lot of work to come soon," Elizabeth agreed. "As for the partners, there is certainly much doubt there as well, though I hope our last meeting solved some of that. Though it brought about one more issue with which I had not thought to have to contend."

"Which is…?" Julia asked.

"Henry," said Elizabeth, rolling her eyes, and then proceeded to tell them about his entry into the bank, how he had found a share for himself, and his vow to bring about her downfall. "How he would do so, I have no idea, but he seems quite intent on winning for himself the senior partnership. Why he would think it is attainable to him, I have no idea. His ideas for the bank, told to me himself, are ludicrous and would destroy everything my grandfather built up. I cannot allow it to happen."

"And you won't," said Phoebe, determination in her eyes as she sat up straighter and poured the last tea that Elizabeth had forgotten.

"Oh, I'm so sorry," she said, reaching for the teapot, but Phoebe waved her away.

"You have much on your mind."

Elizabeth nodded, hoping they were done with discussing her life, but then she caught Sarah looking at her with pursed lips.

"There is something you are not telling us," Sarah said at Elizabeth's returned stare.

"I've told you all," Elizabeth said, picking up her teacup and taking a sip while she attempted to meet Sarah's eye, though she couldn't help but allow her gaze to wander behind her at the pale golden walls where they met the white wainscotting, and the watercolors of every flower in England hanging above them between portraits of ancestors. It would not be Elizabeth's choice of decor, but her grandmother had painted many of the still lifes and landscapes herself, which meant that they would likely remain on the walls indefinitely, for Elizabeth could never bring herself to remove them.

"I don't think so," said Sarah resolutely. "There is more. More to do with how you feel about something — or someone."

Elizabeth placed her teacup on her lap.

"There is no one."

"Aha!" Julia said with a bit of a grin. "That means for certain there is. Who have you even had time to see lately?"

"No one at all," Elizabeth said crisply, though she could feel warmth in her cheeks and knew they were likely turning very bright pink.

"Bank partners and clients," Phoebe said shrewdly, and at that, Julia turned toward her with widened eyes.

"The Duke of Clarence!" she exclaimed, and Elizabeth shook her head, despite the fact her cheeks felt as though they were now flaming red.

"I have seen him, yes," she said in an attempt to dissuade their interest. "But I feel nothing for him."

"After seeing the two of you together in Newmarket, I can certainly say that you feel *something*," said Julia. "Whether you feel hatred or anger or frustration, I am not sure, but I have never seen you act the same around another as you did with him — that you cannot deny."

"That may be true," Elizabeth said with a shrug. "I do despise him, and I have a good reason for it."

They all stared at her, clearly waiting to hear just what, exactly, that reason was.

She sighed, realizing that she could not put it off any longer — she had to share the story with these women, who had shared everything with her.

"Very well," she said, clenching her fingers in her lap so that she didn't tap them distractedly on the table. "Gab— the Duke and I, were young. I was only eighteen, having just had my come-out, he a couple of years older. Our parents were friends, through my father's side, and when we were children, we had known one another. We were reacquainted one night at a party. We… well, we had some type of instant attraction to one another that I never knew was possible. At the time, in my youthful innocence, I thought it was love at first sight, but I know now it was *lust* at first sight. We danced, we flirted, we talked about anything and everything. He was the first gentleman who had ever seemed to actually care about my opinion on anything that mattered. We went for a walk in the gardens, having drunk a great deal of champagne and, well…"

She trailed off, though she was well aware of just how intently the three women were staring at her.

"Well, *what?*" demanded Phoebe.

"We happened upon a gazebo, and our attraction for one another became more than an attraction, which, regretfully, we acted upon. I cannot say that he took advantage of me — I asked him for it all, and he complied. Anyway," she hurried along past that part, for she could see that she had completely shocked three women who were far from likely to allow much to shock them. "He began to court me, and eventually offered to marry me. He only did so because he knew it was the right thing to do. In the meantime, it didn't stop him from having additional *relationships* with other women. When I found out, having quite literally walked into a situation in which he was with one of his other acquaintances, I called it all off and told him to never speak to me again. He complied — until Newmarket."

Even speaking of it once more caused Elizabeth to tremor with anger, hurt, and frustration that the man she had thought she loved quite obviously did not love her in return. How could he have loved her and then treated her so? It was unfathomable. It had been the ultimate betrayal — for him to take up with another woman, especially at a public event, where any and all could have seen him. Not only had he cared nothing for how she felt, but he had cared equally as little for his own reputation. No, Gabriel Lockridge had revealed through his actions exactly what he thought of her, and she refused to give into him again.

Phoebe was the first to regain her wits and asked a logical question.

"But how did he receive his partnership in the bank, then?"

Elizabeth nodded. This, she had no trouble answering. "Once it became obvious that he and I were going to enter into marital bliss, my grandfather Clarke wanted to come to know him better. The two of them enjoyed the company of one another, and became unlikely but fast friends. Thinking the Duke was going to become my husband, when a share in the bank came open, Grandpapa asked if he would be interested. Gab— the Duke said he was, but I'm not sure whether or not he was just being polite. He didn't take much interest in the bank's affairs until this past meeting, and even then he just sat there like a frog on a log throughout the meeting."

"But you still care for him," Sarah said, and Elizabeth turned to look at her, incredulous.

"I certainly do not," she said, holding her nose high in the air.

"Then why does your face take on that expression when you speak of him?"

"What expression?"

"The one in which your eyes slightly soften and yet your mouth hardens — as though you are trying to deny what you feel."

"That is ridiculous," Elizabeth said. "Am I still attracted to him? Of course I am. I will always be attracted to him. Who wouldn't be?"

"I wasn't," Julia said with a shrug, and Elizabeth tilted her head to look at her with a bit of an eye-roll.

"Well, anyway. I still don't know what that was all about in Newmarket, Julia. But I will not forget what happened between me and the Duke of Clarence in the past. I will not risk my heart once more."

"That was a few years ago now," Sarah said softly. "Could he have changed?"

Elizabeth frowned.

"I suppose he could have, in some ways," she said truthfully. "Though I rather doubt it."

"I do have to say," Julia added, speaking slowly, "That there seemed to be more at play than what appeared on the surface when we were in Newmarket. It was as though he knew exactly what was happening, and was trying to… help things along, if you will. I have no idea whether or not that was the truth, but that was how it felt to me."

"He manipulates situations," said Elizabeth with some ire. "He always has. It's some type of game to him, to see how he can use people like pawns on his chessboard in order to reach the King."

"Well, all worked out for me," Julia said with a soft smile. "But I can certainly understand your concern."

"I think you are correct to avoid him," Phoebe said, and Elizabeth looked gratefully toward her. "Can you really trust him? Though, never tell him that I suggested otherwise, for I wouldn't want to ruin his friendship with Jeffrey."

"Of course not," Elizabeth assured her.

"Thank you. And what will you do now?" Phoebe asked.

"I will finish moving into this house," Elizabeth said, waving her hands around her. "I will get to work at the bank, and determine exactly how to keep my cousin Henry from being a problem. If I choose to do so, I can decline his partnership, but that may raise the ire of the other partners, causing them to be concerned about the future. And in the meantime, I will ignore Gabriel Lockwood."

CHAPTER 11

 *hree months later*

ELIZABETH WAS thankful to finally dress in lavender. It felt joyful after so many days of black, over and over. In all honesty, she felt her grandfather, had he been asked his opinion, would have far preferred that they wear color to celebrate his life. But, this was expected, and while the majority of her life these days seemed to be going against what others felt she should do, in this she would follow protocol.

"Good morning," she said as she entered the breakfast room where her grandmother awaited. They had settled into what Elizabeth felt was a delightful routine, having breakfast together in the cream room that reminded Elizabeth of dining on clouds. There was the slightest bit of light blue scattered throughout the room in paintings and upon the upholstery of the chairs, but even the table was in the lightest pine that added to the brightness of the room, while the east-facing window allowed the morning sun to permeate the room.

"Good morning, darling," Justine said, her face wrinkled into her usual smile. Elizabeth knew how much her grandmother missed her husband, but at the same time, Justine had a positive outlook on life and all that it included. "Did you sleep well?"

"I did," said Elizabeth with a smile, though it was a complete lie. Every night she lay in bed, staring up at the ceiling as her mind was in turmoil over all she had to consider following her day at the bank. She hoped her concerns would lessen in time, but for now, she had far too much worry over which decisions were right, who she could trust, and who would prefer not to have a woman leading them. She wished she could ask her grandfather about her choices, but alas, she could only assume what he may think.

Her grandmother looked at her shrewdly now, perhaps guessing everything that was running through her mind.

"Your grandfather brought his worries home too," Justine said, taking a sip of her tea.

"He did?" Elizabeth asked, raising her head from her plate to look at her grandmother.

"Of course he did," said Justine, pulling her wrapper closer around her. She never dressed before noon — she said she had no reason to, so why not be comfortable while she breakfasted and read her papers? "Sometimes he spoke to me of them. He said it helped. I don't want you to feel any pressure to do so, but you are always welcome to; I'd like you to know that."

"Thank you, Grandmother," Elizabeth said. "At the moment, it is primarily gaining the trust and confidence of clients and partners. A female senior partner is not exactly the norm."

"No," Justine agreed. "But your grandfather wouldn't have

named you in his place had he not trusted in you. They will come around — you will know how best to prove yourself."

"Thank you," said Elizabeth with a smile. How different were her breakfast conversations here than with her parents. "I do appreciate that."

"Has the awful business with your cousin now concluded?"

"Henry's contesting of the will? Yes, thank goodness," Elizabeth said with a sigh. "I have no idea why he would ever consider that the will would not be valid, considering who Grandpapa was and how careful he was in such matters. However, after the interviews, it was concluded that there were multiple witnesses present through both the drafting and the signing of the will and, of course, Grandpapa was in a sound state of mind when he made it."

"Well, I am relieved it is finished now and put to rest so that you can continue with what is important," Justine said, and Elizabeth chose not to share her additional fears that Henry would only find new methods to attempt to undermine her authority and her position.

"Now," her grandmother continued. "Have you decided what you will be wearing tonight?"

"Wearing? Tonight?" Elizabeth searched her mind as she tried to determine to what her grandmother was referring.

"To the party your parents are hosting, darling," her grandmother said with a bit of a laugh. "Are you so preoccupied that you have forgotten?"

"Actually, I did," Elizabeth said with a sigh. "I do not think I'm going to attend."

"But you have to!" Justine said, and Elizabeth looked at her in surprise. She never thought that her grandmother of all people would make her attend a party full of members of the nobility. Noting Elizabeth's questioning gaze, her grandmother continued. "Part of being senior partner of a bank is the relationships you develop with clients. It was one of the aspects of his position that your grandfather was best at, and how he grew the bank into one of London's finest. You have to cultivate strong partnerships, allow potential clients to get to know you and trust you. Sometimes what you can accomplish in one night of uncomfortable conversations is more than you could in weeks of meetings."

Elizabeth nodded slowly. "Of course. I should have known that."

"These are things that take time to learn," Justine said. "Soon they will be second nature."

"Very well," Elizabeth said with a sigh. "To the party we go."

ELIZABETH CLIMBED the steps of her parents' home with some trepidation. She had returned a few times, of course, to call upon them and to have dinner. But this was the first event with others in attendance — and, thinking of that, she wondered just who would be here this evening.

Of course, there was one person in particular she was wondering about, but she didn't want to give that thought any credence.

She hadn't seen Gabriel since the partners' meeting, after which they had inadvertently kissed. He had attempted to call upon her one day, but she hadn't been home — which she had been relieved about once learning of his arrival, for she had no idea how she would have greeted him. *Hello, Gabriel, nice to see you. I hope you didn't read much into that kiss, for it meant nothing.* Then he would agree, and all would be back to how it was, would it not? But that conversation would be particularly uncomfortable, and she would rather avoid it, despite the fact that, at some point, their paths were bound to cross again, considering their social circles and involvement in the bank.

Her grandmother squeezed her arm.

"Smile, dear," she said, and Elizabeth complied just as the butler opened the door and led her in to greet her parents, who were perfunctorily polite.

Elizabeth had taken only two steps into the room when her eyes were instantly drawn to one man, the dark, deceptive Duke of Clarence, as though there was a magnet that captured her gaze in its grip. Despite the fact the room was filled with people, all she could see was him. Why, oh why, did it have to be so? She didn't want to feel anything for Gabriel. She didn't want to be inexplicably attracted to him, to long to feel his arms around her and his lips upon hers once more. But she couldn't help her yearning any more than she could keep from breathing.

Which was why, she determined as she tore her gaze away to peruse the rest of the room, she would stay far, far away from him.

* * *

IT WAS AS THOUGH he had traveled back in time.

For when Elizabeth walked into the room, Gabriel was reminded of the moment, years ago now, when he had first seen her in her womanly form as she had entered that party that had forever changed them both. Tonight, as she walked into her parents' receiving room on the arm of her grandmother, Gabriel was once again instantly captivated.

He had hardly been able to rid her from his mind since he had kissed her at the bank those few months ago now. He had attempted to call upon her, but he had received her message clearly — she wanted nothing to do with him. She was a woman with a long memory, one who may have forgiven, but had not forgotten.

Gabriel had long ago accepted the fact that he had ruined any opportunity he would ever have with her, and had moved on. Or so he thought.

Seeing her here now, he was reminded of why she outshone any and every other woman he met.

It wasn't as though she was a stunning beauty. She was pretty, graceful, and had an elegance the likes of which he had never before seen in another. But it was the knowledge of who she was, all she had accomplished, and the confidence with which she carried herself that was unmatched. She walked with the air of a woman who cared not of what others thought, though he was aware that this was truly not the case. Elizabeth cared. Gabriel knew because he had seen the true woman underneath the air of unconcern. He could tell as her unsettling violet gaze surveyed the room that she didn't particularly care to be here, and would likely rather be anywhere else — particularly the bank, he assumed.

This, however, was her parents' party, and she couldn't very well avoid attending — which was why he had chosen to accept tonight's invitation from Lord and Lady Shannon.

He could practically feel when Elizabeth's gaze passed over him, and as much as he knew she had seen him, he could tell she was attempting to pretend she had not. So she was not yet ready to see beyond their past. Very well.

Gabriel had told himself it was probably better that way. How would a woman like Elizabeth, with her position and her disapproval of most within society, fit into his life, anyway?

At one point in time, she had, he reminded himself but shook his head to toss away the thought.

"Clarence." Gabriel turned behind him to see who it was greeting him, pleased to find two of his closest friends, David

Redmond, as well as Jeffrey Worthington, Marquess of Berkley.

"Gentlemen," he said. "A pleasure to see you here this evening."

"Who did Shannon and his wife not invite?" Jeffrey asked with a raised eyebrow. "It seems as though half of the *ton* has gathered in this room."

He was right. The Moreland family had a substantial home within London, though nothing at all like Gabriel's own.

"Are they not still in mourning?" Redmond asked, and Gabriel shrugged. "It has been a few months, it is true, and Lady Shannon continues to wear black."

"Still..."

"Each to their own, I suppose," Berkley said, and Gabriel nodded. As far as he was aware, Lady Shannon hadn't been particularly close to her father in recent years.

"Even Clarke's wife is here!" Redmond continued on, clearly unable to process the fact that the family had disregarded some of the mourning procedures.

"Thomas Clarke was an interesting character," said Gabriel, smiling as he remembered one of his many conversations with the man. "He felt that after the death of someone one truly loved, life should be celebrated. He hated the idea of wearing black, of keeping oneself from any type of merriment. I assume his wife holds similar ideals."

"Interesting," Berkley said, while Redmond raised his eyebrows, clearly still somewhat confused.

"Is your wife in attendance tonight, Berkley?" he asked, to which the man nodded. "Of course. She wouldn't miss this. Far too much to write about — ah, that is, write to Lady Julia about. In letters."

Gabriel smiled. While he was well aware of Lady Phoebe's activities as publisher of *The Women's Weekly* — one of

England's few publications written entirely for women, which often questioned the very ideals of society — Redmond had no such knowledge, and nor would Berkley be wanting to share that information.

"There she is now," Berkley continued. "With Miss Jones. Lady Elizabeth is now joining them."

Gabriel was surprised to see that Elizabeth did not remain with them long, but was soon moving about the room, greeting those who had gathered. So, she was taking her responsibilities as senior partner much more seriously than even he had expected. *Good for her*, he thought, a strange pride filling his chest. Which was ridiculous. He had no reason to be proud of her. He was simply an acquaintance, and she was her own woman, which she had made very clear.

And now that woman was coming their way.

"Good evening, gentlemen," she said with a nod as she joined them. "I am so pleased to see you this evening."

She was a vision. She wore a dress of gray so light it was nearly white, and all he could see was the red of her hair and the violet of her eyes.

"Good evening, Lady Elizabeth," said Berkley. "You look lovely. I have not seen you since the death of your grandfather so I would like to offer my condolences. I hear you are doing well taking his place at Clarke & Co."

"I do not believe anyone can take his place with the same excellence to which he always kept the bank," she said demurely. "But thank you for your kind words."

"I'm surprised to see your grandmother here," Redmond said, and Gabriel wanted to roll his eyes at the man, who had a tendency to say things that weren't particularly fitting for the moment.

Elizabeth, however, ever polite, smiled prettily at him. "My grandmother feels my grandfather would want her to continue to enjoy life. She still mourns him very deeply, I can assure you."

Redmond colored, having been chastened appropriately.

"My apologies, Lady Elizabeth, I never meant—"

"Not to worry," she said. "I would far prefer the question to be asked of me directly than to be spoken of behind my back."

"Fair enough," Redmond said, his wide, well-known charming smile breaking out over his face. Gabriel wished he wouldn't look at Elizabeth with such admiration.

"Would you care to dance, Lady Elizabeth?" Gabriel asked, finally finding his voice.

"I'm not sure..." she said, looking around, clearly wanting to do anything *but* dance with him.

"Just one dance," he said smoothly, and he saw the hesitation on her face, but he could tell by the slight panic that passed over her eyes that she could not think of an excuse.

"Very well," she mumbled, and then offered her hand to him.

CHAPTER 12

*E*lizabeth slowly placed her gloved hand in Gabriel's. So much for her plan to avoid him. But she could hardly have passed by these three gentlemen — one the husband of one of her closest friends, another a bank partner — when she was greeting everyone else in the room.

Gabriel gave her a warm smile, one she would have labeled seductive, but she knew far better than that. It was the look he gave every woman he met and almost all fell for it — with a few exceptions, if his encounters with Julia had proven anything.

Elizabeth vowed she wouldn't give in. The only way around that was to not meet his gaze. She looked straight ahead at the other couples who surrounded them on the dance floor. It was a waltz, of course. She could hardly have worse luck.

Gabriel turned her and took her waist in one hand, capturing her other gloved hand in one of his own. He was dressed beautifully tonight, as he always was. He wore a cobalt blue tailcoat with fawn trousers, perfectly fitted over a white shirt and waistcoat. His hair was expertly coiffed, his dark chestnut curls the envy of most women, including Elizabeth herself.

"You look lovely tonight," he murmured in her ear, and his smoky voice against her neck sent tremors down her spine. Elizabeth was a tall woman, but he was the perfect height beside her — tall enough himself, but not so much so that he dwarfed her. His chin could rest almost exactly on the top of her head if he so chose to tilt it forward.

"Thank you," she said softly, unable to find any witty words to throw at him at this moment. He was being polite, and she would be the same. They could do that, could they not? Be acquaintances, partners of the same business? "You look fine yourself, as always."

"Ah, do you think so, then?" he asked, and she could practically hear his mouth curving into a smile, though she refused to look up at him to see. For then she would be lost in his deep blue eyes, and all of her vows to keep herself from falling for him once more would be forgotten.

"Everyone believes so," she answered deftly. "Tell me, have you been keeping well?"

"I have," he said. "And you?"

"I suppose I have as well. Though it has been a... busy time."

Apparently, he read more into her words, words that were so carefully cultivated within this artificial conversation that was becoming rather ridiculous. When would this dance be over, so that she could continue on her way and take care of her necessary business?

"Have you been having any difficulties with partners and clients?"

"The partners seem to be split about equally on their thoughts of me," she said, not betraying how much it hurt that they would doubt her so, as expected as it was. "I believe they would all come around, were it not for Henry. He has been doing all he can to stir doubt in their minds as to my capabilities as well as the bank's reputation with a woman at the helm. While fortunately, the interrogation into the will's validity proved all was credible, it did create some doubts as to the bank's future, another obstacle to now overcome. I also visited Mr. Mortimer, and he could not remember signing over his share to Henry. His wife does recall Henry coming to visit, but she was not in the room with the two of them. Mr. Mortimer also had no recollection of who I was. His memory is fading fast, but his family has no wish to discuss it. So much so, that they will not come forward and deny Henry's claim, despite their anger at his treachery."

"Do they not want to ensure the partnership stays within the family, despite what that could mean?"

"His wife and two currently unwed daughters have no wish for anything to do with the bank," Elizabeth explained. "They likely would have forfeited the partnership back to the bank, so they are not angry enough to actually take any action. In fact, one of the daughters is not so much angry now, but hopes that Henry might ask for her hand, and then the partnership would be retained within the family anyway."

"Has Henry any inclination to marry the girl?" Gabriel asked, surprise in his tone, and Elizabeth smiled ruefully.

"Likely not. I suspect that he has begun a flirtation in order to win the family to his side, but I cannot prove anything. All I can do now, if I choose, is to deny his partnership, but I'm not sure how the other partners would react."

"Please know that I am happy to help you in any way that I can."

"I appreciate that, Gab— Your Grace, I do, but this is something I must do on my own."

"You are a remarkable woman, Elizabeth."

She wished he wouldn't say such things to her. It softened her resolve toward him, one that needed to be built up.

"I am only doing what must be done," she said. "What my grandfather would have wanted."

"But is this what *you* want?"

She looked up at him finally, then, as she thought on his words and tried to determine just how to best answer them. His eyes met hers, probing deeply, and she felt that connection they had once shared — the ability to talk to him about things that actually mattered, to be able to share her innermost thoughts. She had to be careful, however, for he could now use those words against her.

"It is what I want," she finally answered as she thought of her role with the bank, the fulfillment it provided her. "I enjoy having purpose and, if I am being honest, the power that comes with such a role. It is somewhat frightening, I suppose, to know that decisions I make could so greatly affect many others — especially those who have their entire life savings with us, for however big or small that might be, it is a fortune to each of them. And yet... I do not trust anyone else with such decisions. I must remember that my grandfather asked this of me, and it is important that I follow through."

"So you are happy then?"

"I am. Or, I will be once I feel surer of myself, more at ease that this will not all be wrenched away from me."

"This doubt, this fight," he said, "You must know it will never completely disappear. There have been women in banking before, it is true, but not many. This is an industry controlled by men—"

"Aren't they all?" she interrupted, but he continued.

"—And there will always be men who feel threatened by you, who will not want to see you succeed. Are you prepared to fight that battle for the rest of your life?"

"Are you attempting to dissuade me?" she asked, pulling back from him. "Do you still doubt me?"

"I do not doubt you," he said. "Not at all. I am aware of your abilities. And yet, I wonder if this will be a happy life, always fighting to prove your worth."

"Whether it will be a happy life or not, I cannot answer that, not at the moment," she said, looking back at his chest instead of into his face. "But it is a life that matters, and one that I will not give up on just because there are those who doubt me and want to see to my downfall. In fact, that is all the more reason to fight on."

"Then I offer you my support as well as my admiration once more," he said. "For it will not be easy, but if anyone can do this, it is you."

She nodded, unsure of how she felt about his words. Was he purposefully trying to goad her, or was he seriously unsure of whether she was able to handle this or not?

As if reading her thoughts, he lowered his head so that his mouth brushed against her ear ever so slightly. "I do not doubt you, Elizabeth, never think that. I never have."

Elizabeth nodded, wondering how much longer she had to continue waltzing within his embrace. For she could no longer deny just how attracted to him she was. Yet, how could that be, that she would still want a man who had treated her so poorly years ago? Not only that, but he clearly had conflicting thoughts about her current role. She knew if she were ever to marry — particularly a man like the Duke, though of course not *this* duke — she may have to relinquish much to him, for all of her income would become his. Thanks to her grandfather's wording within the will, the shares and the inheritance would remain hers, but everything else could never be — anything she further earned would be his, as was the law, the injustice of which Phoebe was always fighting against with her paper. Elizabeth didn't want to be another woman who left everything she held important to her for a man, no matter who that man was.

But why did Gabriel have to be not only so devastatingly handsome but also so witty, so intelligent? She had never felt this way about another man and she likely never would again. She reminded herself that for all of his redeeming qualities, he could also be annoyingly infuriating.

At last, the final chords of the song sounded, and Elizabeth stepped away from Gabriel as quickly as she could.

"So eager to be rid of me?" he quipped with a raised eyebrow, and she felt her cheeks redden.

"I must see to the other guests. It is important that they all come to know me."

"Ah, potential clients," he said with a knowing smile. Of course, he saw right through her and her motives.

"I suppose so," she said, raising a silk-clad shoulder.

"May I call upon you tomorrow?" he asked, shocking her as he escorted her off the dance floor.

"Call upon me?" she repeated, sounding like an idiot. "Why would you want to do that?"

"Is it not obvious?" He quirked an eyebrow.

"Well, I suppose it is, but Gabriel ... it has been years. Months since we even last spoke. Why all of a sudden—"

He laid a fingertip on her lips, and she jerked away, aware that they were being watched.

"Hush," he said. "I will explain all — when I call upon you tomorrow. Will you be home?"

"In the late afternoon," she finally grumbled, now simply wanting to be rid of him with all of the eyes upon them. "After banking hours. But do not get any ideas."

He laughed then, a deep, rich chuckle that tickled her very soul. He raised her hand to his lips, kissed it, and then turned away, and she could practically feel the burn where his lips had been, despite the layer of her glove between them.

It took not a minute for Elizabeth to be flanked by Phoebe and Sarah.

"Oh, Elizabeth, I do believe the Duke still has feelings for you," Sarah said, her words coming out in a whisper.

"He is playing a game," Elizabeth said flatly. "I know it. If he actually has feelings, why did he not do the right thing years ago, or attempt to have anything to do with me between then and now? Why now, not long after I was named the senior partner of the bank?"

"Perhaps it is the fact he has seen you again, and you have refocused his energy?" Sarah said as though she were guessing.

"He could have grown up," said Phoebe, and Elizabeth looked over at her, surprised she would be trusting Gabriel's current motives. "What?" she asked, seeing Elizabeth's expression. "I am not saying that is the case, I am only saying it is a possibility. One can never know for sure. Anyway, he is a powerful man, and in your current position, you wouldn't want to turn him against you. Best to play his game, determine what he wants. But Elizabeth," she said, turning and narrowing her gaze upon her. "Don't lose your heart."

"Of course not," Elizabeth said, straightening her spine.

Sarah shook her head at the pair of them, clearly not approving, but what could Elizabeth do? She had a role to play now, and she couldn't let her emotions get in the way.

Especially emotions concerning the Duke of Clarence.

CHAPTER 13

*G*abriel was rather perturbed with himself as he strode up the stairs of the townhouse now belonging to Lady Elizabeth Moreland. His heart was beating in an irregular pattern, it seemed, which was rather ridiculous. Not only was he a well-known, respected gentleman of the nobility, but he was a duke, one of the most wealthy and powerful in all of England.

So why was he allowing a simple attraction to a woman to cause such an unease within him?

It must be because of their past, he told himself. Surely that was it. Elizabeth felt he had wronged her, and though he agreed with her now, he knew that many would argue the fact. A woman, they would say, should be aware that such was the result of entering into a relationship with a man like himself. Many women — most actually — would have little to no expectation that she would remain his *only* woman. In fact, most would expect a man like him to take other lovers.

And yet... he had known of what type of woman Elizabeth was, and, at the very least, he should not have been so entirely obvious in his trysts with others.

He knocked on the door, smiling when Justine's face greeted him.

"Hello, Mrs. Clarke," he said, embracing her with a kiss on the cheek.

"None of that Mrs. Clarke with you now," she said, softly smiling at him. Gabriel had never been sure of how much she and her husband had been aware of when it came to the breaking off of his relationship with Elizabeth, but they had remained kind to him, treating him like one of their own. He hadn't known his own grandparents and enjoyed the time he spent with the Clarkes, particularly when his mother retreated to the country for such lengths of time.

"I expect you are here for Elizabeth?" she asked, and Gabriel smiled at her charmingly.

"I came to see both lovely ladies who reside here."

Justine smacked him lightly on the arm. "You always have the right words to say, do you not?"

She was right — most of the time he did, except when it came to Elizabeth.

"She is in the study, working away of course, and likely attempting to evade your arrival," Justine said, and Gabriel looked at her with mock astonishment.

"Avoid me?" he asked. "Never."

She laughed and led him through the house, knocking on the door to the study before letting him in, leaving him standing within the door.

"Elizabeth," he greeted her as she looked up from the papers in front of her. She blinked a few times as if realizing where she was and who he was, clearly having been within deep concentration.

"Gabriel," she said with some wonderment. "That's right. I had forgotten you were coming this afternoon."

He clutched at his breast with mock pain. "You cause me a

great deal of hurt, my lady, that I would be so easily forgotten."

"I have a lot on my mind," she said with a sigh. "Would you like to sit?"

She gestured to the seat in front of the old scarred oak desk. Clearly, Thomas Clarke hadn't been as concerned about appearances in his home study as he had been at the bank's office. He looked around the dark room before returning his gaze to her weary face and shook his head.

"Actually, I was going to ask if you would like to go for a walk," he said. "The day is lovely and you have clearly spent far too much time indoors as of late."

"Do I really look so terrible?" she asked with a wry smile.

In truth, she did not. But she did look as though she needed someone to take care of her, to ease her worries and be there for her, to provide a means of both support and comfort.

"You look perfectly fine," he assured her. "Despite the fact that you are so pale, I can nearly see through you."

That certainly captured her attention as she looked up with a gasp, and he laughed at the shock on her face.

"I am teasing," he said. "Now, find your bonnet, take my arm, and let us be off."

"Go, Elizabeth," came a voice from the door, and they both looked toward it to see Justine waving her hands toward the front of the house. "You need to take some time to yourself."

Elizabeth nodded, clearly not wanting to argue with both of them any longer. Once they emerged outside, however, her eyes cleared as she took a swift inhale of the fresh air, and Gabriel knew that it had been the right decision to push her to come.

"Where would you like to go?" he asked.

"To the park," she said decidedly, and he held out his arm

to her. She looked at it for a moment, as though trying to determine whether or not to trust it, before finally lightly placing her own hand upon it.

Her touch sent a strange tingle through him, one which Gabriel did not particularly welcome. She was somewhat stiff beside him as they walked, her gaze forward and her face hidden from him by her bonnet.

"How do you find working within a world of men?" he asked her, and she shrugged.

"I am used to being at the bank, so it is nothing new to me, I suppose."

"Well, I, for one, do believe that more institutions might be better off if more women were involved."

That caused her to turn her face toward him.

"Do you really now?"

"Well, yes," he said. "It can help men be less idiotic sometimes."

"Some would argue the opposite — that women distract men from their rational thinking."

"Then they would be wrong," he said in his arrogant manner, and she raised an eyebrow.

"You do realize you are speaking of your own kind?"

"Elizabeth, yesterday at White's two of *these kind* had a bet over which of them could drink the most whiskey before passing out. They both ended up in such a drunken stupor that by the time they got to that point, neither of them remembered why they had been drinking in the first place."

She laughed at that, a tinkling noise that he enjoyed. It had been some time since he had heard her laugh. The last time he had heard such from her was likely the last time he had called upon her before she had found him with another woman. Now that he thought about the time, he couldn't even remember which woman it was, that was how unremarkable she was in comparison to Elizabeth.

"So that is how you spend your days — with such men at White's?" she asked.

"There and in Parliament," he said with a bit of a sigh. "Which are the same men, unfortunately. I appreciate the opportunity to hold such a position, and yet sometimes lords feel the need to argue simply because they are expected to be on opposite sides — even when their true thoughts on an issue are exactly the same."

"It is rather silly, isn't it?" she said. "I had always thought you were a Tory."

"I am," he agreed. "But that doesn't mean I cannot share similar ideals with gentlemen of both parties."

"That makes sense. It is much like the bank itself. Some are known to have a political leaning, but my grandfather was always careful to ensure that he appeased both sides," she said.

"Your grandfather was always a wise man," Gabriel said. "He named you his heir."

"Your argument today has changed from when you first came to visit me at the bank," she said and he shrugged.

"Perhaps my thoughts have changed somewhat."

She raised an eyebrow, and he realized she may have understood that he had slightly manipulated the situation, but thankfully she didn't pursue it.

"Gabriel… will you tell me now, what happened with Julia in Newmarket?"

Ah, so the situation *had* upset her. Inwardly he smiled that she still cared.

"Your friend, the lovely Lady Julia, and her jockey love, Eddie Francis, clearly cared for one another very much, and yet it seemed that they weren't quite taking the next step to share their feelings with one another. Sometimes one just needs a bit of a push in order to reach for what they so desire. Lady Julia is an interesting woman, to be sure, but I quickly knew we would not make a suitable match. I never intended to marry her, nor even to court her. I only intervened because I found the entire situation rather intriguing, and saw the opportunity to help her and Francis realize the extent of their own feelings."

"I see," Elizabeth said contemplatively. "How soon did you realize that Julia was riding Orianna?"

Gabriel grinned. "After the very first race," he said with a laugh. "It is interesting that I was one of the only ones to determine the truth. But people see only what they want to unless they know enough of others' motivations to look deeper within."

"That is very cryptic," Elizabeth said. "Why did you not say anything?"

Gabriel shrugged. "It was an interesting situation, one in which I wanted to see just how the lovely Lady Julia would extricate herself, and how Francis would help her to do so. I say, the man nearly bungled the entire situation, but he found his way in the end."

"With your help," she said, an eyebrow raised, questioning his motives perhaps.

"I only helped the situation along, ensured that all went according to plan." Upon her look, he added hastily, "Their plan, not mine. I was an observer, a spectator if you will."

"Knowing she was my friend?" Elizabeth had to ask.

"Because she was your friend," Gabriel responded, and Elizabeth remained silent for a moment, clearly not knowing exactly how to respond to this revelation. It was more than Gabriel felt he should tell her, and yet he needed her to know that he had never pretended to court Lady Julia for any reason other than in the interests of those involved. He also had enjoyed seeing Elizabeth's reaction, determining that there was, if nothing else, still a sense of jealousy within her.

"That is rather manipulative," she finally said. "But at the same time… I must admit that it worked, and I have never seen Julia as happy as she is now."

"Aha, so you admit that my methods are not as untoward as you originally made them out to be."

She tilted her head toward him and eyed him warily out of the corner of one eye as they neared the park.

"I still do not entirely approve. You have a tendency to become rather too involved in many a situation. I am well aware that you played a part in ensuring Phoebe's publication remained viable last year. And yet your motives seem pure, I suppose."

Gabriel pretended to be affronted. "My motives are always pure, my lady."

"Mmm hmm," she said, raising an eyebrow. "So why this sudden interest in the bank?"

"I have always been interested in the bank."

"You have been interested, perhaps, but I don't recall you taking an active role when my grandfather was alive."

"I attended meetings."

"Sometimes."

"Sometimes," he said with a bit of a sigh, wondering how much to tell her. "The truth of it is, Elizabeth, after we broke off our courtship, I was unsure of what your grandparents knew of the reason for it. I was too ashamed to face them for some time, and then it was difficult to know what to say later on. I must admit I was a coward."

She stopped on the path they were walking, a gentleman behind them fixing them with a glare before continuing around them.

"Those are the last words I ever thought I would hear from the Duke of Clarence."

"Well, hear them you have," he said, chuckling self-consciously. He himself had never thought to make such a confession to her, but he supposed she deserved to hear it.

"Gabriel," she said, dipping her head before tilting it up toward him, and he led her ever-so-slightly off the path, out of the way of others walking by. His heart quickened when he saw how wide her eyes were, her emotions open to him now, bared in a way he didn't think they ever had been before — at least not to him. "I must ask you…"

When she hesitated, he said softly, "Yes?"

"Why wasn't I enough?"

He looked down at her, her violet eyes probing into him as though searching his own might provide her with the answer she was looking for.

"I thought we would be married," she continued, breaking their gaze for a moment, giving him a glimpse of the sheen of tears that covered her eyes. "I know our tryst in the garden was certainly not planned, but when you offered for me, I had thought that it was more than you simply feeling you had to do the right thing, but that you actually desired to be with me. And then, when I saw you…"

Her voice broke, as did his heart at the despondency in her question. He yearned to tell her that she was enough, that she always would be, and that it was himself who had been lacking. But how to put that into words without becoming completely vulnerable?

"Elizabeth…" he said slowly, carefully. "I was young. I was… having fun. It wasn't you at all. I suppose I just wasn't ready to settle down."

He had been young, yes, foolish, and interested in the world open to him, a world full of women who were eager to please him. At least, that's what he had been telling himself for so long now. The more time he spent with Elizabeth, however, the more he realized that there had been more behind his actions. He, the Duke of Clarence, the man afraid of nothing, had been a coward. For the truth was, he had been so full of questions, so afraid of disappointing her, that he had subconsciously destroyed their relationship before it had barely begun. He had always been confident in himself, knew his strength, his intelligence, and his ability to take on most things that had come his way.

This, however, was one area in which he doubted himself. Would he have — *could* he have — made a good husband? He realized now how insecure he had been. How, instead of telling her all of this, he had done the unthinkable, at least in her eyes. He had rationalized it all by telling himself she was too cold to care, but that had been wrong. He knew he should tell her this even now, but he couldn't seem to find the words to admit such a thing.

"And now you are ready? To stop 'having fun,' as you say, to settle down?" she asked, raising an eyebrow. "Is that what this is all about, why you have suddenly decided to pay me attention once again?"

"I am intrigued by you," he said honestly. "You are one of the most proper, respectable women I have ever met. And yet the position you have taken on is nearly unheard of, particularly for a woman of your station. The way you handle it all is a marvel."

"So you are spending time with me in order to slake your boredom?"

He supposed she was particularly right in his initial interest in becoming more involved with the bank, with her in particular. But it had become more than that. He felt as though he now had a vested interest in her success, in the bank's success. And at the same time, he couldn't help the affection and attraction he felt toward her.

"I am spending time with you because I enjoy doing so," he said, finally settling on what he knew to be the truth.

She didn't seem particularly inclined to entirely believe him, but she didn't question him any further, for which he was grateful. He hadn't partaken in a conversation of such intelligent wit in some time, and it was rather taxing.

"Very well," she said. "I believe I am ready to return home."

"Just one question," he said, taking her arm once more and walking her toward the fountain in the corner of the park, where they were slightly more secluded from others walking nearby.

"Yes?"

"Could we at least be friends? I do enjoy your company, and I must say that I miss it."

She hesitated before nodding slowly, then returned her gaze to him. "Very well, Gabriel. Friends once more."

She reached out a gloved hand, and he took it within his own fingers. Only he didn't stop there. He couldn't. He grasped her hand, pulled it toward him, and then took her warm, pink lips with his own.

CHAPTER 14

*E*lizabeth could feel the breeze fluttering the edges of the bonnet around her face, the warmth of the sun upon her back, and the softness of the grass beneath her boots. She could hear the water of the fountain trickling down over the stone, the murmur of voices far away from them.

And oh, she could smell Gabriel's scent, the musk of the cologne he had always worn that was so distinct she could recognize it anywhere. He tasted of oranges and whiskey, a strange yet delectable mix.

It wasn't as though he were kissing her senseless — no, it was rather that all of her senses were heightened. If she opened her eyes, she thought that even colors would be brighter, but she was loathe to do so for then, perhaps, she would remember where they were, who they were, what they were doing, and rational thought would once more overcome her and force her to push away, to quit this kiss and all the promise and potential it held.

Gabriel never did anything halfway — all he did was with purpose, including this kiss. One strong, warm hand cupped her face, tilting it just so, his other splayed across her back as he held her close against him.

Why, oh why, could something that felt so very right be so wrong?

His tongue swept within her mouth, tasting, teasing, and she nearly wept with how adept he was, how skilled he was, that he could cause such pleasure to course through her very soul.

A skill that was well practiced, she reminded herself, which slightly colored this moment with a different lens. Yet, her body still begged for more.

If footsteps hadn't approached, Elizabeth had no idea what she would have done — if she would have continued to accept his kisses and caresses, to forget herself, as she had five years ago in that garden gazebo. She was typically a decisive, practical woman who used her mind rather than emotion to make decisions.

But with Gabriel, everything was different.

Before she could allow him to convince her otherwise, Elizabeth finally pushed him away and stepped back quickly, feeling her cheeks flaming as she turned from him and looked down so as not to meet the gaze of the gentleman approaching. Instead, she simply nodded her head and walked back the way they had come, feeling Gabriel at her elbow.

He said nothing for a few moments as they walked, and Elizabeth found her heightened senses remained. The grass smelled fresher, the sun seemed brighter, and the birds chirped a cheerier song. But it wasn't only everything around her. Elizabeth's own body seemed to be nearly humming with life. It was as though she could feel the blood pumping from her heart and rushing through her veins. Her lips were tingling as the pressure of Gabriel's remained.

"It's beautiful out here," Gabriel said, and Elizabeth

nodded, unsure of what else to say. When she stole a glance at Gabriel, he was smiling as though he had not a care in the world, while she was in turmoil.

Why had she let him kiss her? She was well aware from the last time it had happened that it would only confuse her all the more. Even now, as he began to make light conversation once again as he returned her home, her mind, which she had always so relied upon, was unable to properly grasp a thought.

And as he walked her to her door, brought her hand to his lips, kissing it with his eyes intent upon hers, she knew with certainty that she was tearing herself in two — for as much as her head told her not to give in to his charms once more, that she was better off without him, her body was resisting the fight against her attraction to him. And her heart — well, that she had decided to completely ignore, for it wasn't to be trusted at all.

ELIZABETH WOKE the next day with new resolve to ignore any thoughts of Gabriel — for now, at least, until she was on smoother footing at the bank. It would only be a few more months, she consoled herself, and then she was sure she would feel more confident, would have a more solid foundation to work from. How long would it truly take many of the partners and clients to realize her abilities?

Perhaps not as soon as she thought, she realized as she sat down at her desk, finding the correspondence atop it. She noted one of the first envelopes was from one of their wealthiest clients, a baronet involved in shipping, and she broke the seal and opened it with fingers of trepidation, for she had been attempting to call upon him for some time, but had been rejected time and again.

Her stomach sank as she read the words within, and she closed her eyes, hoping that when she opened them the words would have transposed themselves on the page. But, unfortunately, it was not to be.

For the letter, addressed to her, clearly stated that the man had no desire to remain further involved as a client with the bank, and could he please meet with the manager, Mr. Bates (certainly not her, she inferred), to discuss removing his funds from the bank in order to invest elsewhere?

Elizabeth dropped her head on the desk, fighting the headache that threatened — and the day had only just begun. Why, oh why, had Sir Hugo not even given her a chance?

She knew very well why. Because she was a woman, which some men would never accept.

Such as this one, entering her office at the very moment.

"Henry," she said warily. "What are you doing here?"

"I am a partner of the bank," he said, smoothly sliding into the chair across from her and crossing one leg over the other. "Can I not come to meet with the most senior partner with my pressing concerns?"

"Of course you can, Henry," Elizabeth said, summoning all the patience she had ever held as she regarded him across the desk. "However, most first make an appointment, as I have previously requested of you."

"But we are family," he said with what Elizabeth was sure he thought was a charming grin, while in all actuality, it made her skin crawl. "Does that not count for something?"

"Of course, Henry, family counts for many things," she said with icy politeness, "such as loyalty, does it not?"

"It does," he said with a smile. "And honesty."

"As we have always found with one another?"

"Of course," he said, with a cool smile. "I believe I have made my feelings about your new… position well known."

"Yes, Henry," she said, straightening in her chair, placing

one hand over the other upon the desk in front of her. "In fact, I am actually glad you came, as I must speak to you about this. Your contestation of Grandpapa's will has not helped matters, and we have been forced to spend much of our valuable time ensuring clients that the bank, and our family, are not at odds with one another. While I *appreciate* you being honest with me, as partners within the bank, we must all speak with one voice and appear unified to our clients. We cannot have anyone dissenting the position of another, or it weakens us as a whole. Do you understand what I am saying?"

She said the words slowly, as though he was a small child, but he only sat back in his chair smiling smugly.

"Let me guess, Elizabeth," he said. "Did you receive a letter recently from Sir Hugo?"

"I did, actually," she said, narrowing her eyes at him. "I do not suppose you had anything to do with his decision to leave the bank?"

Henry emitted an exaggerated sigh.

"I actually sat down with Sir Hugo just last week. We happen to frequent the same club, you know," he said with a wink. Elizabeth actually didn't know, and that was one of the problems she faced — while she may belong to some of the same social circles as these men, she would never frequent the same clubs, would never find herself within the same rooms following dinner, partaking in conversations with one another. It left her at a great disadvantage to someone such as Henry, who could insert himself into those very same situations.

"And what, pray tell, did Sir Hugo have to say?"

"Only that, unfortunately, my dear Elizabeth, he feels the ways of women can be fickle. While he knows the bank continues to run efficiently and effectively with the same managers involved as during Grandfather's time, he says that women may make sudden, impulsive decisions for no particular reason. That the bank is not safe nor under control when a woman could create an irreparable situation, such as distrust one of the partners who has been so confidently appointed."

He was quite clearly speaking of his own appointment, of course, but Elizabeth could not call him out upon it when he would only continue to use her words against her.

"And I am sure, *dear Cousin*, that you absolved him of his fears?" she asked pointedly.

"Alas, he was rather sure in his opinions of you," he said, lifting his hands, not answering her question. "And to be honest, *dear* Elizabeth, he is correct in his assumptions. For how much longer are you going to continuing playing this game? It is getting rather foolish and you are only going to embarrass yourself if you keep at it much longer. Women do not belong in a business such as a bank."

She stood from her desk, placing her palms flat upon it as she leaned over toward him, her anger, for once, getting the better of her. For she was tired. It had been far too long since she had slept well overnight, as she continued to question herself and all of her decisions. And she was tired of the opinions of the men within this banking world. Particularly her cousin, a man she wished would disappear from her life forever.

"I will have you know, Henry, that women have been partners in far more banks than this one. And they have been active partners. If you spoke to anyone besides those within your circle, you would know that many of the country banks can list women as partners, as have a few within London. But you wouldn't know. For you care for nothing more than seeing your own bank accounts fill. Do not think I am not aware of your deception of Mr. Mortimer. I cannot even imagine what Grandpapa would think if he was aware of all you have done. Furthermore, Henry, Grandpapa named *me* his heir, and—"

"If I hear you say that one more time, Elizabeth, I swear I shall fall asleep in boredom," said Henry, leaning back in his chair with a grin, enjoying her tirade, which only made Elizabeth even angrier, but forced her to remember herself and hold her tongue. "Besides that," he continued. "Grandfather was a senile old bat who didn't know what he was doing by the end."

"Get out."

Her words were short, clipped, and lacking the emotion she truly felt as she pointed to the door.

"Oh, Elizabeth, come now, I—"

"I said, get. Out. Now."

"Cousin—"

"I will not ask again."

"And if I don't?" He asked, rising to his full height. "Just what are you going to do?"

"Perhaps," came a voice from the door, a deep, smoky voice that Elizabeth well recognized, "she will decline your partnership, which she would be fully within her rights to do. Now, Clarke, when a lady asks you to leave, I have it on first-hand authority that it is typically in your own best interests to do so."

CHAPTER 15

*G*abriel had waited long enough in the corridor outside Elizabeth's office.

He knew she would far prefer to handle a situation such as this one with her cousin alone, but poor old Henry clearly wasn't hearing her words, despite the fact she had delivered them in quite a clear and concise manner.

If Gabriel had any hesitation to enter her office, it was for fear that her cousin might provide her with the idea that there had been a deal struck between them — albeit one that he had no intention of ever honoring. But would Elizabeth see it that way? That he was only attempting to hold off her cousin while staying close to her?

Finally, he became concerned that tensions were becoming slightly too heated in the office, and he pushed the door open, only for neither Elizabeth nor Clarke to even notice him for a few moments.

"Clarence," Clarke said now with a bit of surprise as he turned to look at him after Gabriel spoke. "What are you doing here? Is there a partners' meeting of which I was not aware?"

"Not at all," he said. "I am simply here to pay a visit to Lady Elizabeth. It seems that you and I had a similar idea this morning."

He gave Clarke a pointed look, one that he hoped the man interpreted as, 'Get out of this office in order to allow me time alone with Lady Elizabeth.' Clarke would assume he was doing so for purposes other than the truth.

Of course, Clarke was slow to catch on, and it took a few moments for recognition to spark within his eyes as to why Gabriel may perhaps be here to call upon Elizabeth. Clarke began to slowly nod with a smile, and Gabriel could only hope that Elizabeth couldn't see her cousin's face, or she might suspect something was amiss.

Fortunately, she seemed otherwise occupied — on him. Her angry stare had swung from her cousin to Gabriel, and he nearly jumped at the intensity of it, though he was aware that her ire was primarily directed at Clarke.

"What are you doing here?" she asked in a heated tone.

"I am here to do as I said," he responded, "to meet with you. I have some things to discuss."

"Very well," she said, sighing as she turned away, some of her anger dissipating, and Gabriel nearly laughed at the forlorn look she cast upon the pile of correspondence on her desk. For who actually welcomed attending to such drivel?

Finally, Henry rose, casting a look upon each of them before sauntering to the door.

"When you change your mind, Elizabeth, you know where to find me."

She only shot him one more unimpressed glance before he left with a chuckle.

"Henry," she said, throwing down the pen she had been twisting in her fingers upon the desk with some force, "is a rat."

He said the words at the same time as she, and the two of

123

them looked at one another in some surprise. Finally, he chuckled, and soon enough she reluctantly joined in, the two of them, at least, finding some mirth in their shared opinion of her cousin.

"You must laugh more, Elizabeth," he said, and her smile slowly faded.

"It's been somewhat difficult," she said with a sigh, making her way to the circle of chairs and resting her head in her hands as she leaned over the round table in the middle. "Everything I do seems to be erroneous. Whichever way I turn, it seems to be the wrong direction."

She waved toward the pile of letters upon the desk. "One of our largest clients has just decided to take his business from the bank, and I have no doubt that much of it was Henry's doing. Honestly, I don't even understand why he wants to be the senior partner when he would hardly step foot in the building for it might require that he actually do some work."

"Would it be so bad, to allow him to take over, to take some of the pressure off yourself? For as you say, I'm sure he would rely on others who are currently working at the bank."

"Absolutely not," she said, shooting him a vehement glare, her violet eyes practically glowing. "The ideas he has to apparently save money would only run this bank to the ground. Ideas that he was already spouting mere days after my grandfather's death."

Then recognition dawned.

"You are goading me. No more manipulations please, Gabriel."

"Elizabeth," Gabriel said, softly now, seeing she needed to calm somewhat. "Come here."

He crooked a finger, beckoning her closer, but she only crossed her arms over her chest as though she were defending herself.

"Why?"

"Can you just come here… please?"

He lifted his palms up now in supplication, and she sighed, dropping her own arms and stepping closer to him. Gabriel stood, moving behind her. He brought his hands to her shoulders, but when he set them down, she jumped a step away from him.

"Shhh," he whispered in her ear, coming closer once more, and this time she shivered, likely from his breath on her neck. He slowly replaced his hands and began to carefully knead his fingers into the tight muscles of her shoulders and upper back. She tensed for a few moments until she finally gave into his touch.

"How does that feel?" he asked softly.

"Heavenly," she admitted, her head rolling slightly back and forth as she now not only accepted his offering but silently requested more of it. Continuing his massage, he steered her over to one of the Gillows elbow chairs, helping to set her down upon it while he sat on the arm of the chair to provide himself some leverage.

He wasn't sure how long they stayed in such a position, him applying the pressure she so needed upon the warm skin he could feel through the silk of her dress, but finally it seemed as though she were leaning back against him. When he looked over her shoulder, her eyes were beginning to shut, as though she were nearly falling asleep.

"Elizabeth?" he whispered. "Are you still awake?"

"Of course!" she said, sitting up with a jerk now, and he shook his head, knowing that soon enough she would be tensed up back over the desk, and all of his hard work would be for naught.

"I'm so sorry… I have forgotten myself," she said, her voice just over a whisper, and he shook his head despite the fact that she couldn't see him.

"Do not apologize, Elizabeth, for taking a moment to yourself."

"What was it you wanted to speak to me about?" she asked him now, and he sighed at how quickly she reverted back to business. Did the woman never take any time to actually enjoy life?

"I actually have something for you. A gift, if you will."

"Oh, you really shouldn't have," she said, and he knew they were more than just words — she likely sincerely felt that he should not have brought a gift of any sort. For that would mean that he was expecting something of her, courting her — of which she was clearly not accepting.

"I wanted to," he said softly. "And you deserve it."

She eyed him somewhat warily but took the offered box from his hands, and he felt a jolt when their fingertips brushed as she took it. It was as though he were a young lad in the first blush of love around her. How was he letting a woman affect him so?

But affect him she was.

She took the box in her long, elegant fingers, carefully unwrapping the twine and then the brown paper, before carefully folding it on the desk beside her. Gabriel couldn't seem to bring his gaze away from those hands, as he pictured them on his neck, running down his chest, and further, down to—

"Oh, Gabriel."

Her voice, low and throaty, brought him out of his reverie. Her gaze was in her lap, staring into the box she held, now open to reveal the contents within. Slowly, she reached inside, lifting out a writing set. She set the items upon the desk — the feather quill pen, nib pen, ink well, and blotter, arranging them just so.

She picked up the pen, running her fingers tenderly over the blue-green feather.

"This is beautiful," she whispered almost reverently. Gabriel resisted the urge to smile in satisfaction. "Is this from a peacock?"

"It is," he nodded, steepling his fingers together in front of his face.

Elizabeth was about to return the pen to the holder when she eyed it more carefully, turning it one way and then the next.

"Gabriel," she said slowly, "This feather is from a right wing, is it not?"

When she turned to look at him now, he nodded.

"As much as you try to hide it, I am well aware of your tendencies to write with your left hand — a practice your parents surely attempted to change?"

"They did," she said, her cheeks coloring. "I am perfectly able to write with my right hand but... you are correct. I do prefer the left. It is easier. How did you know?"

He shrugged. "By watching you. Whenever you think no one is looking, you write with your left hand, and then when you know others are watching, you switch to your right. You also tend to use your left hand in other actions as well, though you likely do not even know it."

Her face turned even redder at his words, which somewhat disconcerted him.

"I apologize, Elizabeth, I didn't mean to offend you—"

"Oh, you didn't, not at all," she said with a wave of her hand. "I suppose I simply wasn't aware that you — or anyone — had actually noticed at all."

"Of course I noticed," he said softly. "I notice everything about you."

She looked up at him then, catching his eye, and he tried to determine what her gaze was telling him. It seemed to hold partial respect for his observations, and yet some wariness as well — as though it concerned her that he kept such a diligent eye upon her.

While she stared at him, Elizabeth was absently running her fingers over the holder, and she must have felt something beneath the skin of her fingertips as she broke their gaze to inspect it further.

"What is this?" she murmured, and she turned the ink well for a better look.

"Elizabeth Moreland, Senior Partner," she read, then, feeling a matching engraving on the other side, turned it around quickly. "Thomas Clarke, Senior Partner," she read, followed by the years her grandfather had been senior partner of the institution.

She looked up at Gabriel once more, and now her eyes were slightly shiny with the tears within.

"Where did you find this?" she asked, her voice nearly breaking, though she was able to maintain control.

"I had it commissioned," he said with a smile. "I thought it would be a reminder to you of the connection you had — and still do — with your grandfather. He would be very proud of you, Elizabeth."

"You sound like my grandmother," she said with a bit of a laugh, though he could tell she was trying to swallow the tears that threatened.

"I will consider that a compliment," he returned, "For your grandmother is a very wise woman."

They shared a smile at that, and then she turned to look back down at the set in front of her. As she did, her eyes must have rested on the letter below the set.

"Gabriel," she said, her voice a bit desperate now, "What am I to do with this bank? With having to answer the questions coming my way, proving myself, protecting my family after Henry's inquisition, and mollifying the clients you wish to leave?"

He stood and took a few steps forward before leaning overtop of her. He lifted his index finger to rest underneath her chin, tipping it up to look at him.

"You continue to do what you are doing, Elizabeth," he said fiercely. "Be the woman you are — the strong, confident woman who has this in hand. Prove your worth. Meet with clients. And demonstrate that people like your cousin are wrong. Clients will remain with this bank. If they choose not to, it is their loss, and then more will come in their place. Whatever you do, do not let rats like Henry Clarke destroy your confidence."

"If this bank fails," she said slowly, "then we will all lose, more than just the bank, but our very livelihoods outside of it. You have the most to lose."

"I know that," he said, keeping his gaze intent upon her. "I knew that when I accepted the partnership, and I am aware of it still. However, I am not at risk of losing everything, not with the small size of my share. You, however, could very well lose all."

"Until a few months ago, I had nothing," she said. "Now it seems everything is at risk."

He paused for a moment, unsure of whether she meant anything further than what her grandfather had bestowed upon her. She couldn't have meant anything to do with him — could she?

She smiled at him now, the smile of a woman who had lost some of the tension of the worries she held. Whether or not she completely believed in what he had said to her, he had no idea, but he hoped so.

"Thank you, Gabriel," she said. "For everything."

He withdrew his finger, though only to slowly stroke her cheek with it, and while she didn't lean into his caress, neither did she turn away, offering him a bit of hope. He was falling for this woman all over again, which both excited and terrified him in equal measure.

He knew she didn't trust him, and he was worried that if he pushed too hard to win her hand, she would push back in equal measure, creating a chasm he would never be able to cross again. He would have to win her back slowly, a little at a time. First, however, he had to determine if that was his goal at all. Did he truly want her again? Could he, after all they had been through together? For if he did, it would be forever. He would have to forsake all others, and there would be no turning back.

Before he did anything further in the here and now that either of them might regret, he carefully extricated his hand, nodded his head, and wished her good day before he strode to the door. He paused with his hand upon the handle, took one final, long look back at the confusion now reigning upon her face, and then strode out the door.

CHAPTER 16

Gabriel became a frequent visitor over the next few weeks — and Elizabeth was as confused as ever. She waited for him to attempt to steal another kiss or to vocalize his intentions toward her, but he did nothing of the sort, which disconcerted her more than any actions actually could. For she didn't know what to expect, nor how to respond. So, she did what she always had — responded with the politeness with which she was raised.

Quite often she accepted his calls with her grandmother, who welcomed Gabriel's visits. Justine, along with her husband, had been aware that Elizabeth's past relationship with Gabriel had ended abruptly, though they had never questioned why, for which Elizabeth was glad. As much as she had wanted nothing to do with the man she considered to have betrayed her, she had no wish to end the friendship he had developed with the two of them.

Now her grandmother had welcomed him back excitedly, and Elizabeth didn't miss the looks she sent her way, in both question and encouragement.

At the parties Elizabeth chose to attend, Gabriel was

always there. He would request his two dances, one always a waltz — nothing improper, and yet Elizabeth was well aware of the many questioning gazes upon her at his continued attention. Some of them were curious, yet there were many others laced with jealousy as well as undisguised ire and dislike bordering upon hatred. She knew Gabriel was a prize which many women were clamoring to win — for themselves or for their daughters — but really, it was not as though she was stealing him from under their noses. He was the one who, as far as she could tell, seemed to be pursuing her. The issue was, she wasn't entirely sure how she felt about it all.

Which was precisely the question being posed to her at this very moment by Sarah, who had arrived to call on Elizabeth before she planned to visit the bank to take care of the day's business.

Justine was out of the house having tea with an acquaintance, leaving Elizabeth and Sarah alone and free to converse of whatever they wished.

"I am not entirely sure what to think of his advances, for I'm not even certain I could call them that," Elizabeth said truthfully. "He visits now and again, and we dance, we see one another at the bank on occasion, but since the day he gifted me with the pen set, it has all been quite… cordial."

Sarah laughed lightly at that and raised an eyebrow.

"Is that not what you prefer — *cordial* relationships?"

Elizabeth was well aware of what Sarah was doing, and she smiled at her friend's tone, for she knew Sarah was attempting to draw out Elizabeth's true emotions.

"Perhaps I do," she said with a slight shrug. "But I find myself in a state of quandary as to how to react when I am not entirely sure of what the path forward would be. If he were to make a statement of courtship, then I would have the ability to rebuke him. But as it is, I cannot simply ask him to remove himself from my doorstep or refuse his arm when he offers it, now can I?"

Sarah leaned forward, her deep brown eyes as perceptive to Elizabeth's emotions as always.

"Why would you choose to take such action?" she asked. "Do you not want Gabriel Lockridge, Duke of Clarence, to court you?"

Elizabeth sighed as she stared at the sandwich platter in front of her, which she had barely touched since she and Sarah had begun to speak of this subject.

"I cannot deny how much I am inexplicably attracted to him," she said, biting her lip. "I have never been able to lose that enchantment, no matter what he says or what he does. He is a handsome man, and every time I look at him all I can think of is… well…" she felt her cheeks warm. "I have rather improper thoughts, if I am being honest. If we hadn't the past that we do, I would not be afraid to follow through to determine if there are still emotions lurking there, but as it is, I cannot trust him, nor myself. For it would be too easy to fall for him, to allow myself to forget everything that happened before and be right back in his arms. And then where would I be? Once again, I would be with a man who had eyes for not only me but for other women as well. I could very well lose my heart, but even more than that — I could, perhaps, lose all my grandfather has built, for would a duke truly want a wife who was also the senior partner of a bank?"

Sarah smiled softly and tilted her head to the side as she studied Elizabeth.

"I understand your dilemma, truly I do," she said. "Once trust is broken, it is a very difficult thing to regain. It can only come with time, and with proof that it should be reinstated. As for what the Duke would want, well… that is a question that only he can answer. And I don't recall saying anything about marriage."

Elizabeth cleared her throat, realizing her blunder. She shouldn't be thinking about marriage to Gabriel, for she was not the type of woman willing to stand idly by while her husband took lovers or mistresses. And yet, she could not deny that the thought of forever with him had crept in once more.

"I only mentioned it because courting typically leads to marriage, does it not?"

"It does," agreed Sarah. "And while I am happy to discuss all of this with you, I must say, I think there is someone else with whom you must speak."

"You're right," Elizabeth said with a sigh. "I hate to admit it, but you are."

"Come, now, Elizabeth, you are the senior partner of a bank. How difficult can it be to have one small conversation with a man?"

Elizabeth chuckled ruefully.

"You have no idea," she said as the image of Gabriel came to mind. "No idea at all."

* * *

WHEN SHE SAW him the following night at a small party of about thirty people, Elizabeth knew it was not the time for such a discussion. No, she would save it for another day, when there were far fewer people about and she had time to collect her wits.

Though it would have to be soon, for she wasn't sure how much longer she could take questioning what she was to say, nor how he would respond. How many times had she rehearsed the words over and over within her mind? And then there was the longing... the longing she wished she could ignore, but lingered there, tempting her, taunting her as though it were alive and whispering in her ear.

This was why she had decided to keep her distance. And why she had determined that if he wasn't going to make his intentions clear, then she would just have to take the initiative to tell him that his attentions were, unfortunately, not required, nor were they wanted.

She just wouldn't explain that it was only her mind that had decided such things, while the rest of her was yearning for him and all that he could offer her.

But her mind was strong, she reminded herself — and it was determined.

She set her chin resolutely, lifting an invisible shield before her as she perused the attendees at tonight's party. She noted one or two clients, with whom she would be sure to converse. There were a few who could potentially become clients as well, ones she was determined to bring to the bank to prove her worth to the rest of the partners.

Not that it was required.

Her thoughts were arrested, however, when Gabriel walked through the door. Once her eyes came to rest upon him, it was beyond her to tear them away, for it was as though they belonged upon his person — as did the rest of her.

Elizabeth remained rooted on the spot despite the fact she knew she looked a fool. She was sure she wasn't the only woman to note Gabriel's arrival, nor his dark chestnut locks, or the way his breeches and deep navy jacket fitted so perfectly to the planes of his body. A sculptor would so love to have him as a model, she thought, before her thoughts wandered to him as a model in the nude — a sight she hadn't seen with her eyes in the dark of the gardens that night, but had felt underneath her fingertips.

When Gabriel caught her eye now, his own widened just a touch, and then, accompanied by his slow, seductive smile, he winked at her. Heat rushed into Elizabeth's cheeks as she realized just how obvious she had been in her perusal of him, how she was undressing him with both her eyes and her imaginings here in the middle of the receiving room. She had to get a hold of herself before she was made a fool.

She nodded at him primly before she turned, picked up a glass of lemonade from the table beside her, and fled as quickly and as she gracefully could, out the doors and into the night air of the garden for some cool, blessed relief.

* * *

GABRIEL WATCHED HER GO, pleasure coursing through him at her reaction to him. She wanted him.

It had been a slow dance, this courtship, one that was frustrating him to no end. For he, a man who had once taken pride in his ability to capture nearly any conquest he endeavored to chase, had been unable to see anyone but Elizabeth since he had come to her rescue the night of her grandfather's funeral.

He knew she fought her own feelings toward him — he could see it in her eyes when he called upon her, when he danced with her. He could see it when she let down her guard — when she laughed at a joke he told, became entranced in a story he relayed, or widened her eyes in shock at a piece of gossip she swore she didn't want to hear yet eagerly listened to anyway.

For then he would make the smallest motion toward her, and she would instantly tense up, as though she were remembering all of the reasons she had promised herself she would never allow him to become close again. It killed him, but he understood. Now he just had to make her forget the past and move into the future.

For as much as it pained him to admit that one woman

alone commanded his attention, it seemed he could do nothing but attempt to capture Lady Elizabeth Moreland.

Now she ran from him. He tilted his head when she contemplated her exit. Was she running from him, or wanting him to chase after her?

Gabriel sensed another gaze upon him, and he turned to find Miss Sarah Jones, Elizabeth's friend, studying him. She could be described as plain, he thought, with her brown hair and brown eyes. But there was something interesting about her look. Her hair was soft around her face, and unlike Elizabeth's nearly hidden freckles, those of Miss Jones were clearly speckled across her nose and over her cheeks. She didn't look at him as most did, as though they wanted to devour him whole one way or another.

"Your Grace," she said demurely in that strange accent of hers once she saw that she had been caught, though she didn't seem embarrassed by the fact.

"Miss Jones," he greeted her, deciding that he could spare a moment to learn more from a friend of Elizabeth's. "I apologize for the fact that we have not yet before met, despite the fact that we share some mutual acquaintances."

"Primarily Elizabeth," she said, and it seemed to Gabriel that this woman was somehow able to read beyond what a person said and into his inner thoughts — which was ridiculous, but she certainly seemed more insightful than most.

"Perhaps you can help me, Miss Jones," he said.

"I can try."

"As you well know, Lady Elizabeth and I have been spending time together as of late. What do you suppose she would say were we to officially court?"

Miss Jones said nothing for a moment, instead tilting her head to the side as she looked at him.

"I do not believe I am the one to whom you should be asking such a question," she said with the slightest of smiles.

"Does she feel anything toward me?" he asked, attempting to infuse his voice with an air of nonchalance, though he knew he was opening himself up to extreme vulnerability in front of this woman, a woman he hardly knew. But he felt he could trust her, for some strange reason.

"Of course she does," Miss Jones said, before a wicked smile across her face. "Everyone feels some sort of emotion for those they have become close with. I doubt Elizabeth would continue to spend much time with you if she felt *nothing*."

He nodded, knowing her words to be true yet unsure of what to do with them.

"Elizabeth…" she continued with some hesitation, as though she was unsure of whether to say anything that might betray their friendship. "As much as she tries to portray otherwise, she looks at everything with both her heart and her mind — they work in concert, so you must appeal to both of them."

"Understood, Miss Jones," he said with a smile and a mock salute before he turned and followed Elizabeth out the garden doors.

CHAPTER 17

*G*abriel found the scent of lilies nearly overwhelming as he strode through the gardens in search of Elizabeth. He knew she would come here. Did she realize, as he did the moment he walked through the doors, that they were in the very same building where they had discovered one another all those years ago?

Likely. She was not one to miss such details.

He rounded a wall to spy her in the distance. She was sitting on the marble border of a small water feature, her light blue gown flowing around her, making it seem as though she were meant to be part of the tableau surrounding her.

On this late spring day, the sun was just beginning to set, casting a brilliant light of pink and gold, glistening off the reddish hues of her hair as he neared. Clearly not expecting anyone else in the gardens at this early hour of the party, she had removed her gloves and was trailing her fingertips through the water of the fountain next to her, leaving ripples behind them as they moved through.

Gabriel stood there, taking it all in, not wanting to say

anything to startle her and ruin the moment. After a couple of minutes, however, she must have sensed his presence, for her head jerked up and she looked around her until her eyes finally came to rest upon him, causing them to narrow.

"How long have you been standing there?" she asked, her voice, despite its accusatory tone, calling to him from across the courtyard as he began to walk toward her once more.

"Just for a moment," he said before coming to stand before her. As she began to rise, he reached a hand down, and she reluctantly allowed her fingers to wrap around his. He paused, reveling in their touch, before he gently pulled her to her feet.

"You followed me?" she asked resignedly, and he slowly smiled.

"I knew where to find you. Do you recognize these gardens?"

She turned her face away from him, he knew, to hide her blush.

"I suppose I do," she said, shrugging her shoulder as though it was of no consequence. "I have been to Lord and Lady Holderness' a time or two before."

"I remember these gardens well," he said with a sigh, wandering away from her around the stone courtyard, slowly circling the fountain within the middle of it. "I made one of my finest discoveries here on a night long ago."

She snorted, so unlike her usual polite tendencies.

"'One of,' being the pivotal point of that sentence," she said, but he shook his head as he watched her while she continued to move.

"No, that night was my *very* finest discovery," he said. "A discovery I lost but continue to search for, but to no avail."

"On that note, there is something of which I would like to speak to you," she said, holding a finger in the air, but he quickly rounded the corner and took that very finger within the palm of his hand, before curling his own fingers around hers.

"I know you do, love," he said, smiling at her once more, the smile that had been proven to charm that coldest of the *ton*. Elizabeth only stared back at him, her jaw set and her brow furrowed. He reached out to cup her cheek. "But can it wait?"

"No," she said, shaking her head, as though she was convincing herself as much as she was him. "It cannot wait any longer. I have been wanting to say this to you for some time, and I need you to listen and to understand. I wasn't going to do this here, but it seems to me as though I have no other choice."

She paused, taking a deep breath, and he used that moment to move in toward her, filling the space between them. He brought a finger up, placing it gently on her lips.

"Why do we not go somewhere quieter, where we are less likely to be happened upon?" he asked. "I would like to speak to you as well."

She looked as though she was going to protest, but instead, he was relieved when she nodded her head. Gabriel bent and picked up her gloves, but kept them in his own hand instead of returning them to her as he took her other hand in his and led her over to a bend in the path where a bench was hidden within a small alcove of the fence, covered by brush on one side and out of view of the house from the other side.

He helped her to sit before taking his own spot on the bench beside her.

"I know what you are going to say, Elizabeth," Gabriel said before she opened her mouth. "You are questioning what we are doing together, about whether or not you feel we should continue to see one another. That is it, is it not?"

"In fewer words than I would have used, but yes, I

suppose it is," she said, her face in profile to him, backlit by the setting sun as she looked out over the elaborate gardens around them, the flowers beginning to bloom with the beautiful awakening of spring.

"I understand why you feel that way, truly I do," he said, cupping her face and turning her toward him. "I wronged you, Elizabeth. You did not deserve to be treated that way. I was a young fool. I didn't realize how fortunate I was to even have an opportunity to be with you. I squandered all and for that, I apologize. But, Elizabeth..."

Gabriel paused for a moment, stunned at the fact that, for once, he lacked the words he required. How could he make her understand what he was feeling without his words sounding trite?

"Elizabeth, I am falling for you," he said, letting out a low chuckle at himself when he heard the words. He knew he sounded ridiculous, like a lovesick pup, but he didn't know what else to say to her but the truth. "I can no longer see myself with any other woman but you, and it's driving me mad keeping myself away from you."

She was turned toward him now, her violet eyes wide, and he knew he could lose himself within them for days. He could read the confusion there, in the way she desperately ran her eyes over his face, as though she was searching for proof of his words. She opened her mouth, but Gabriel found that he could not, at the moment, hear a refusal from her.

"You don't need to say anything right now," he said before she could get a word out. "Take some time and think on what I've said. I know you have much on your mind, and I do not wish to add to your burdens, but actually want to do what I can to take away from them."

"Burdens are to be expected," she said with the smallest of

smiles. "Particularly when one is part of an enterprise such as a bank."

"You take on much, and you do not ask for help," Gabriel said, raising an eyebrow. "It is to be commended, true, but it can also become more than you can bear."

"And you, oh wise Duke, do you ask for help with your burdens?"

He laughed at that, knowing she had him there.

"I suppose not, although I have many good men in place to share the responsibility."

"But ultimately, it all rests on your shoulders, does it not?"

"It does."

"Then so this must on mine."

"Well, in that case, you know I am always here to help release the tension of them."

She looked down at the toes of her cream kid slippers at his mention of his intimate caress so many weeks ago within her office. It was the last time he had touched her in such a way, besides the odd brush of fingertips, and he longed to do so once more.

Risking the moment, he brought a hand to the back of her neck, gently massaging, stroking, loving the elegant lines of the length of it. Instead of recoiling, she leaned into him, welcoming his touch, for which he was grateful. He shifted slightly, lifting a leg to straddle the bench so that he was sitting behind her, and he pulled her back against him so that she could lean on him. While she wouldn't give him any of her responsibilities, perhaps he could ease some of the load she carried with a few moments of peacefulness.

His hands wandered from her neck to her shoulders, before running down over her cap sleeves to where her arms were bare, her gloves still lying on the bench beside them. He trailed his fingers over the softness of her skin, and he could feel the gooseflesh rise behind his touch. An unexplainable sense of pride filled him that he could cause such a reaction within her, and a sudden possessiveness enveloped him, as he wanted to ensure that he was the only one who would ever cause her to feel such a way.

Gabriel leaned down and brought his lips to her neck where his fingers had previously caressed. He trailed kisses from behind her ear, down her neck to where it met her collarbone; then he neared her shoulder, to where the sleeve of her dress began. He brought his arms around her, pulling her back against him, nearly groaning from the feeling of her lithe body as she pressed back against him, where he ached for her.

He knew that Elizabeth, for all of her refined elegance, had fiery passion buried deep within her, and he was determined to unleash it.

As his lips continued to explore her neck, Gabriel's hands roamed over her body. They began at her slim waist, ran down over the curve of her hips then back up again, where he cupped her ribs within the span of his hands. He slowly, cautiously, brought his fingers higher still, running them over the swell of her breasts, which strained against the fabric of her gown. The silk was sleek beneath his hands, and he cupped her soft mounds, which were the perfect size — while not overly large, he couldn't have asked for any that would be better than hers.

"Elizabeth," he murmured, and then he rose slightly, picking her up and turning her around so that she was now straddling his hips, the skirts of her gown spilling around their legs as she now tilted her head down to meet his lips while her cool fingers lightly brushed his jawline. He met her kiss hungrily, the desire for her that had been building for weeks now pouring through where their mouths met.

His tongue touched the seam of her lips and she opened to him, allowing him in. She was so warm, so sweet, and he wrapped his arms around her, pulling her close as he explored her velvety softness, finding within her all that he had been looking for.

When she moved restlessly against him, he bucked slightly, and he knew what she was seeking. But he was no longer the foolish youth he had been the last time the two of them had been alone in these gardens. While he was able to better control his impulses, he was also a man with much more experience, and right now, he only sought to make Elizabeth happy.

Gabriel took one of his hands from behind her back and found her ankle, which was resting against his side. He stroked around the soft bone, then began to trail his fingers along her leg underneath her gown, lifting them higher and higher as he continued to love her with his lips and his tongue. Finally, he reached her inner thigh and he went higher, gripping her hip. As she seemed to be fully capable of holding herself up against him, he now brought both hands around her bottom, squeezing the firmness of her cheeks.

Oh, how he longed to undo the fall of his breeches and bring her down upon him, finding the sweet softness within her. But he wouldn't do that to her in these gardens, not again. Instead, he brought a hand around to the front of her, finding her curls, reaching through them for the bud he knew was awaiting him.

She gasped into his mouth when he found her, and he began to stroke in circles. She was restless against him, moving with him, and he brought his left hand up to tease one nipple and then the other through her thin silk dress.

Elizabeth broke her lips away from him for a moment to cry his name, and then suddenly she was gripping him tightly, her fingers digging into his shoulders as she rode the waves he knew were engulfing her.

They stayed still where they were for what must have

been a few moments, holding one another, until finally she leaned back ever so slightly. Gabriel was surprised to see a slight sheen of tears over her eyes, but before he could question them, she whispered, "Thank you."

She began tugging at the fall of his breeches, but he stilled her hands.

"No, love," he said softly. "Tonight was for you."

He looked down at her dress, ensuring she was properly covered once more, before fixing a few silky strands of hair that had fallen out of her chignon.

"You could be a lady's maid," she said with a short laugh, and he winked at her, easing her apparent sudden nervousness.

"I'm at your service anytime you need," he said, and she shook her head with a smile on her face as he lifted her up to her feet.

"Tomorrow," he said, cupping her face, "Will you be home?"

She blinked a few times as though clearing her thoughts, and then nodded. "Until early afternoon, yes."

"Very good," he said. "I shall call upon you, for I have a question. Goodnight."

And then, with one last quick kiss, he left her there, as he had to make his way out of this party to his home — for if he stayed here for one moment longer, he would lose all control and take her to that very same gazebo he had five years ago.

CHAPTER 18

*W*hat had she just done?

Elizabeth had had full intentions of telling Gabriel tonight that they could no longer see one another, that their time together must come to an end. And then she had found herself being ravished once more in the very same garden as she had years ago! Was there some sort of potion within the scent of these lilies that caused her to lose her senses? Or was it Gabriel himself?

Elizabeth was rubbing at her forehead, perplexed at all that had just occurred, when she walked back into the party room, looking around for Gabriel, but it seemed he had vanished. Instead, Sarah found her.

"Elizabeth?" she asked, looking up into her face. "Is something... amiss?"

"Everything," Elizabeth said with a rueful laugh.

"Oh dear," Sarah responded, biting her lip. "The Duke just wandered through here looking rather pleased before he made his excuses and left for the evening. Our host was quite agitated, though the Duke assured him it was nothing of his doing, but instead complimented him on his beautiful gardens. I don't suppose..."

"That I ruined myself once more, with the same man, in the same place?" Elizabeth asked, arching an eyebrow, and when Sarah looked worried, she waved her hand in the air with a little laugh.

"It's fine, Sarah, it is a legitimate concern. Particularly because that is nearly what happened."

"You and the Duke..." Sarah breathed, and Elizabeth sighed in response, looking for a drink much stronger than her previously untouched lemonade. Finding a glass of champagne, she took it in hand and tilted it back, emptying half the contents of the glass.

"I don't know what happened," Elizabeth said, lifting her hands in front of her, the golden liquid sloshing in the long glass, threatening to spill over the edges, but she was too agitated to care.

"I had every intention of telling him that I no longer had any wish to be together, that we would have to spend our time apart, with the exception of business meetings. But then... but then... he was kind and understanding, and I allowed my emotions and my attraction to him to overcome all else. Oh, Sarah, I am falling for him once more, and I have no idea what to do."

Elizabeth sank heavily into a chair at the side of the room, and Sarah took the seat next to her in a far more graceful manner.

"Why are you so upset?"

"Pardon?" Elizabeth asked, turning toward her, puzzled.

"I only mean that, perhaps, this might be a good thing," Sarah said with a shrug. "Perhaps you and the Duke might find that you are no longer the same people you were years ago and that if you explored this attraction for one another further, you might be very well suited for one another."

Elizabeth was already shaking her head before Sarah finished speaking. She couldn't give in — she wouldn't. She had decided that she could not be with him for a multitude of reasons, and tonight only further proved why it would be a disastrous decision. For if he could distract her from all rational thought with one simple touch in the gardens, what would that mean for everyday life?

"He's calling upon me tomorrow... with a question," Elizabeth told Sarah now, and she saw her friend's eyes widen in joyful surprise.

"Oh, Elizabeth, do you think—"

"I hope not," Elizabeth cut her off, already anticipating Sarah's question. What would she say if Gabriel did propose? A large part of her jumped in gleeful anticipation at the thought, but the other part — the rational side, which typically won over — was much more cautious. For there were many more concerns with marriage. It was a lifetime decision and one that she certainly couldn't take lightly.

"Why not?" Sarah asked once more, and Elizabeth rolled her eyes at her friend.

"Oh, Sarah, I know you always see the best in people, and I love that about you, truly I do. I wish I could be much the same way, but, unfortunately, I am far the opposite. You see—"

Elizabeth's words were cut off by the appearance of red skirts in front of them, and she looked up to see a woman staring down at her. She was beautiful, her dark, shining hair perfectly coiffed, her ample breasts pushed up over the bodice of her elaborate gown. She had a black circular mark over her lip and Elizabeth wondered whether she had put it there on purpose.

"Lady Elizabeth," she drawled. "How lovely to see you. And who is your little friend?"

Elizabeth felt Sarah bristle beside her, but she took her

elbow and drew her up next to her so that they stood in front of the woman, allowing Elizabeth to look down upon her, which she far preferred.

"Lady Pomfret," she greeted her, and she felt rather than saw Sarah startle next to her, recognizing the woman's name. "Please meet my dear friend, Miss Jones."

"How lovely to make your acquaintance," the woman said. "My, it has been far too long, Lady Elizabeth," she said. "I heard the silliest rumor the other day — that you were running a bank!"

As she tittered, Elizabeth felt her ire toward the woman growing. She told herself that it was because of her rudeness, and not because of the fact she was the very same woman Elizabeth had seen Gabriel with many years ago, but she knew she was lying to herself.

"I am the senior partner of Clarke & Co., actually," she said, and Lady Pomfret fanned herself. The widow was a frequent guest at parties such as these, unfortunately, for she was a favorite of many of the *ton* — particularly the gentlemen, as she was generous with her favors. "Perhaps you have heard of it?"

"Oh, I'm not sure," the woman said with a shrug. "I do not bother myself with such issues but have my solicitors and stewards and the like care for it all. It allows me to spend my time on other matters that are far more interesting."

"I actually find bank matters more interesting than most others," Elizabeth said dryly, and Lady Pomfret laughed as though Elizabeth had told an amusing joke.

"Oh, Lady Elizabeth, darling, you are silly, are you not? Now, I must ask you about your growing acquaintance with our darling Clarence. It is on the tongues of everyone, as you must know. I do recall you were close some years ago, were you not? He has always been such an enjoyable man."

Her words were warm, but her blue gaze was ice, and Elizabeth felt her spine grow stiff as she stared her down.

"We are friends," she said, which was the truth. They were. She enjoyed their time together, enjoyed talking to him. She would just never admit to this woman that there might be more than that between the two of them.

"How lovely!" the woman gushed, then leaned in, resting her fingers upon Elizabeth's bare ones.

"Oh, whatever happened to your gloves?" She looked back up at Elizabeth with a knowing glance.

"I spilled a drink upon them and they were ruined," Elizabeth said, unconcerned, suddenly wanting to be anywhere but this room. "Now if you will excuse us, Lady Pomfret, but I promised Miss Jones that I would introduce her to a friend of mine. Farewell."

As they turned away, Sarah murmured, "Nasty witch," and Elizabeth could only nod in agreement, though her stomach was in turmoil at all she had been reminded of through her conversation with Lady Pomfret. Was Gabriel still involved with the woman? Or any other women? She felt as though she was going to be sick and she took a few deep breaths as she brought a hand to her belly.

If — *if* — she were to accept Gabriel, or, at the very least, further whatever it was that was currently between them, these would be the types of women, the types of circumstances she would have to endure.

"Are you all right?" Sarah asked, placing a hand on Elizabeth's arm, and she managed a nod. She would love, more than anything, to return home and leave this party behind, but that was not to be. For she had clients here who would find it rude, would consider it odd, would say that this is what a fickle woman would do — attend such a party and then leave the moment she felt emotional or ill. No, she would remain and do what she needed to do. She took a deep breath, pasted a smile on her face, and went to work.

* * *

GABRIEL SANK into the broad leather chair in front of the fireplace of his study, his brow deeply furrowed in concentration as he studied the item he held between his fingers. The gold of the band glinted in the reflection of the orange flames, while the three diamonds in the center reflected a brilliant light around the dark walls of the room.

The ring had been his mother's. Years ago, when her health began to decline, she had become too thin for the ring to fit any longer, and it kept slipping off her finger. It was then she had given the ring to Gabriel, making him promise to find a woman worthy to wear it.

It was not so much that the woman had proven difficult to find, Gabriel thought as the longcase clock in the hall chimed midnight. No, it was Gabriel himself who had not been prepared to offer it to anyone. Even when he had asked Elizabeth to marry him the first time, all of those years ago, something had kept him from offering such a gift to her. It was as though he had known that it wasn't meant to be — at least, not at that time, at that moment. For the truth was, had they married five years ago, it never would have worked between them. He was not ready to be a husband, and he would have disappointed her at every turn.

But now… now he was sure that he could be the man she needed. He just had to determine that this was the right step to take — for both of them. For once he went down this path, there was no turning back. Gabriel refused to fail at anything in his life. Especially at this.

He nearly jumped at the knock at the door, and he turned toward the voice of his butler.

"Your Grace," came his gravelly voice. "You have a visitor."

Gabriel stood, confused, and shock coursed through him when Elizabeth walked through the door — alone. Never before had Gabriel felt so fortunate that his butler had been loyal to him and his family for years now. He was a man who could be trusted to keep the secrets within these walls. He nodded at him as Elizabeth took a step into the room, requested, "A towel?" and then bid him to close the door.

Gabriel then looked to Elizabeth, who remained standing there within the first few feet of his study.

"Is it now raining?" he asked.

It was a stupid question, for her entire being was sopping wet. Her hair was pressed against her face underneath a nearly ruined headdress, water dripping down the strands onto the plush deep green carpet at her feet. She looked down upon it, as well as at her now-ruined slippers and the damp folds of her silk gown, as though she was recognizing the water stains for the first time.

"Oh, dear," was all she murmured, before finally looking up at him. "I've ruined your carpet."

"Not ruined," he clarified. "Marked slightly, perhaps. It seems you forgot your trusty umbrella this evening."

"I am so sorry," she said, biting her lip. "Forgive me?"

"Always," he said, and at that moment so much more was spoken than what was said aloud.

CHAPTER 19

*H*e had said he would always forgive her. At least, that's what Elizabeth thought he had meant as he watched her standing there ruining the beautiful, likely very expensive, carpet beneath her.

He would always forgive her, whereas she could not seem to find it in her heart to do the same for him — though, one could hardly compare a wet carpet to a tryst with Lady Pomfret — and perhaps others — now could one?

Elizabeth took the subtle headdress with its humble ornamentation of a few small jewels from her head, rolling it in her bare hands, though she was aware she must look like a wet dog with her hair hanging in cloying chunks around her face. Her auburn locks were typically nearly straight, but once they became wet, they sprang up into a curl that was now most likely out of control.

Meanwhile, Gabriel was the vision of perfection, slouched back once again in the wide, comfortable chair, his legs splayed, without a jacket or cravat, his shirt open to reveal the dark skin of his chest beneath it. The sight of him made her knees tremble ever so slightly, and a slow heat began to rise through her body.

She sighed. Coming here had been a terrible idea. In fact, she wasn't sure why she had even had the idea at all, or what had ever possessed her to act upon such a thought.

Gabriel crossed one leg over the other as he leaned back in his chair and casually folded his hands in his lap, perusing her. "What are you doing here?"

Elizabeth nodded. It was an appropriate question. What *was* she doing here? It was after midnight, and when she left Lord and Lady Holderness' party, she should have gone directly home. When Justine had decided to leave, Elizabeth had offered to accompany her — in fact, she had more than wanted to do so; but her grandmother urged her to continue her conversations, reminding her of just how important they were. They lived not far, and Justine promised the carriage would return for her shortly and would await Elizabeth for whenever she was ready.

It didn't take long until she was impatiently waiting for it, but the moment she was in the carriage, the thought of returning home caused a feeling of restlessness to course through her bones.

She had looked down at her hands, remembered her loss of gloves and Gabriel's possession of them, and then determined that she must travel to his house to see them returned.

And, perhaps, they had some unfinished business to discuss.

Of course, Elizabeth wasn't completely foolish. She had returned home and then found a hack to take her to the Duke's house. It wouldn't do for her driver to know her late-night whereabouts, nor for anyone to see her carriage take her there or be waiting in front of Gabriel's spectacular Mayfair home. They might receive the incorrect impression of what it meant.

Now that she was here, standing in Gabriel's study, with him sitting so nonchalantly in front of her, she felt the complete fool, despite her earlier conviction that she was far from it.

Just then the door opened slightly more than a crack, and the butler passed her a couple of pieces of cloth, which she gratefully took to dry her hair before removing her cloak to replace it with a towel to cover her dress. She had asked the hack to drop her off down the street so no one returning home would see her, but she hadn't realized just how hard the rain was coming down.

"I, ah…" she cleared her throat, looking around her at the deep masculinity of the office that bespoke of the same characteristics as the man himself. "I came for my gloves."

"Your gloves?" he questioned, raising an eyebrow, his expression causing her insides to turn to warm liquid. "Unfortunately I cannot aid you in your quest."

"Did you not take them home?" she asked, narrowing her eyes as she attempted to determine what his current ploy was. For he took every situation and turned it around to suit his own purposes. Including something as simple as when she had removed her gloves to feel the water on her fingertips.

"I did, but I gave them to my valet in order for him to have them laundered," he said, spreading his hands wide. "So you see, you will have to wait. But Elizabeth," he drew out the syllables of her name in that deep, sultry voice that made her tingle all over. "I could have returned them to you in the morning. Don't tell me I now hold your only pair of which you are currently in desperate need."

"I have more pairs," she murmured, looking down at her hands now, which she folded within her navy blue cloak.

"Yet you felt the need to come all the way to my lodgings in order to find your gloves."

Oh, she wished he would stand, instead of leaning back and watching her with that smug expression on his face.

"I did," she said with a nod, holding her chin high, refusing to back down. "For you see, Your Grace, I also needed you to know something. What happened at the party tonight should never have occurred. I became lost in my senses and did things... *allowed* things, that should never have happened. I no longer want nor need any ties to you. You said you would call on me tomorrow, but the truth of the matter is that this cannot go on."

"No?" he asked, seemingly unaffected by her words. "And why would you say that?"

"You and I are different people," she said, all of her fears and worries flowing out now. She didn't know if it was the late hour, or the intimate atmosphere, or the few glasses of champagne she had drunk that night in order to get through it, but suddenly all of her inhibitions fled, and her true thoughts came pouring out. "I will not discuss the past, not again, but it's more than that. I love the bank, despite how difficult some days may be. You are a duke, and no matter what you say, your wife will have expectations placed upon her. I certainly would not meet any of them. You care nothing of what anyone thinks, but to me, it matters. It has to, due to the role in which I've been placed. And yet, you know that I am attracted to you, an attraction that I cannot seem to deny. Therefore, the only thing to do is for us to no longer see one another, besides during times for business and social engagements."

He uncrossed his arms now, bringing them to the sides of the chair as he slowly began to rise and step toward her. His gaze had darkened, his expression unreadable, and Elizabeth swallowed hard. But she wouldn't back down. She had come here for a purpose, and now that she had delivered her carefully practiced message, it was time to go.

"Good night, Gabriel," she said, but as she turned, he crossed the room in an instant and reached out, catching her fingers in his, turning her around to face him.

"That's not why you came here tonight," he murmured, and her eyes widened.

"What are you talking about? Of course it is," she said, indignant that he would so question her.

"No, that's what you are telling yourself," he said, still holding one of her hands in his, the other coming up to lightly stroke her face. She told herself to move back, to tell him to stop, but somehow she found herself leaning into him once more.

"Look me in the eye, Elizabeth, and tell me that you came here only for your gloves, that you truly no longer desire my company, and I'll see the truth," he continued. "Say the word and I will walk you to the door, say farewell, and have nothing further to do with you besides our business at the bank. But first, you must convince me, Elizabeth."

As he spoke, he inched ever closer, his lips nearing hers, and she could feel his breath upon her cheek. He smelled slightly of brandy, but it was the musky scent of his cologne that was so distinctly him that overwhelmed her. She closed her eyes for just a moment, losing herself in the sensations that came over her just by his nearness.

Her rational thought was fighting against her instincts, telling her to do as he told her, to tell him that she must go and he should leave her be.

But when she opened her eyes and stared into the deep blue of his, they drew her in, pulling her closer, and all thought fled. She reached up, wrapped her arms around his neck, and with one hand entangled in his thick locks of midnight hair, she tilted his head down toward her and stood on her toes to press her lips against his.

He instantly responded to her invitation, taking the kiss

and expertly deepening it. His tongue swept into her mouth, and she matched him stroke for stroke. Never before, even with him all those years ago, had she felt such a yearning to come ever closer to a man. His hands came around her back, wrapping the two of them more tightly together, their bodies flush against one another, his hard and unyielding.

She slipped one hand from the back of his head to place it on the opening of his shirt, over the bronze skin at his neck where her gaze had been lingering for so long, feeling the warmth of his skin on her fingertips. She moved her hands lower, trailing her fingertips along the bristle of dark hair that dusted his hard chest, and it seemed as though his breath was coming ever faster. It gave her a feeling of heady power to know she could have such an effect on him, but at the same time, it wasn't enough. She wanted more. She wanted to see all of him, to know him as she had once before.

Elizabeth knew they could never truly be together — not in any way that would be longer than what had already come before. But she would give herself this one night. One more night to know him, to love him, to have a memory she could forever cherish.

She broke her lips away from his, unsure of how to tell him, to ask him for what she wanted.

"Gabriel..." was all that came out on a throaty whisper, but it seemed to be enough for him to understand what she was seeking.

"Are you sure?" he asked, his forehead against hers as they remained locked in an intimate embrace, their breath mingling together.

She nodded against him, feeling the hard set of his jaw beneath her fingertips.

"Very well," he said, his voice full of smoke and promise of more to come. "But tonight, love, tonight I will show you exactly how it should be done."

He nudged the towel off of her shoulders, allowing it to pool on the floor at their feet, and Elizabeth gasped as he suddenly bent at his knees and scooped her up in his arms, her own hands wrapping around his neck.

"Where are you taking me?" she asked, to which he smiled seductively.

"My bedroom, of course," he responded, but as he began to carry her out of the room, Elizabeth protested.

"Your servants," she said, "whatever will they think? Can we not stay here, away from prying eyes?"

"Most are abed, except the butler, and he is as loyal as they come," Gabriel said, clearly not concerned in the least, and for a fleeting moment, Elizabeth wondered whether this was the first time he had carried a woman through the house to his own chambers. "I can promise you, Elizabeth, the utmost privacy."

"I am soaking your clothing."

"It will wash."

He paused for a moment, a thought clearly entering his mind.

"Is your carriage out front?"

"Of course not," she said, indignant that he would even suggest she wouldn't have thought of such a thing.

"Good," he said, a slight smile teasing his lips. "Then we have all the time in the world."

What he was going to do with that time, Elizabeth had no idea. When the two of them had previously come together, it was quick, hurried, with him finishing in the bushes beside them in order to "protect her." She knew he had been remorseful afterward, which had hurt more than the actual act in itself.

Now, he carried her through his home, and Elizabeth knew that if she had to find her way out alone, she would become lost through the dizzying array of corridors and rooms within. Gabriel possessed wealth of which most people could only dream, and his London home was more expansive than many country estates she had visited.

Her heart began to beat so quickly and loudly that she thought he surely must be able to hear it as they climbed the stairs to the upper level. He strode down the carpeted hallway as though she weighed nothing, stopping in front of a door at the end of the hall. He nudged it open with his shoulder, revealing his chambers within.

As he stepped out of the corridor and into the room, he finally set Elizabeth back on her feet, and she looked around her in awe.

There was no question of the masculinity of the room, and it bespoke Gabriel at every touch, from the dark stone surrounding the fireplace from where a dim glow fell over the room, to the dark gold drapes pulled over the windows on the wall beside. In front of them sat a writing desk, where she supposed he often worked in order to see out to the view beyond, though what was beyond the curtains, Elizabeth had no idea, so turned around she was.

The canopy over the bed matched the curtains, and Elizabeth gasped at how massive it was. The ornate wood carvings within the headboard were rather ghastly, though she certainly wasn't about to remark upon them at this moment. The thought, however, did ease her beating heart somewhat, at least for a moment.

Until Elizabeth remembered just what they would be doing upon the bed, and then she became slightly nervous once more.

Gabriel must have sensed it, for he walked over to a sideboard next to the fireplace, and picked up a glass.

"Would you like a drink?"

"You keep brandy in your bedroom?"

He shrugged. "It helps me sleep."

Elizabeth took a step toward him, reaching for the glass after he had poured a bit into it.

"Very well," she said, thinking it couldn't hurt, and drank it down quickly, welcoming the burn in her belly.

He took the empty glass from her, deliberately allowing their fingertips to brush against one another, then placed the glasses back down before turning to her.

"Now, Elizabeth," he said, his voice sending tingles down her spine. "Let your education begin."

CHAPTER 20

*W*hat was this woman doing to him?

It was all Gabriel could do to keep himself under control, to prevent himself from tossing Elizabeth on the bed, ripping the buttons of her dress as he divested her of it, and entering her with all of the passion he had been attempting to hold back.

But that was not what a woman such as Elizabeth deserved. Nor what she would welcome, as far as he could gather.

So, instead, he had allowed a brief respite between them before he came toward her, forcing himself to be slow and tender. He brought his hands to her slim shoulders, turning her around so that her back was to him. Gabriel removed one pin, and then another from her hair, allowing the wet tresses to trail down her back. He had never before seen her hair disheveled, and it enticed him. He had imagined this moment for some time, of what it would be like to have her before him, beneath him.

Once he had released her hair, he began on the buttons of her dress. They were dratted things, tiny and not made for large fingers like his own. But he managed well enough, and soon her gown gaped open at the waist. He fitted his hands inside the silk, around her chemise, drawing her back toward him between the V in his legs. When her bottom came against him, he nearly groaned aloud.

He helped her sleeves down her arms, trailing his fingers along her skin behind the silk. Remembering how much she had seemed to enjoy his mouth on her neck earlier this evening, he repeated the motion, satisfaction filling him when he heard her sigh in response.

Her gown soon fell down her slim body to the floor, and he took a moment to appreciate her form in only her stays and chemise. He quickly unlaced the stiff garment about her waist, allowing it to join the clothing beneath them. He picked up her clothing and laid it before the grate to dry. He turned back for her chemise but she stepped away from him, her eyes teasing as she waved a finger in front of him.

"Not yet," she said. "It's your turn now."

He grinned at her challenge as she stepped back toward him, undoing the remainder of his shirt buttons. Thankfully he currently wore far less clothing than she, and soon his shirt followed her own clothing to the floor while her hands came to the fall of his pants, freeing him in a few swift motions.

He stepped out of his breeches, coming toward her now, and she backed up until she was against the bed — exactly where he wanted her.

Gabriel now found the hem of her chemise, and in one motion it flew off of her.

Before Elizabeth had time to even feel any embarrassment due to her current state of undress, Gabriel picked her up and placed her gently on the bed. Instead of following her, he took a moment to step back and appreciate what lay in front of him. Elizabeth squirmed uncomfortably once she realized what he was doing, but he leaned over and stilled her with his arms around her.

"You are the most beautiful woman I have ever seen," he whispered, and she raised an eyebrow.

"Do you say that to all the ladies?" she asked, and her words cut into him for a moment, but he shook his head truthfully.

"Never before," he said, fully meaning it, and he could see she was fighting back a slight smile.

But when she spoke, her words made him laugh more than anything, for they were so practical, so Elizabeth.

"I'm cold," she said, narrowing her eyes when he chuckled, and he sobered, nodding as he pulled back the blankets and she crawled in.

He followed, bringing a hand forward to cup her cheek.

"That's what you get when you chase after a man in the rain at midnight," he teased, and she pinched him.

"I was not chasing you," she said, and he chuckled as he leaned in, ready to capture whatever words were coming next with his mouth.

"Say what you want," he said, "but either way, Elizabeth — you've caught me."

He didn't allow her to respond, but fused his lips upon hers, stroking, loving, and promising what was to come. Her hands were upon him, seemingly everywhere, and he grasped them in his own as he wasn't sure how much longer he could take her touch.

He trailed his lips down her neck, over her collarbone to the swell of her breast, where he began to lavish his attention upon first one pink bud and then the other. She bucked up against him, and he grasped her hips in order to still her.

Elizabeth, however, was having none of it, and she positioned herself beneath him, begging him to enter her. He slipped a finger between them to ensure she was ready for him and finally gave in to what she wanted, filling her in one swift stroke.

Elizabeth cried out in pleasure as Gabriel stilled for a moment, unsure of just how long he could restrain himself, to keep control over his pace.

He had imagined this moment over and over again for the past few months, but nothing could have ever prepared him for how it would feel to join with her again. It was indescribable magic, and nothing in his life had ever felt so right.

Gabriel always seemed to be reaching for something, trying to entertain himself through his schemes, his plans, his... well, yes, his manipulations, though they were always for the right reasons. It was the only way he seemed to be able to find satisfaction in his life. Until now. Now he knew that everything else was just a facade, and this was the truth he was looking for.

At Elizabeth's urging — damn, the woman was impatient — he began moving back and forth in long strokes, intent on providing her with all of the raptures he was feeling himself.

Her hands seemed to be everywhere — in his hair, over his back, sliding along his hips and down his thighs.

"Elizabeth," he groaned, and when he didn't think he could hold back any longer, she tightened around him, crying out, though what she said, he had no idea, for he let go himself.

After a moment of recovery, Gabriel rolled over to take any weight off of Elizabeth but stretched an arm behind her head to draw her in close to his side.

She lay there next to him, her head on his shoulder, and yet he could sense the tension that remained within her body as she didn't allow herself to completely relax against him.

But that was his Elizabeth, he thought with a smile. Never completely allowing anyone in, keeping her guard raised for fear that without it, she would be hurt.

"Elizabeth," he murmured, leaning down to kiss the top of her head. "You are magnificent."

She chuckled slightly and placed a hand on his chest. "I can't say I did much of anything."

"You were here," he said simply. "You came to me."

"I shouldn't have," she said, her voice just above a whisper now. "I didn't even realize what I was doing, if I am being honest. It was as though something drew me here, something... unexplainable."

It was their desire for one another, he wanted to tell her, but he knew that too much explanation would only scare her and drive her away. Gabriel could already see that passionate fire beginning to ebb, to be replaced by the cool exterior she used as a shield. He wanted nothing to do with it. He wanted her to be open with him, to allow him to know her thoughts as he had known her body. But it was clear that Elizabeth wouldn't be having any of that tonight.

She was silent for a moment, and Gabriel readied himself for the words that he knew were coming next.

"I should go home."

"Of course you should," he said, smiling slightly, and then winked at her, knowing it would only irk her. "That doesn't mean you have to."

"Gabriel!" she exclaimed, pushing herself up now and looking at him with wide eyes. "Of course I have to. I shouldn't even have come here to begin with. It was foolish. It was impulsive. It was—"

"Perfect," he finished for her with a grin, and she sighed in exasperation.

"What?" he asked, bringing his other arm behind his head in over to prop it up to look at her. "Do you not agree?"

Her cheeks flushed a very pretty pink as she swatted at him. "I will never forget it."

Gabriel bristled slightly at her words — words which

suggested that this was a one-time event with little chance of recurrence. But that, he determined, would certainly not be the case. No, his decision had been made the moment she stepped through the door of his study. Lady Elizabeth Moreland would become his wife. Even if it did take some time for her to realize it.

* * *

ELIZABETH SETTLED into the comfortable seats of the carriage as it conveyed her home. While she had refused to allow Gabriel to accompany her, when he found out she had hired a hack to bring her to his house, he had insisted that she return home in one of his many carriages — one, he assured her, that was nondescript, with no suggestion of who might be the owner. She had finally relented and now, with the cool night air flowing through the open window onto her flushed skin, she had a moment to consider all that had just happened.

Gabriel had been right when he had said it was perfect. In all honesty, Elizabeth had little remembrance of the first time they had come together, so hurried and hasty they had been that night in the gardens. But she would never forget tonight for the rest of her life.

Elizabeth knew there was little chance she would ever marry. Not now, not when she was so focused on her role at the bank. She would not marry someone who wasn't of her choosing — and so far, no one had fit such a role.

No one but Gabriel. A duke. A man who had broken her heart. A man who could not be trusted — not only for his indiscretions but for the fact that life was a game to him, everyone within it pawns for him to move around on his chessboard. Elizabeth didn't like to be played and, if she were being honest, she was worried that Gabriel would soon become bored with her, as he was with everything else in his life after a time.

But tonight, for one night, she had forgotten all of that. She had given in to her desires, the longings that she had been unable to quench. She knew part of her would always love Gabriel, no matter what else had occurred. And that part had better be satisfied now, for this was never happening again.

CHAPTER 21

*H*aving only found sleep by the early hours of the morning, when Elizabeth finally rose the next afternoon, she felt as though she had wasted an entire day. There was so much to be done, and here she had squandered most of the working hours in bed. Though now that she was awake, she was unsure of just how productive she would be, for her mind was in a fog and her limbs seemed to feel heavy as she dragged them down the stairs. She had slept a bit, true, but it was a restless sleep, one filled with thoughts of Gabriel and the uncertainty of her future. Would she continue to relive this memory with him over and over, both her body and heart aching over the fact that this would never happen again?

After a quick conversation with the housekeeper about making up a plate for a late lunch she would eat at her desk, Elizabeth began to make her way into the study but was stopped by a voice from the drawing room.

"Elizabeth?" her grandmother called. "You have a visitor."

A visitor? Elizabeth began to follow her grandmother's voice, wondering if it would be Sarah, or perhaps Phoebe, and she contemplated whether she should tell them about last night.

Then she stepped into the drawing room and her jaw dropped.

For there, in the pink corner chair, sat Gabriel, leaning back into the velvet, a smug smile on his face as she walked through the door and took him in.

"Lady Elizabeth," he said, standing. He placed his cup of tea on the table in the middle of the room and walked toward her, stopping in front of her and taking one of her hands in his. He lifted it to his lips, pressing a kiss to the back of it, and Elizabeth's cheeks warmed as she remembered where else his lips had recently been.

She quickly regained her composure, hoping her grandmother hadn't noticed the brief lack of it, though Gabriel was already looking at her knowingly. When she glanced up at him, he held her gaze for but a moment before he slowly, subtly winked at her.

Had he not heard anything she had said to him last night? Of course more likely, knowing him, he had completely disregarded her words, instead, simply doing as he pleased.

Elizabeth narrowed her eyes at him as she tried to assess just what he was up to this time, but he quickly released her hand and returned to his seat, picking up his small teacup as he went. The fact that he, a big, broad-chested male, looked so at ease sitting in the dainty chair with a tiny cup of tea in his hand was not lost on her. Was there anywhere he didn't look as though he naturally belonged?

"Well," Justine said, looking back and forth between the two of them, clearly sensing the tension now thick in the air. "I suppose I will leave the two of you. The door will stay open just a crack so that no can ever suggest that I was anything but a proper chaperone."

Elizabeth did laugh slightly at those words, for her grandmother was far from a chaperone, nor had she ever any intentions to be one. But it did help to maintain appearances, though with whom, Elizabeth had no idea. When the door shut nearly all the way, leaving the two of them alone, Elizabeth rounded on Gabriel, who had made himself quite comfortable, crossing one leg over the other as he reclined in the chair.

Elizabeth's grandfather had rarely frequented this drawing room, and so her grandmother had decorated it as she chose. The walls were a pale gold, the curtains cream, and some of the accents — including the chair upon which Gabriel sat — were a decidedly pinkish color.

Not that it seemed to bother Gabriel.

"What are you doing here?" she asked pointedly, remaining standing herself so he would know that she was expecting him to be leaving shortly.

"I told you I would be coming," he responded, raising an eyebrow at her.

"Yes, you did, but that was before…"

"Before we made love?"

Elizabeth didn't think her cheeks had ever before flamed so hot. She cleared her throat. "Before I explained to you why I felt it was best that we didn't see one another anymore."

"Elizabeth," he said, drawing out the syllables of her name in a way that made the hairs on her arms stand on end and a tingle begin in the center of her belly. "I told you I was going to call on you and call on you I have. Yes, I did hear you when you told me you no longer wanted to see me. However, that was not how we left things between one another. If anything has changed between us, last night would only have brought us closer together, would it have not?"

Elizabeth crossed her arms over her chest and began to pace across the room, unable to bring herself to sit down.

"Gabriel, before… before anything happened, I told you

how I felt, what my thoughts were regarding our relationship with one another. You heard them, did you not?"

"I heard them," he said, his face unreadable. "However, I have never taken you for the type of woman who would be with a man to whom she wasn't… committed."

Elizabeth couldn't meet his eyes. Somehow in the sober light of day, all that had transpired between them seemed almost like a dream, and she could hardly believe it had occurred. Now she had difficulty even speaking of it. Whereas Gabriel… Gabriel didn't seem to have a problem with anything. It seemed as though everything came easily to him, for there was nothing with which he struggled.

"I am also not the type of woman to say things of importance if I do not mean them," she said, stopping and turning on her heel to look at him.

Gabriel finally stood and slowly sauntered across the room. He had a nearly predatory look in his eye, and with every step he took, Elizabeth took one away from him in equal measure, until her back came flush against the wall and she jumped, startled. A satisfied grin came over Gabriel's face as his step never faltered, and when he was but inches from her, he leaned over her, one arm stretched out above her, his hand on the wall, trapping her in front of him.

Elizabeth's heart pounded, but not with fear — oh, no, it was with anticipation, despite the fact she had vowed this would never happen again.

He lifted his other hand to cup her cheek, and he stroked her skin with his thumb.

"Elizabeth," he repeated, his face inches from hers, though he made no move to kiss her nor come any closer. "You have reservations, sure. I understand them. I gave you reasons to distrust me in the past. You have responsibilities now. No one is aware of all of this better than I. But," he slid his finger down to rest under her chin and tilted her face up so that she had no choice but to look into his deep blue eyes, where she was afraid she would become lost. "Can you truly tell me that you have ever felt anything close for another man to what you feel for me? For I can honestly say that never before have I met another person — man or woman — with whom I enjoy conversing with so much, for in you I have met my match. Your sensuality, although hidden, is incomparable to any I have ever encountered before. In short, Elizabeth, you fit my every need, and I cannot imagine a life with anyone else."

Elizabeth swallowed hard. He was correct in everything he said. She had never felt for another man what she felt for him, and he was as coolly intelligent and as hotly passionate as she could ever ask for in a man. Yet, while he had asked her of her feelings toward him, he had said nothing about what was in his heart, what he actually felt for her. Did he love her? *Could* he love her?

And with his words, he certainly couldn't mean — but then a hard, determined look flashed in his eyes as his jaw tightened, and she realized that yes, he clearly did.

He pushed back from the wall, took her hand in his, and sank down to his knee in front of her. Elizabeth wanted to pull him up, to put a finger to his lips, to tell him not to say the words, but she found she was stunned into shocked silence. She could only stand there mutely looking down at him, like a deer who had sighted a torch.

"Be my wife, Elizabeth," he said, his voice more demanding than pleading, for he was a man for whom nothing was ever denied. "Marry me, have my children, be my duchess."

Elizabeth remained frozen. *Say something,* a voice in the back of her mind urged. She opened her mouth, but nothing came out. She closed her eyes, gathered her thoughts, parted her lips and tried again, but still, no words came.

"I believe the appropriate response is, 'yes,'" Gabriel said, clearly not pleased at having remained bent upon the floor for so long.

Elizabeth tugged at his hands, and a dark look crossed his face as he rose, though he kept a tight grip on her fingers.

"I know that, Gabriel, and I want to say yes, truly I do," she said, her heart at war with her mind.

"But?" he asked, releasing her hands now, and she felt bereft without his touch upon her. "I simply do not understand what could be holding you back."

"The reasons I gave you to keep distance between one another — they still stand," she said, hearing the desperation in her tone, and she vowed to keep such emotion from it for the remainder of the conversation. "If I marry you, I will give up everything that's important to me — *except* you. Your life would be nearly unchanged. You could participate in the same activities, attend the same clubs, keep the same hours. All that would be different is that you would not only hold your own fortune but mine as well."

"I would never—"

She lifted a hand, stilling his words. "I know that you are not asking to marry me for my income nor my partnership — and you should know that my grandfather ensured my inheritance would remain untouched. You are many things, but you are not a fortune hunter and while you enjoy your games, I know you are a man who would far rather earn his own riches than inherit them from his wife. But part of the law is that all that is due to come to me in the future would become yours — and I would no longer have a say over any of it."

He took a step away from her, a wall having come up between the two of them at her talk of finances and legalities.

"Your grandfather provided you the partnership and all of his fortune not for your husband but for you, and I understand that," he said. "I would allow you full control over all of your income."

"And that's just it!" she exclaimed. "You would allow me. It is not something that I could choose any longer for myself."

"So you are telling me that you would rather spend your days alone, with only your independence to keep you company, than share a life with me?"

"I implore you not to say it like that, for you well know that is not what I mean. But can you tell me that as a duchess, I would still live the life I am living now?"

"You would have a few more social obligations, of course," he responded. "But you will have your partnership well established, and the title of Duchess of Clarence would certainly do well to solidify partnerships and clients, would it not? I do not see it as anything but a boon for the business you currently conduct, and it would, perhaps, convince you to share some of your responsibilities with others."

"I do not wish to share the responsibility," she said, her jaw set, and he wrenched his gaze away from her, walking over to the window and looking out beyond, his hands upon the windowsill and his shoulders hunched, likely in cold, reserved anger.

"Why did you come to me last night?" he asked, his voice steel now, and Elizabeth's stomach turned in turmoil.

"I wanted to be with you," she said softly.

"But just for one night?"

"I suppose... yes... no. I don't know. I cannot deny what I feel for you, how I do want you. But..."

But she was scared that one day he would turn from her, and she would be left with nothing. How could she make him understand what she feared? She spoke to him of finances and her independence, but she knew the truth, even if she couldn't say it aloud – she most feared allowing herself to be vulnerable before him once more.

He turned around now, crossing his arms over his chest as he leaned back against the window. He was a man slow to anger, but once he did…

"How is it," he asked slowly, "That in everything else in your life, you are so decisive, so sure in your decisions, and yet with me you are entirely contrary?"

"I ask myself that question constantly," she said honestly.

"The last time I asked you to marry me, you said yes rather quickly," he observed.

"Things were different then. *We* were different."

"So what is it, Elizabeth?" he asked, pushing away from the windowsill and walking toward her until he was a foot away, carrying himself with the imposing ducal power he knew how to wield. "Should I take this as a 'no'?"

Elizabeth refused to be cowed by him, to back down or allow him to make her feel anything less than what she was.

"I would ask that you give me time to think on my answer," she said. "Would you *allow* that, Your Grace?"

His eyes narrowed ever so slightly, but otherwise, he seemed unaffected.

"Very well," he said, then reached into his jacket and pulled a small box out of his pocket, which he slammed it down on a small end table beside him. "This was for you. It still is, I suppose, if you choose to accept it. It was my mother's and is for the woman I will one day marry. Good day, Lady Elizabeth."

And with that he was out the door, pulling it shut firmly behind him before Elizabeth could even whisper, "Good day, Gabriel," as her eyes began to fill with tears.

CHAPTER 22

*G*abriel hadn't meant to be so heavy-handed with Elizabeth, to show such anger nor try to intimidate her. He could hardly tell her, however, just how much her denial had hurt him, and instead he had lashed out at her.

She had fortitude, though, not giving into his words nor showing any sort of emotion herself. But she frustrated him to no end. If she didn't want him, why not just come out and say so? Why hide behind all of these excuses? For what else could he possibly give her, or could she want from him? He had told her she could keep her banking position, and even her bloody fortune, for goodness sake. Most men would not be nearly so generous. Most men likely wouldn't be able to afford to be either, although that was beside the point.

And what kind of woman would prefer to be alone than to marry — and a *duke* no less? He could knock on the door of any house within Mayfair — hell, within all of London — and ask for the hand of the eldest daughter and none would deny him. In fact, he was sure even a few married ladies of the house would gladly leave their husbands for him if they were able.

Why, oh why, for all that was good, did he have to fall for Lady Elizabeth Moreland — not once, but twice? And why had he made such a disaster of things the first time so that now she would think of any and every excuse not to be with him? She was scared of being hurt again, he reasoned. That must be it — and so she had hurt him first.

All of these thoughts circled around his head as he entered White's Gentleman's Club later that evening. He didn't know why he was here, nor what he expected from the men within these doors, but it had to be better than sitting in his study ruminating on Elizabeth's words as he looked to the door where she had entered only the night before to fulfill all of the fantasies that had been flowing through his mind.

Gabriel was relieved to find that both Redmond and Berkley were in attendance this evening. Thank goodness, he thought, for he didn't think he could stomach the company of any other men tonight. He was well aware of just what a foul mood he was in, and he hoped a drink and a win at cards could help raise his spirits.

"Gentlemen," he said, taking a seat between the two of them and they nodded, though he noted Berkley's raised eyebrow and he realized how surly his greeting had been.

"Troubles, Clarence?" Berkley asked nonchalantly, and Gabriel shrugged, not interested in telling them of Elizabeth's near-denial, though he was aware that Berkley had found himself in such a situation not long ago. Berkley seemed to read his mind, however, as he laughed at Gabriel's reluctance to answer the question. "Do you not recall telling me that you were interested in finding yourself a woman such as Phoebe, one who would keep you on your toes?" Berkley asked. "Just how is that going for you?"

Gabriel couldn't help but chuckle, aware that Berkley spoke the truth.

"It certainly is a question to ponder, whether one should prefer to be kept interested or at ease," he said with a sigh, and Redmond looked between the two of them before shaking his head.

"Or you could just stay single and enjoy all that the world has to offer you," he said with a grin. "*That* would be my preference."

"A fact of which we are all well aware, Redmond," Gabriel said dryly, though his remark did not seem to bother his friend, who rather embraced his role as an affable rake.

Gabriel would have preferred to enjoy an evening with just the three of them, but it seemed that tonight White's was a particularly popular choice, for soon the room was crowded with men milling about, and the chairs throughout the room were filling so that other men were close enough to converse with the three of them.

"Clarence," came a voice from Gabriel's right. "How are you this evening?"

"Fine, thank you, Sir Hugo, and you?"

"Very good, very good," the man said, his round cheeks flushed, a cigar firmly clamped between his teeth. "Though I was hoping to find you here this evening. You are a partner at Clarke & Co., are you not?"

"I am," Gabriel said, suddenly wary. "Though typically I find myself to be more of a silent partner."

"Yes, well," Sir Hugo continued, leaning in closer, though he didn't lower his voice. "Clarke — Henry Clarke, that is — tells me that you are working from the inside, which I admire. It is not the rightful place for a woman to be at the head of the bank, I'll tell you that — not at all. Good on you to work with Clarke in order to determine how best to remove ol' Thomas' granddaughter from her position. I respected the man, I did, but it seems his heart was a little too soft when it came to the woman."

Gabriel's heart began beating in panic, though he kept his composure. He had nearly dismissed the lies he had told Clarke, but he hadn't expected the man to share with others to what he had agreed. If Elizabeth happened to hear of this, well... the consequences could be dire.

"I would not say that is entirely the way of it, Sir Hugo," he said carefully, and the man looked at him conspiratorially.

"Well, it is not as though she is the type of woman you would otherwise court!" he said with a laugh, and his companion, Lord Baxtall, joined in.

"I'm not entirely sure what you mean," Gabriel said, his countenance frosty, and Sir Hugo began to look slightly concerned as he realized that Gabriel might not be entirely pleased with what he had thought was an entertaining joke.

"Only that a potential duchess is certainly not a woman like Lady Elizabeth Moreland, who is more concerned with business than anything else — especially one who may see herself as above you!" Sir Hugo exclaimed. "Why, if a woman thinks she can tell others what to do within a business, I can only imagine what she might think within the home!" He laughed at his own joke, a long, loud chuckle, and Gabriel's expression didn't change.

"She doesn't know her place," Baxtell said with a wave of his hands, his mustache bobbing with his head as he agreed with his own sentiments. "A woman should be in the home, providing for her husband. If she does not yet have a husband, then she should be preparing for one. Women in places of business are nothing but trouble — for everyone involved."

"Lady Elizabeth is certainly not the first woman to find herself a partner within a bank, and I have heard hardly a word of ill regarding the prospects of other such banks,"

Gabriel responded, his words clipped. "Why do you believe in the toxicity of women in such a position?"

"Women are a distraction," Baxtell continued, his voice annoyingly pompous, as though he were providing a lecture to the rest of them. "How is a man supposed to concentrate on matters of the day when he has a beautiful woman sitting in front of him? And how is a woman — particularly an unmarried one — supposed to even attempt to look into matters of business when she is surrounded by potential husbands? If she is married, how can she focus on the important work she must do if she is also concerned with matters regarding the household? It is not natural, Clarence, and I, for one, am glad you are doing something about it."

Gabriel said nothing as he sat and stewed on their words. They were unfair to Elizabeth, that he knew — she was one of the most intelligent people he had ever met, far more so than these fools at the table next to him. Though he hated to admit it, he could see their point regarding her role as a duchess. The fact was that there was much to attend to, with various social events as well as philanthropic efforts and households to manage. Not that he couldn't hire someone to see to such activities, but to have a completely absent wife would be difficult. Particularly if he had to attend to matters in the country — could Elizabeth leave London for a spell? Not likely.

Besides all of that, the woman didn't seem to want him anyway.

"Tell me you are not actually listening to all of that horse-shit," Berkley murmured from across the table, taking a sip of his drink. "I can tell you, man, I thought that way for far too long and it got me into nothing but a heap of trouble. Allow your woman to be happy and you will be too, I can promise you that."

He tipped his drink toward Gabriel, who gladly accepted

his own once it arrived. That was one thing about White's —
it was predictable.

Unlike Elizabeth.

"Let me ask you something, Berkley," he said now,
moving the glass back and forth in front of him. "Is your wife
always questioning you? Does she try to undermine you? It is
one thing for a woman to have her own passions in life, but
at the same time, a man must still have the power within his
own home. What does that say about a man — a duke — if he
cannot even control his wife?"

"It's not about control," Berkley reasoned. "That only
spells more trouble. I do hope you are not actually working
to remove her from the bank."

"Not at all. I was actually trying to protect her from
Clarke, though I'm not sure she would see it that way. You do
not listen to your wife in *all* matters, do you?" Gabriel asked,
slightly incredulous, and Berkley only smiled.

"You have a lot to learn, son," he said jokingly, and Gabriel
rolled his eyes at his friend.

"Or," Redmond chimed in, "Perhaps you need to determine if you're asking the right questions. You are all talk of
business and control. There are many marriages, however,
that are convenient for many purposes but do not mean
joining your entire lives together. For instance, would your
woman mind you taking on a mistress or two, to keep things
interesting?"

Gabriel turned his stare toward him. "She absolutely
would mind. And I would never do such a thing — not
again."

Redmond held his hands up in the air. "Just a question!
No need to be angry with me. Then, Clarence, what I would
ask you is whether you really want one woman — one
woman only! — for the rest of your life? I tell you, I can
hardly imagine it. There are so many options out there

awaiting you, the thought of giving all that up... I couldn't do it. Not a chance."

Gabriel smiled now, a slow, knowing smile.

"If it's the right woman," he said, thinking of Elizabeth — in his bed, in the boardroom, in his life — then absolutely.

But he would not grovel. He was a duke, and if he allowed her to make him beg before a true relationship even began, then he was only setting himself up for a life in which he would be brought lower than he was.

Gabriel wanted her, that much was true. But he had far too much pride to allow her to bring him to his knees once more. He had bent for her once already — in order to ask the question — but now it was up to her. He wouldn't be made a fool, not again.

* * *

GABRIEL DIDN'T STAY LONG at White's — only long enough to finish his drink and brood in the company of friends, before Berkley finally told him to go home and think on things with only his own miserable company. Gabriel readily agreed, but as he walked out the imposing dark doors, he jumped at a presence suddenly appearing at his right.

And like the rat he was, Henry Clarke snuck out of the shadows to latch onto Gabriel's side.

"What do you want, Clarke?" Gabriel practically snarled as he continued walking toward where his carriage awaited.

"I needed to talk to you — alone. I went to your house, but was told you were not in residence."

"No," Gabriel said. "I was not."

"Right," Clarke said, seemingly not affected by Gabriel's snappish tone. "Which is why I came here. As far as I can tell, Clarence, you have done nothing to further our plan. Elizabeth remains firmly entrenched in her position, and any progress made has been entirely of my own doing."

"Progress?" Gabriel turned to him with a raised eyebrow, and Clarke nodded proudly.

"Did you hear of Sir Hugo's defection? That was me — all me!" he crowed. "In addition to the fact that I am a partner now, which I also did of my own accord. You have done nothing of any note."

Gabriel shrugged. "It's too much effort, Clarke. To be honest, I don't really care for your schemes any longer, nor for you. Consider our agreement broken. Now, leave me be."

He had reached his waiting carriage, and now he waved Clarke away as though he were brushing away a flea, but the man was just as persistent.

"You've fallen under her spell, haven't you?"

Gabriel looked at him for the briefest of moments, a look that told Clarke he wanted nothing further to do with him.

"My cousin is a spider," Clarke said, and Gabriel was taken aback at his vehemence. "I know when you tried to further your relationship at the beginning, you had good intentions, which I appreciate. We could use that. You must realize that she is weaving a web around you, drawing you in, bringing you to her side. I tell you, Clarence, you are better off without her. Escape from her clutches before she poisons you, I beg of you. Otherwise, you will be nothing but her prey." He laughed suddenly. "Oh, I can see it now. You, one of the most powerful men in England, falling victim to my cousin, the Lady Elizabeth."

He paused for a moment, obviously collecting his thoughts.

"Well, I will tell you this, Clarence. You have a choice. Come on board with me, or fall down along with Elizabeth. For I have no problems in telling the board of your deception to the bank."

"That would be revealing your own ploys," Gabriel said dryly.

"I am a favored son!" Clarke said, mockingly defending himself. They had come to a stop outside of Gabriel's carriage, and Gabriel was loathe to board with Clarke so close in case the man should attempt to follow him and Gabriel would have to resort to physically removing him. Not that he couldn't do so, but he would prefer not to sully himself. "I am the grandson of their most revered patron. I will defend my cousin to no end, tell them all of how you have been manipulating her in order to get your hands on her fortune and the bank itself. It's not the most far-fetched story, as I'm sure you are aware."

"I hardly think they will believe that a duke with five manors and estates to call home would be so desperate as to marry a woman for her fortune."

"Yes, but a man who enjoys power?" Clarke asked with a sly, knowing grin, "He can never have enough. And what speaks power more than control over one of the largest banks in all of England?"

With that, Clarke finally continued down the street, whistling a tune that made Gabriel want to run after him and shut the man's mouth for him. But instead, he let out a growl of words that would not be fit for the ears of most company and hoisted himself into his carriage.

Gabriel vowed he would not let a man like Clarke question him nor bring him down. He was not afraid of what others may think, nor whether they would believe Clarke — words such as his had never bothered Gabriel in the past, nor would they ever in the future.

No, what he was concerned of now was what Elizabeth would think if she found out about his pact with Clarke, as insincere as his own promise had been. For it would be his word against Clarke's, and while he knew how much Elizabeth reviled her cousin, he also couldn't deny that he had, in fact, made something of a promise to him.

Gabriel was well aware of what Elizabeth thought of his past manipulations, despite his best intentions. This would only solidify her stance to distrust him and deny him.

For once, Gabriel found himself in the thick of a situation from which he did not know how to extricate himself. And he didn't like it. Not one bit.

CHAPTER 23

*T*wo days later, Elizabeth was not in her best form for the partner's meeting. She hadn't heard from Gabriel since he had left her house after his proposal, nor had she expected him to reach out once more. She knew how proud he was, and after thinking on it, she realized that while he was angry, he was likely also hurt as well. She understood why, and it ate at her, knowing that she was the cause of his pain.

But this decision was one that would affect the rest of her life, and she couldn't take it lightly.

As her boots hit the marble floor of the bank's lobby, she managed a smile and a "good morning" for the clerks she passed along the way. Elizabeth had made a careful study of each of their names, a practice to which she knew her grandfather attributed the loyalty of his employees over the years, and one she vowed to continue.

Elizabeth had ensured she would arrive at least an hour before the first partner might venture through the doors. She knew her punctuality was, perhaps, slightly ridiculous, but by the same token, she couldn't help the anxiety she felt whenever she thought she might be late — or later than her guest. Arriving before any others put her at ease, allowing her time to prepare herself for whatever was to come.

And there would certainly be much to come today.

Elizabeth took a seat behind her desk, reviewing the papers before her, upon which were names and words she had carefully written out herself. In addition to Mr. Bates, the manager of the bank, she wanted to accolade one other clerk who had been with the company for many years, as she felt both men had showcased their loyalty and should be commended as well as rewarded. She had final say over the naming of the partners, but she hoped the remainder of the current partners would be in agreement.

And then there was the issue of Henry. Elizabeth was still unsure of how to best approach his removal. If she gave no reason for it, then it would seem there was discord within the Clarke family, which would be unsettling for the reassurance of the bank's partners and clients. But she refused to provide the reason for Henry's manipulation of Mr. Mortimer, for she had given her word to his family that she wouldn't share his current struggles.

She sighed, reviewing the remainder of the agenda next to her, which included salaries as well as client accounts. She wasn't looking forward to sharing the loss of a few of their key clients, nor did she have any new additions to provide as of yet.

And then there was Gabriel. Elizabeth thought of the ring he had left her. It was beautiful, of course. But more than that, she remembered seeing his mother wearing it years ago and knew the significance of him bringing it to give to her. Elizabeth hadn't been able to help trying it on after he left. Once she had blinked away the flood of tears that threatened, she could see that it fit her perfectly, the firelight reflecting off the diamonds to shine around the room. She had admired it for a moment or two until she had to remove it in order to regain her wits and not make a decision based solely on emotion.

She wondered if Gabriel would attend today as she strode down the hallway, her head held high as she vowed to keep control of the meeting, no matter what Henry would challenge her on.

Elizabeth attempted to maintain some positivity when the partners arrived and the meeting finally commenced. The partners, at least, still looked to her as their leader, which she determined was promising.

Henry wasn't in attendance, for which Elizabeth was both surprised and relieved. Nor, however, was Gabriel.

He wasn't, that is, until ten minutes into the meeting.

Elizabeth halted mid-sentence as the door opened, emitting his imposing frame.

"My apologies," he said, his eyes meeting each of the partners at the table before settling on her, a strange look within them. "I was tied up with other business."

"Ah, I'm surprised you made it here at all, Clarence!" one of the partners, Mr. Donahue, said with a bit of a cackle. "A man like you has many important matters to which to attend."

"Clarke & Co. remains one of those matters," he said, taking a seat. "I can assure you of that."

And just then, Henry strode through the doors, greeting them all as if he had arrived on time, taking a seat across from Elizabeth at the other end of the table.

"Lovely to see you all!" he said as though he were the one hosting, and Elizabeth gripped her pen so hard it nearly snapped. She was losing control, all thanks to these two men who had seemingly taken hold of her life, and she was not at all happy about it.

"Now that we are all here," she said, her tone admonishing them without being overly critical — at least she hoped not, "Perhaps we can get on with business?"

"Of course, Elizabeth," Henry said with his sly smile. "Is that not why we are all present today?"

She ignored him, continuing on with the discussion that would lead to her suggestion of new partners.

"I would like us to review the salaries of some of our key employees," she said. "You have each been given copies of what they are currently making. I would suggest, in order to provide both rewards and incentives, that we slightly increase those who have been showing exemplary performance."

A few heads began to nod around the table until Henry began to speak.

"And just where would these additional funds come from?" he asked.

"The bank has seen some growth in profits in the recent years," she responded.

"Perhaps the partners would like the rewards of these profits for themselves instead of giving them to employees!" he exclaimed, and then the heads that had been nodding at Elizabeth's previous words began to pause as the partners contemplated what Henry said.

"We will all see increased profits, Henry, if our employees are content and working to increase the fortunes of the bank," she said through gritted teeth, and she noted that the partners' heads were turning back and forth between the two of them, awaiting each of their responses.

"That may be so, but they are already making a healthy sum compared with some of our competitors," he countered.

"I would suggest that we stay ahead of our competitors instead of matching them," Elizabeth bit back.

The two of them stared at one another, their gazes

locked, until finally Henry smiled and waved a hand to her as if conceding.

"You are the senior partner, Elizabeth, so I suppose what you say will have to go anyway."

Elizabeth didn't miss some of the disgruntled looks around the table, and she knew what Henry was doing, making it look as though she were making poor decisions to which the rest of them would have to agree.

"This may be the case; however, I would like to have the support of the partners," she said, her smile brittle. "Perhaps we should put it to a vote?"

Elizabeth's suggestion narrowly passed, and she moved on to the next issue, after she had asked Mr. Bates to leave the room for a moment.

"As you are all aware, Mr. Larkin and Mr. Bates have been with Clarke & Co. for over twenty years now. They began in small roles, but have been promoted through the years and have proven both their loyalty as well as their competence. I would like to suggest that they are made partners in the bank, as it could only help grow the company."

This statement was met with some contemplation on behalf of all the partners in attendance, and Elizabeth knew it was one area she may lose, but she had to try.

"More partners means a greater division of the partner revenue." Henry – of course – was the first to speak across the table, and Elizabeth nodded, willing herself not show any sign of chagrin, for any emotion she displayed could be used against her.

"This is true," she said, and keeping a pointed look at Henry, she continued. "Which is why my second suggestion is that we could hold their partnerships in lieu until we have room within our partnership group to include them."

"Do you mean until one of us croaks?" asked one of the elderly partners, his eyes wide.

"No, Mr. Donahue," Elizabeth said with the slightest of smiles, which she hoped was reassuring. "Until there is financial space to add them, or until one of the partners chooses to leave of his own accord."

She returned her gaze to Henry, as though suggesting he be the first to do so, but he looked away from her.

"I have no issue with having them in wait," said Mr. Cartwright, and Elizabeth nodded, noting the response on the page in front of her.

"Although…" Henry spoke up from across the table, and Elizabeth inwardly groaned. Why could the man not keep his mouth closed? "Perhaps there is more advantage to be had from partners with connections. The Duke of Clarence, for example, has furthered our relations within the nobility. What could these two men do for us?"

"They would exemplify to other employees the merits of working hard for the bank. In addition, they would bring expertise and knowledge on the inner workings of our business," she responded.

"Should that not be the role of the senior partner?" Henry challenged, and Elizabeth clenched her teeth so tightly that her jaw began to ache.

"It is a combined effort," she finally said, and Henry nodded, in satisfaction this time, for he knew that he had won that round.

"On that note," he said, "I would like to discuss some of our current — and former — clients."

"That is the next topic on the agenda," Elizabeth said. "Perhaps we could wait to conclude our current discussion?"

"Oh, I think it is all one," Henry said. "Partners… clients… do they not go hand-in-hand?"

"All of the business of the bank could be considered to be of one entity," Elizabeth said. "However, I find it more efficient to review one item at a time so that we do not become disorderly."

"Oh, no one could ever suggest *you*, Lady Elizabeth, of being disorderly," Henry said with a smile, as though he were complimenting her. "Since you have all in order, perhaps you could share what has happened to one of our largest clients, the shipping baron, Sir Hugo? He was a significant account, both personally and commercially. It is a shame he has left."

"Sir Hugo has left?" asked another partner, Mr. Lang, and Elizabeth felt rather than saw discontent beginning to rise around the table.

"Yes," she said, cutting through the murmurings surrounding her. "Sir Hugo has decided to bank elsewhere, unfortunately. However, I am diligently working on securing clients of equal wealth and status in his place."

"If Sir Hugo has left, have any others as well?" asked Sir Gray.

"Only a few small clients."

"Have we replaced them?"

"Not yet."

The murmuring intensified, and Elizabeth wanted nothing more than to rise out of her chair and run from the room. Her grandfather had taught her many things but never had he instructed her on how to handle a group of unruly men.

Although… her governess had taught her how to handle children, for her mother had hoped that Elizabeth would have a great deal of them. Elizabeth had been fighting the fact that she was a woman, but perhaps, now, she could use it in order to aid herself.

Elizabeth pushed back her chair, clasped her hands in front of her, and stood, waiting for them all to notice her. Finally, a few of the men observed that she was standing, and hastily moved to do so as well, for one should never permit a lady to stand while he remained sitting — whether said lady be the senior partner or not.

In a few moments, they had all risen, awaiting her next movement.

She smiled, enjoying the fact that there was some power that came from being a woman.

"Thank you, gentlemen," she said. "Now, within the pages in front of you is a listing of our largest clients and the status of their accounts. As you can see, I have confirmed with most of them that they will be remaining with the bank. It is to be expected that my grandfather's death has caused change, and I am well aware that the fact that I am a woman may cause some concern. However, I am sure that you can all attest to the fact that I have proven my ability thus far, and am committed to this bank. There are many potential clients I have been meeting with who are interested in coming aboard. I would ask all of you during this time of transition to put the bank's interest first and also be on the hunt for anyone who would like to bring their business to Clarke & Co."

She sat now, and the rest of them followed suit.

"I do have one question, Elizabeth," said Henry, of course. "You say you are dedicated to the bank, but what happens when you marry? Then we will have yet another face, another transition, and perhaps the loss of more clients."

"Perhaps I will not marry," she said, refusing to look at Gabriel as she did so. "Or perhaps I will, but then I will maintain my current position. I am the head of this bank, and you must all understand that."

They seemed appeased by her proclamation, and Elizabeth finally allowed herself to meet Gabriel's eyes. His expression told her nothing, although she knew those eyes well enough to sense that they looked... haunted. Contemplative. Unsure.

"Thank you all for coming," she said finally, unable to take the scrutiny any longer. "We will return to some of these matters at our next meeting in four weeks' time. Good day."

And with that, they began to file out. Elizabeth herself escaped before the lot of them. It was unlike her, but she had no wish to be left alone with Gabriel. Not now, not yet.

But as she entered her office, she heard a step behind her, and she knew she had no choice.

CHAPTER 24

"*Y*ou did well in there."

"Congratulations, I see you have found your voice."

Elizabeth took a deep breath after hearing the bitterness within her tone. She must ensure she remained calm and composed, despite the fact that inside she was still churning with anger. She was frustrated over her lack of control and seething over the fact that Henry had managed to not only undermine her credibility but to also cause damage to the bank. She wasn't succeeding in properly protecting the bank, as she had vowed to do when her grandfather passed it onto her, and that caused a great deal of guilt to fill her.

And, as ridiculous as it was, she was angry that Gabriel hadn't come to her defense in the meeting. Oh, she knew what it would look like if he had — that he was defending her because there was something between the two of them, or that he was trying to win her affections. But at some point she had needed *someone* to stand up for her, to show her that she wasn't alone.

She whirled around now, aching to take it all out on him, to tell him how angry she was, how upset she was, but she couldn't. *Don't show any emotion, Elizabeth*, said the voice in her head, which for so long had been her mother's, but was now her own counseling her. *It will only portray your weakness.*

So instead she stood there, trembling within, her jaw set tightly and her hands in fists by her side.

Gabriel stood by the door, staring at her. Finally he turned, and she thought he was blessedly leaving, but instead, he shut the door and turned around, leaning back against it with his arms crossed.

"Let it out," he said, his voice commanding.

"What are you talking about?"

"All that you're feeling — let it out. Tell me what you are thinking. Be angry. Let the emotion flow. For God's sake, do something besides standing there looking at me as though I am speaking nonsense!"

"If you don't like it," she said, the words clipped, "then you are more than welcome to leave. In fact, I would prefer that you did."

"Is that what you want, Elizabeth? To be alone? To never have to rely on anyone else so you can say that you did it all by yourself?"

Elizabeth felt her ire rising, but she knew he was doing this on purpose, trying to goad her into saying something she shouldn't.

"That has nothing to do with anything personal," she responded. "You had your opportunity to rescue me if that's what you wanted to do so badly. You could have ridden your white horse into that meeting with your shiny suit of armor and told the rest of them, 'I agree with Lady Elizabeth. As a duke, I have seen the way she has consulted with the nobility, drawing them in as potential clients. I have full faith in her abilities.' But no. You arrived late, disrupting me, and then you simply sat there and allowed Henry to sway the rest of them in his direction."

Gabriel stared at her for a moment.

"Do you have no faith in your own abilities?"

"Of course I do."

"You didn't need me to do that for you, for you did it yourself. There are times when you need help, need someone to lean on, and then there are times in which you must show strength. Which you did in there."

He paused now, and Elizabeth could say nothing, for she could feel her chest rising and falling rapidly as she struggled to hold back the tears that threatened.

"I have to apologize," he continued.

Well, this would be interesting. Gabriel never, ever apologized.

"Go on."

"When you first took over this senior partnership, I came in here and I questioned your abilities. That was not right of me to do. For I knew you were able to take on the position your grandfather had left to you. I was simply pushing you to make sure that you believed the same. I knew that you would want to prove yourself if I questioned you, and so I pushed."

Elizabeth's expressionless wall finally broke, and she could only chuckle at Gabriel's words, though he now looked at her as though she were slightly crazy.

"You find that funny?"

"I should have known better," she said, turning around and beginning a slow pace of the room, looking down at one foot moving forward, and then the other. "You are a master manipulator. Nothing you do is ever straightforward. Even now, how am I to know that what you say to me is the truth?

Perhaps you are being honest. Perhaps you are not. Perhaps this is all part of some new game that you are playing to pass the time, to keep from boredom. How am I to know?"

"I would never manipulate you, Elizabeth," he said quietly.

"No?" she asked, rounding on him, flinging her hands widely. "Did you or did you not manipulate Julia and Eddie?"

"I wasn't manipulating anyone," he defended himself as he remained standing stoically. "All I did was feign interest in order for them to realize how important it was that they find one another."

"But you were lying."

"I wasn't lying—"

"Were you being honest?"

"Not quite."

"And with Phoebe's newspaper, did you not play a game in order to ensure she would be able to keep her secret?"

"That, I am proud of," he said, his expression hardening. "Are you questioning the actions I took — in concert with Berkley — which ended in your friend finding happiness?"

"I am not questioning the action," Elizabeth said, exasperated that he was completely missing her point. "I am only proving how much you enjoy these games, using people as pawns in order to find the result you are looking for. It doesn't matter that your end goal is a noble one, don't tell me you do not enjoy this type of deception."

"What I enjoy, Elizabeth, is using my position to help others find what they are looking for. For that, I will not apologize."

"Of course you won't," she said, shaking her head. "But whether or not I believe you…there's something else."

"Yes?"

"What happens… what happens when you no longer want only me?"

"Elizabeth," he said, his voice suddenly harsh. "You are not like any other woman. I could never be bored of you."

Elizabeth swallowed. She wanted to believe him, truly she did, but she just didn't know any longer what to think. She was hit with sudden exhaustion as it all seemed to be raining down upon her at once. She allowed herself to fall back into one of the chairs that surrounded the small conversation table in the corner as she placed her head in her hands.

"I don't know what to think anymore, Gabriel," she said, her voice low, just over a whisper, and he walked over to the chair across from her, likely to better hear her than anything else. "All I know is that I don't want to spend my life questioning every word you say to me, wondering if it is all part of some ploy. I want honesty, straightforwardness. I have enough deception here at the bank. I want to be able to trust you."

Gabriel reached across the table and took her hands in his. "You can trust me, Elizabeth. That, I can promise you."

She roamed her eyes over his face, taking in the strong jaw, the patrician nose, the deep blue of his irises. If only she could see what was behind it all, to peer into the depths of his mind and understand him. He was intelligent, sure — more so than any other man she had ever met. She knew it intimidated many, for he always seemed to be able to read through the words of others to come to the proper conclusion. She liked that about him. She always knew she could converse with him and not have to explain herself.

But it also scared her. For she could hide nothing from him, while he seemed to have perfected the facade that kept everything from her.

"What do you want, Elizabeth?" he asked, far more gently now, to the point that his words nearly brought tears to her eyes.

"I'm tired," she said, her voice nearly a whisper. "I'm tired of fighting for everything. I'm tired of not knowing if anything I am doing is ever going to come to anything. I'm tired of having to prove myself simply because I'm a woman. And I'm tired of my own indecision when it comes to you."

He stood then, stepping over toward her, his hard thighs beneath his tan breeches filling her vision. Before she even knew what he was doing, he picked her up as he had the night at his manor, holding her close against him. But instead of any suggestion of passion, he turned around, sat back in the chair she had just unwillingly vacated, and held her close against him. His chin came to rest on the top of her head, and he simply held her.

"No one can do anything alone, Elizabeth," he said in a low voice, as she unconsciously clutched at his shirt, drawing strength from him.

"You do," she said, hearing her own voice so small and vulnerable.

"It may look that way," he conceded, "But that is not necessarily true. I have many people working for me — people who care for my households, my estates, my business matters. Do I oversee it? Yes, of course, I do. It helps, though, to know that you can offload some of the work."

"You still retain that responsibility as though it is of no consequence."

"It may seem that way, but it is not entirely the case," he said, and she could feel his smile upon her hair. "I lean on others just as I ask you to lean on me. Ask Berkley how many times I have come to him with my complaints. Even my mother... she may be slightly sickly, but she was a great source of wisdom and comfort for my father, and she remains so for me."

"I didn't know that," Elizabeth said. "When I met her those years ago, she seemed so... reserved."

"She is, typically," he said, his voice warmer now than

Elizabeth thought she had ever heard it. "When she has something important to say to someone she loves, however, she is not afraid to express her opinion. Similar to another woman I know."

"Are you referring to me?"

"I am. You know how to make a statement without resorting to emotion that will color others' responses toward it. I admire that about you."

"My mother always told me that emotion was a weakness."

"It can be. It can also be a strength."

"That is rather perplexing."

"Decisions and actions based on intellect alone may seem like the right choice, but in the end, they can lead to heartache — for you, or for others. Sometimes emotion is necessary when dealing with other people, for it is the only way you will know if you are making the right choice."

"Just when did you become so wise?"

"It's taken a few years," he said with a low chuckle. "It's also included a good deal of life experience, and learning lessons the hard way."

"That, I can understand," she said, sitting up now on his lap, knowing she had to begin to take action to do what was best for herself, and for this bank. "Thank you, Gabriel. And I am sorry, for my words against you earlier."

"It's not as though I am completely blameless," he said as she stood and he followed suit, his hands behind his back. He remained motionless, saying nothing for a moment, and despite the closeness they had just experienced together, there was underlying tension in the air, and she knew the cause of it. He still needed his answer. He was waiting, some-what patiently, but he would want to know sooner rather than later. She needed just a little more time.

"Can we speak further tomorrow?" she asked, looking up

at him with some pleading in her eyes, and he nodded at her, clearly fully aware of what she spoke.

"Of course," he said. "I look forward to it."

"Thank you, Gabriel," she said, her voice nearly breaking, though she managed to retain a hold of it. "Thank you very much."

CHAPTER 25

*G*abriel left the bank with a slight bit of weight lifted from his shoulders. Elizabeth would come around — he was sure of it. In the moments when she had allowed him in, he could see how much it helped her to have someone there with her — someone to talk to, with whom she could share her burdens. On the surface, she was calm, reserved — some would say cold. But he knew better. Gabriel knew the fire that was inside of her, which she needed to learn how to release. It bothered him that she thought she could ever bore him, for that was far from what could ever be true. He just didn't know how to make her see that.

As Gabriel walked toward his waiting carriage, he saw Henry Clarke standing with another of the partners, sharing a laugh. Oh, what Gabriel wouldn't give to tell the little fool exactly what he thought. But there were far better ways to deal with someone such as Henry.

"Clarke!" he called out, passing by the man, who seemed somewhat pleased to see Gabriel. "Good day."

"And to you, Your Grace," Clarke said with a satisfied

smile, pleased that Gabriel was acknowledging him amongst peers.

"Say," Gabriel said slowly, knowing Clarke's preference for certain establishments within London, "I don't suppose you have been to The Red Dragon lately?"

"Ah," Clarke said, his cheeks turning slightly red as he stepped away from the other man and closer to Gabriel. "Why do you ask?"

"Only because I had heard a rumor about the place that I was hoping to dispel — or to warn you about."

"Oh?" Clarke's eyes darted back and forth rapidly at Gabriel's words.

"It's been said there is a disease spreading from within, so I wanted to caution all of my friends to avoid the place — for the time being, anyway. If you do go, stay away from the blonde." He lowered his voice conspiratorially and leaned in toward Clarke as though he were sharing a secret. "I've heard she was with a man who was the initial source. They say once the itch begins, it's impossible to be rid of."

He straightened now, smiling at Clarke, who was standing still with a bead of sweat beginning to drip down his forehead. Gabriel placed a hand on his shoulder. "I know it's not something of which we gentlemen normally speak, but I thought you frequented the establishment and did wish to warn you. Well, good day to you Clarke. I hope to see you again soon!"

Gabriel permitted the smile to cross his face once he turned, and he chuckled to himself all the way to his carriage.

* * *

FOR ONCE, Elizabeth left the bank early, and when she returned home, instead of ensconcing herself in the study, she decided a bit of fresh air might be helpful to clear her mind. The house had a small garden in the back, well enough away from the mews. It wasn't overly large, but her grandmother had always ensured it was kept in beautiful condition, and especially with the green leaves budding on the trees and the flowers beginning to bloom, Elizabeth had always found it a particularly peaceful place.

She let herself out the garden doors, settling herself on the small bench, breathing in the scent of her grandmother's roses around her, appreciating the beauty of the red petals. Gabriel was right about one thing — she had allowed the responsibility of the bank to rest far too heavily on her shoulders. She was taking on this position because she enjoyed it, not because she wanted further burden within her life.

If only her cousin would leave her be. Why he cared so strongly about seeing to her downfall, she had no idea. Was it the money? If so, perhaps she could pay him off. She knew, however, it was likely more than that. It was his pride, and jealousy that she had received what he somehow felt was rightfully his, despite the fact that her grandfather had never promised Henry a thing.

She closed her eyes as she tilted her head back to feel the sun upon her face, but started when she heard the door opening. She smiled as she opened her eyes, expecting to see her grandmother, but her countenance turned to one of great disappointment when she saw exactly who it was.

"Henry," she said warily. "Have we not already traded enough barbs today? I would ask that you give me an afternoon of peace and then we can resume them another day."

"Oh, Elizabeth," he said with feigned affection. "I certainly do not wish to fight with you. I am only trying to help."

"If that is the case, then I kindly ask that you bestow your assistance upon someone else," she said. "I have no need of it."

"You require far more help than you realize," he said,

coming to sit on the bench beside her, leaning back against the arm of it, making himself comfortable. "It is a cruel world out there, Elizabeth, particularly for a woman such as yourself."

"What is that supposed to mean?" she asked, raising an eyebrow.

"A woman in a man's world, of course," he said. "One who is subject to questioning and disagreements. It is only fortunate that I have been able to avail myself of a partnership so that I am able to look out for you."

"You stole your partnership, and are only trying to bring about my downfall," she said, no longer veiling her words, for Henry would likely miss any subtle hints. She had to be straightforward with him. "What is it you want, Henry?" she asked, exasperated now. "Do you want money? Do you want a silent partnership? What will it take to convince you to leave me be?"

"Elizabeth, I am hurt," he said, bringing a hand to his chest. "You are my family, and I want nothing but the best for you. In fact, I am here to protect you from others."

"There is no one else who so greatly wishes to bring about my downfall but you, Henry," she said, rolling her eyes. How naive did he think her to be?

"Do you truly think that?" he asked. "There are snakes in the grass, Elizabeth. Ones you cannot see."

"None as venomous as you, Henry."

"Oh no? Well, you think that *I* have gone to great lengths in order to be close to you? Not nearly as great as another, I tell you."

"And you would know this, how?"

Elizabeth didn't want to listen to him speak anymore, for she knew that nearly all of his words were fabricated in order to cause her to question all that she knew to be right and true. Yet as he was sitting right next to her, she could hardly completely ignore him, as much as she wanted to.

"I have my ways."

"Mmm hmmm."

"It is true. Do you ever wonder how I know your every forthcoming action, and the inner workings of the bank? It is because I am friends with someone who knows you well, Elizabeth, who provides me the information I seek, who is looking forward to you eventually stepping away from the bank even more than I am."

"There is no one close to me who would do such a thing," she said, though her mind began to race, as much as she attempted to prevent it from doing so. Was there any truth to what her blasted cousin said?

"Oh no?" he asked, his smile smug. "Is there anyone in your life, Elizabeth, who has become particularly close to you since good old Grandfather named you his heir, since you decided to take an active role in Clarke & Co.? Anyone who would particularly benefit from your newfound wealth, but not so much your newfound position? Anyone who is smart enough to know and understand just how to convince you to leave the bank by your own decision?"

There could only be one person to whom Henry was referring, but Elizabeth knew that Gabriel would never do such a thing. He couldn't. Not only that, but he had just spent their entire time within her office encouraging her to continue in her role, to be strong and uphold what she knew to be true.

"Stop, Henry," she said. "You are making a fool of yourself. There is no one who would do such a thing but you."

"Not even your duke? Tell me, Elizabeth, why Clarence's sudden attraction to you, when he left you years ago, yet has remained within the same social circles since that time? What would so greatly interest him after so long?"

"Our paths crossed again," she said simply, folding her hands in her lap, refusing to allow him to see the effect his words were having upon her.

"They *conveniently* crossed," he continued. "At the bank. Where, suddenly, the Duke has taken an interest once more."

"Not only are you incorrect as to where we initially reacquainted ourselves with one another, but he had been a partner in the bank for years, since receiving the partnership from Grandpapa."

"Yes, but only recently has he taken an active role," Henry continued. "How do you explain his sudden interest in you?"

"His interest is not sudden," Elizabeth said calmly. "He asked for my hand in marriage years ago, long before there was ever a chance or a thought of me inheriting a fortune or becoming a partner in the bank myself, let alone the senior partner."

"He left you years ago."

"It was my choice — not his."

"Say Clarence truly is interested in you," Henry said, though he rolled his eyes to tell her that he clearly didn't believe such a thing could be true. "Do you really believe he would want his wife to remain the senior partner in the bank?"

"I do."

Elizabeth realized then that she did — she did believe that what Gabriel had said to her was true, that he would support her. To what extent, she wasn't sure, but she had a renewed hope that they could determine the best path forward.

"You would give him a pretty fortune."

"I keep my own inheritance, as you may recall. As for future income, he doesn't want it. He has enough of his own."

"No one ever has enough," Henry said with a sneer. "Not even your pretty duke."

"Careful, Henry — you are stretching now."

"I am stretching nothing," he said, standing, as though he thought that if he towered over her, he could become much more imposing, but she still saw him as nothing but a little rat she could fit underneath her boot. "I know with complete certainty that the Duke has no desire to see Clarke & Co. run by Lady Elizabeth Moreland. He has been spying on you, Elizabeth — for me. I just never thought he would go to such great lengths to do so. I suppose he thought to get a little action as part of the deal. Which is smart. I certainly would!"

He cackled at that, as Elizabeth stood up in anger. "You're lying!" she said, her hands by her sides in fists.

"I am not," he said, holding his head high, obviously pleased to see that he had finally managed to anger Elizabeth. "Ask him yourself if you'd like. I know he is a well-practiced liar, but at some point, he must admit to what he has done. It isn't as though he would indeed marry you. Or… oh no, you poor thing. You thought he actually would?"

He began to laugh at that, not a low chuckle this time, but a long laugh. Elizabeth felt as though she were ready to explode, and all she could do now was raise her arm and point her finger to the door of the gardens.

"Get. Out."

"Elizabeth..."

"Get out, right now," she seethed. "Before I find a footman and have you thrown out. Go right to the front door, march yourself down those steps, and do not return here. Ever. Do you understand me?"

"I—"

"I said, do you understand me?"

Her words were now low and threatening, and Henry visibly blanched, providing Elizabeth with a moment of slight satisfaction.

"Very well."

He sniffed, turned, and let himself out the door, but not

before he sent a small, knowing, smug smile over his shoulder toward Elizabeth. It grated on her to admit it, but he had achieved his goal.

For the moment he was out of sight and out of hearing, she collapsed back onto the bench, laid her head in her arms, and began to weep.

CHAPTER 26

*I*t had been over four days since Gabriel had asked Elizabeth to marry him — for the second time in their lives. He had been understanding, he felt, the first day. Patient the second. Slightly frustrated the third, the day she had promised to provide her answer. And now, four days later, he decided he was no longer waiting. Surely by now, she knew what she wanted. At the very least, she owed him a response of some sort.

It was a matter of principle, he attempted to reason. A man of his stature could not be so affected by a woman. Truth be told, he would never have expected himself to be a man to wait for a woman's decision. If she didn't want him, then so be it.

But as he crossed the threshold of the bank, nodding to Anderson, he sighed. He had allowed Elizabeth into his being. It was more than physical. He was tied to her, connected in a way he couldn't explain, and he didn't want to let her go. He wouldn't.

He climbed the stairs determinedly, surprised for a moment when he found that the anteroom outside of her office was now filled with a desk, a young man sitting behind it.

"Good afternoon," Gabriel said, as he walked past the man to Elizabeth's door beyond.

The young man looked up at him, stood hastily, and began to tap his fingertips nervously on the table. "Your Grace, good afternoon," he said, bowing slightly to Gabriel, which caused him to smile. Such circumstance.

Seeing that Gabriel was about to enter Elizabeth's office, the man rushed from behind his desk to stand between Gabriel and the door. There wasn't much room, and Gabriel raised an eyebrow at him, not pleased with his close proximity.

"Ah…" the lad, who looked as though he had only recently reached his twentieth year, stuttered with a sheepish smile, "M-my apologies, Your Grace, but ah, Lady Elizabeth is not accepting visitors at the moment."

As much as he wanted to, Gabriel didn't step back, attempting to cower the man to allow him to pass.

"She will accept me."

A bead of sweat broke out on the man's brow.

"Unfortunately, Lady Elizabeth asked that no one enter — in-including you."

"I see," Gabriel said, stepping back slightly, feeling the rejection as though Elizabeth had physically pushed him away. Not that he would allow this man to see how it had affected him. "Well, please tell *Lady Elizabeth* that I was here. And that I will be expecting to speak with her very soon."

A storm beginning to rage inside of him, Gabriel turned on his heel and strode back down the corridor. If she was anyone else, Gabriel wouldn't waste another moment of his time. But this was Elizabeth, and damn it all, he couldn't leave her be.

* * *

Which is how he found himself, two hours later, sitting in the drawing room of Elizabeth's home, having tea with her grandmother. Apparently, Elizabeth hadn't extended her ban of his presence as far as her residence, or at the very least, she hadn't informed her grandmother of the fact. Mrs. Clarke was as lovely as ever, asking after his family and questioning him about his time in Parliament and with what other activities he was keeping busy.

It was clear where Elizabeth had received her intellect from, that was for certain. In her grandmother, Gabriel could see Elizabeth's identity fifty years in the future.

They spent nearly an hour in companionable conversation until Gabriel finally heard the opening of the door down the corridor at the front of the house. The beat of his heart picked up, likely due to the amount of tea he had drunk in the last hour. For surely, *surely* a woman's footsteps couldn't cause it to be so?

But of course, they were. Gabriel had to admit that he was both aching in anticipation to see Elizabeth, and also nervous about what the confrontation may bring. Would this be the last of their meetings? Would she tell him she wanted nothing to do with him any longer, that she was turning down his proposal of marriage? For why else would she have no wish to speak with him any further?

The frustration that had simmered down low through his conversation with Justine began to rise as Elizabeth's footsteps grew ever louder, and Gabriel took a breath to calm himself.

Perhaps he should have gone to her father first to ask for her hand in marriage. Was that why she was concerned? No, he chastised himself. What a stupid thought. A woman like

Elizabeth would want to have the opportunity to choose herself, and she and her father hardly got along as it was.

Gabriel had no idea who this contrary, unsure-of-himself person in his head was. If this was what it meant to be in love with a woman, he wanted nothing to do with it.

Love? He hadn't meant in *love* with her. Interested in her, perhaps.

But before he had time to contemplate the frightening idea any further, Elizabeth stepped into the room. Gabriel could feel the tension radiating off of her as her eyes came to rest upon him first. She stared at him, hard, her gaze unreadable, though she was nearly trembling with the emotion coursing through her — emotion she was attempting to hide, of course.

Mrs. Clarke stood, looking between the two of them.

"Good afternoon, Elizabeth," she said, and Elizabeth finally turned and saw her, a clearly forced smiling emerging.

"Good afternoon, Grandmother," she said. "You look lovely as always."

"Thank you, my dear," Mrs. Clarke said, walking over and placing a hand upon Elizabeth's arm. "I have to see to some correspondence, so I shall leave the two of you for a moment. I won't be far."

Elizabeth nodded, then took the seat her grandmother had vacated. She gripped the arms of the chair as though she were holding onto the edge of a boat to keep from drowning, though she sat as tall and regally as any queen ever had before.

She was dressed in a deep purple gown, the color so dark and the fabric so stiff that it almost looked as though she were in mourning. Perhaps she was.

"Elizabeth—" he began, but she cut him off.

"No more speeches," she said, her words clipped. "No more fancy words, nor lies, nor stories from your lips. I have a question for you, and I ask you to answer it truthfully."

He nodded, sitting back in his chair, rather stunned. Her lips were pressed tight together, her face so pale it was nearly white.

"Did you collude against me with my cousin?"

Gabriel's mouth dropped open in shock. Damn Henry. Damn him and his big mouth and his slippery ways. He couldn't imagine what the man might have said to Elizabeth, but he knew it wouldn't have been anything good.

"No."

She tilted her head, as though she could read what he was actually thinking.

"I know Henry is as dishonest as they come. But I am also aware that you look very uneasy, and you, Gabriel, are never uneasy. Please, please do not lie to me."

"I never actually colluded with him," Gabriel said reluctantly, his gaze upon her, seeking out her eyes as he needed her to understand.

"Did you agree to help him in any way? Is there any truth to what he told me?"

Gabriel sighed.

"Yes, but—"

She stood then, walking to the door, holding it open.

"You can leave."

"Elizabeth—"

"Please," she said, her voice and her expression desperate now, and he knew she was on the brink of losing control of her emotions, which he actually wanted, needed her to do.

"I am not leaving until you listen to what I have to say," he continued, standing himself as he walked over and looked down at her. "I told him I agreed to his schemes, but I only did so because I thought then he might leave you alone. I thought if he was of the impression that I would partake in his collusion against you, that he would leave you be. Clearly, I was wrong."

"Clearly. He is certainly of the impression that you have helped create my downfall, which also includes the downfall of the bank — of which you are a partner. You should only be trying to build it up."

"Elizabeth, I was trying to *help* the bank."

"How could helping Henry possibly help the bank?"

"I would never do anything that Henry requested."

"I don't understand—"

"Elizabeth, can we please sit down and discuss this, instead of standing here as you hurl accusations and I attempt to defend them? Come, you are smarter than this. You know your cousin, know the lengths he would go to in order to cause discord."

He could see her fists clenching and then unclenching at her sides, and she looked away from him, over his shoulder to the other side of the room.

"Gabriel," she said, her head dropping now to look down to the floor, her shoulders sagging in defeat. "I'm tired. Yes," she said holding up a hand when he began to speak, to protest that it was partially her own fault for taking it all on her own. But apparently, she already knew what he was going to say. "I know, I should share my burden. But at the moment, what is most tiring is the fact that I do not know who I can turn to and who is against me. I am tired of your manipulations, Gabriel. You may not have schemed against me, but you become interested in the bank, interested in *me*, at the same time. Whether it was or is a game to you, I have no idea, but this is not just a game. This is my life. And if you marry me, it is forever. Sure, I may provide you stimulating conversation, but marriage is more than that. It's a pact to be together, with only one another and no one else. You've made your promises, I know that, but it is hard to know what to believe when it seems like everywhere I turn there is one lie and then another. Yes, at the moment you are interested in the bank, in me, but what happens when that interest wanes? Do you turn to another scheme, another business, another *woman*?"

Gabriel could feel his chest rising and falling rapidly at her words, at the emotions roiling within him.

"There is no other woman like you," he said, but she was too far within herself to listen any longer.

"For now," she said, her hands falling to her sides. "Gabriel, five years ago, you promised me a life together. A marriage to the man I loved. I could hardly believe that a future duke wanted *me*, though the fact of your title had nothing to do with it. It was you, the man, Gabriel Lockridge, who I wanted. You were the man every woman wanted, though for different reasons than I. And I thought that you chose me. When I saw you with Lady Pomfret, I could hardly believe my eyes. I wanted to deny it, to tell myself that I was seeing someone else, something else, but of course, it was you. You knew how much loyalty meant to me, that I could never be with a man who took anyone else. You broke me then, and just when it seemed that trust was beginning to heal, it has been called into question once more."

"So what, then?" he asked, angry with her refusal to listen to him, for not having any faith in him, for not realizing that he was a different man than he had been five years ago, for her hold on past hurts and past sins. "That's it? We are to go our separate ways?"

"I suppose so," she said her voice small, and Gabriel was filled with a feeling of despondency like nothing he had ever experienced before.

He had known, from the moment he had asked her to marry him, that this was a potential outcome, but never had he thought that the result could have such an effect upon him. Part of him — his heart, he realized – longed for him to keep fighting, to beg her to reconsider, to listen to him, to allow him to prove to her the man that he was.

But the other part — his ducal mind, his pride, his very being — would not allow him to do so. That would be admitting defeat, which Gabriel would never, ever do.

"Are you sure that is what you want — what you really want?" he asked one last time, hearing the harshness in his voice but unable to prevent it.

"I… think so."

"Well, you better be sure, Elizabeth, because I will not be asking you to marry me a third time. So answer me, and answer me now. Is your final answer to my proposal a no?"

She finally looked up at him, and when she did, a glaze of tears covered her eyes.

"I can hardly agree to marriage in such circumstances!"

"A no then," he said, hardening his heart in an attempt to protect it from the pain that was currently coursing through it. "Very well. Goodbye, Elizabeth. I hope your ledgers keep you warm at night."

And with that, he brushed past her and out the door, refusing to take even one glance behind him as he stormed out of the house.

CHAPTER 27

*E*lizabeth gave herself one day. One day in which she stayed at home, lay in bed, moped around the house and ate far too many sweets. At first, the despair was nearly overwhelming, encompassing her to the point that she was nearly incapable of doing anything else. When it threatened to overtake her, she set her jaw and determined that she would not give in.

Instead, she let the misery simmer, and in pushing away the grief, it began to turn, to take shape as something else entirely.

It began with anger. All of the frustrations that had been building inside Elizabeth, that she had refused to acknowledge or discuss, burned inside of her, to the point that the fire threatened to consume her. She didn't wholly blame Gabriel — her own stubbornness, her life's circumstances, her fickle heart was as much to blame.

And so, she decided to do something about it.

After her day of melancholy, Elizabeth woke with purpose. That morning she dressed in brilliant green silk, so unlike the somber, careful colors she had selected until now so as not to stand out or garner any particular attention as a woman. No, today she had much to see to, and she would use her femininity to her advantage.

She strode through the doors of the bank with purpose, climbing the stairs, saying her hellos, but with less of a smile than usual. When she found her office, she nearly jumped in surprise, as she had almost forgotten about Mr. Brant, who she had moved from downstairs to be her secretary. Her primary goal for his appointment had been to keep away unwanted visitors, but on his first day, he had proven quite resourceful.

"Good morning, Lady Elizabeth," he said, jumping up from the desk, an eager smile on his youthful face. "I trust you had a lovely day yesterday?"

It was difficult to keep from responding to his enthusiasm, and Elizabeth returned his smile despite her mood.

"It was a necessary day, Mr. Brant, that much I can say."

He seemed confused but nodded.

"I have correspondence awaiting you on your desk. I was unsure of whether or not I should open it, but I am happy to respond to anything you would like me to. There are a few urgent memos regarding clients of the bank who wish to speak to you."

"Thank you, Mr. Brant. Can you please arrange a meeting for me with Mr. Bates and the senior clerks for later this afternoon?"

"Yes, of course."

"Thank you."

The correspondence, fortunately, was primarily good news, until she came to the last letter. Another client had chosen to leave the bank. Elizabeth sighed and placed her head in her hands. She hated to admit it, but Henry might be right. She may not be the best leader of this bank after all or, perhaps she needed to start doing business differently — for otherwise, she may allow it to fall to ruin. Her grandfather would be so disappointed.

Elizabeth heaved a sigh, drumming her fingertips on the tabletop. Perhaps she should find someone else to take her place. But it certainly wouldn't be Henry.

Later that afternoon, she sat at the table with Mr. Bates and the senior clerks in front of her. It wasn't a particularly strange request to have them all meet with her, though typically she provided them with more notice.

"Thank you all for coming here today," she said. "I have a question to pose to you, and I would ask that you keep our conversation here confidential." At their nods, she continued. "I wish to confirm that as the senior partner, I have the power to confirm, deny, or replace any other partner of the bank."

Shocked expressions stared back at her. Whether or not it was within her ability was one thing — the fact that she was actually considering such a thing was clearly another.

Mr. Bates was the first to regain his voice.

"Certainly, you have the power to do so, Lady Elizabeth," he said. "You may name or remove any partner you like. When your grandfather named the Duke of Clarence partner, he used his own authority to do so. He also at one time asked a similar question as you are posing now, though I cannot recall what the outcome was, nor did he ever tell me which partner was in question. He did, however, discuss the possibility of termination."

Elizabeth thought back to her conversation with him all those years ago, of a partner who was working against the bank along with one of the clerks. She wished she knew what had become of that situation. Was either of them still within the bank, other Brutus-like turncoats working against her? The problem was, she had no idea who she could trust, who she could ask. Perhaps her grandmother might know.

"There are two partners who I wish to remove," she said, and the four heads swiveled back toward her, each man clearly uncomfortable with her words.

"Will these partners be replaced?" Mr. Larkin asked.

"They will," she confirmed. "I will name the replacements in due time. We will first deal with the dismissal. Tell me, what is the protocol?"

They outlined the procedure for her. She would first draw up a written dismissal, then meet with the partners in question to provide it to them or send it by messenger if a meeting was impossible. All of the bank's partners would then need to be informed of the decision and sign the final paperwork for it to become official. In the meantime, the clerks would draw up the necessary documentation.

"If the partners are being replaced," Mr. Larkin continued, "The partnership passes on to the replacements. If not, then we must determine how the appropriate shares will be allotted to each remaining partner."

"Thank you, Mr. Larkin," she said. "That is all very straightforward."

Mr. Bates cleared his throat, looking slightly uncomfortable. "This could cause some discord, Lady Elizabeth. In no way do I mean to question your decision; however, I simply want to ensure you are aware that it could have some unfortunate questions come upon the bank."

"I understand that, Mr. Bates," she said with a nod of her head. But no longer would Elizabeth be afraid, be unwilling to do what she knew was the right action because of what others may think. She had done what she thought was right for the bank, had stayed true to the course and been the woman all expected her to be, and look where that had gotten her — rid of two clients whose business she sorely needed. "This must go ahead regardless."

"Understood."

"Very well," she said, rising. "Thank you all for your attendance this afternoon, and for your wise counsel as always.
Mr. Brant," she looked over to her secretary, who had been
sitting to the side of the meeting, taking notes for her —
which was actually quite helpful, she realized, to not have to
make notes for herself, allowing her to concentrate on the
meeting at hand. "Please arrange two meetings for me. One
with Mr. Clarke, and the other with the Duke of Clarence."

This time she actually heard audible gasps resound
around the room.

"My lady..." she heard one of the clerks say, but she
refused to provide any explanation. She was the senior partner, was she not? Therefore, she could make the decision
without having to explain herself.

"Are you able to do so, Mr. Brant?"

The young employee had turned very white, but he
nodded mutely.

"Very good," she said, gathering her papers in hand and
striding to the door. "And a good day to you all."

* * *

Henry came that very day. Gabriel, it seemed, was far too
busy to speak with her.

"Thank you for coming, Henry," she said as he took a seat.

"Of course, Elizabeth," he smiled. "I hope the news I
shared with you the other day was not too distressing. I felt it
was important that you were aware."

"Yes, I am sure that was the case," she said, picking up her
quill pen and looking down at the paper in front of her, in
effect to tell Henry that her conversation with him did hold
significant importance to her. "Henry, I asked you here for
another reason, entirely, however. As you know, I am the
senior partner of the bank, which affords me some powers

and responsibilities which are over and above those of the other partners."

"I am aware," he said, his voice and his smile dropping.

"One of those powers is the ability to name or dismiss partners," she said. "And so, I am effectively dismissing you as one of the bank's partners. Immediately. Here is the letter of confirmation. Your dismissal will be become official upon the next partners' meeting."

He stared at her in shock.

"I would ask you now to leave," she said with the slightest of smiles, as though she were sending him away him after a congenial tea together.

"You cannot be rid of me!" he said, his face distorting to one of anger.

"Actually," she returned, maintaining calm, "I can."

Rage stretched across his face, but instead of feeling any sort of threat or fear, it was as though a great weight had been lifted off Elizabeth's shoulders and was now floating away, up over the bookshelves, to the ceiling, and out of the room completely. She should have done this ages ago.

"If you do this, Elizabeth," Henry seethed. "You will be ruined. Ruined, I tell you! You, and this damn bank."

"I do not think it is appropriate to swear in front of ladies, Henry," Elizabeth said, the smile across her face real now. "You were raised better than that."

"Were you not raised to be a genteel lady, one who knew her place?" He asked, standing now, spittle flying from his mouth as he spoke.

"I was," she confirmed, standing herself but taking a step backward to put space between them. "I do know my place. It is here, in this bank, where our grandfather believed I would fit. Where you certainly do not."

"You do not want all to know of Mr. Mortimer's condition, do you?"

"I do not," she confirmed. "But nor do you — for then others would know how dishonestly you came by your partnership. It would only show how prudent and protective we are of those we consider to be like family."

"I shall tell your mother!"

"Go ahead and do so, if you choose."

"Who are you, Elizabeth?"

"I am the senior partner of Clarke & Co.," she said proudly. "An establishment of which you, Henry, will no longer be a part. Now please leave my office, or I will ask the clerks to help you do so."

Scowling, he turned to leave, but then with one motion, he turned back around, sweeping an arm across her desk in anger, knocking over not only all of the papers that filled it but also her quill pen set — the one that Gabriel had given her. As she watched the ink slowly leak out of the well, she froze, staring at the liquid, which reminded her of her own relationship with him, spilling all over the floor.

Elizabeth didn't even realize that Henry had left or that Mr. Brant had come rushing in to ensure that all was well.

"Lady Elizabeth!" he exclaimed, bringing her out of her reverie as he rushed over to tidy the mess Henry had created. "Are you all right?"

"I am, Mr. Brant, thank you," she said, bending now. "Here, let me help."

She picked up the pen set, running her finger over the inscription that Gabriel had commissioned, causing the ache in her heart, the one she thought she had defeated, to begin anew.

Once all was righted, Mr. Brant cleaned up the ink, which thankfully had spilled only on the wooden floor below, missing the carpet entirely.

"I received word from the Duke of Clarence, Lady Elizabeth," he said. "It seems he is indisposed and will not be able to meet with you for the foreseeable future."

"Very well," Elizabeth said, somewhat relieved that she didn't have to see Gabriel again, though she realized how cowardly she was behaving. "Please send him the necessary documentation."

Mr. Brant nodded, turned smartly on his heel, and left. While Henry's termination had left Elizabeth feeling free, letting Gabriel go was heavy on her heart. But she couldn't see him again, couldn't have him remain such an intricate part of her life. For every time she thought of him, it was as though she had been stabbed in the chest. This was the one instance in which she would allow emotion to rule her. Others may criticize her for it, but it was what she had to do.

Elizabeth had to move on. And that meant cutting Gabriel from her life completely.

CHAPTER 28

*G*abriel took the piece of paper between both of his hands and ripped it down the middle before throwing it into the fire licking at the grate in his study.

Dismiss him as a partner? What was Elizabeth thinking?

It was one thing to turn him away as a suitor, as a man. But to be rid of him as a partner in the bank was utterly foolhardy. All she was doing was proving others right — that a woman could be far too overcome by emotion to make the proper business decisions.

But as he sat there, staring into the flames that overtook the paper, he put himself in her place to consider her decision, and wondered — would he have done the same? If their roles were reversed, would he have chosen to see Elizabeth as often as each partner's meeting, knowing what it would be like to see her, to know she was so close and yet so far from him?

No, he would not. But it would be far easier to explain the dismissal of a woman than it would a duke. He was interested to see just how she would play this one, to explain herself and keep from losing the support and confidence of the partners.

Gabriel picked up the drink he had been nursing and walked to the window, looking out onto the dark night below. The truth was, he was a coward. He hadn't even been able to bring himself to respond to her meeting invitation. And here he was, judging her.

He snorted, downing the rest of his drink now in one gulp as he turned from the window and the people he saw beyond it. They all looked so merry from up here, the couples returning to their homes, arm in arm, or within carriages pulled by magnificent horses. He probably looked the same himself, he supposed, despite the fact he was now miserable. It was all a matter of perspective.

Gabriel poured himself another brandy as he sat back down, this time in the leather chair in front of the fire. He could have gone to White's or another club tonight — perhaps one of the seedier ones, where he could lose himself in drink and women. The only problem was, the thought of any woman other than Elizabeth left him feeling nothing but disgust at himself and his current situation. He wanted her, and only her. He just didn't know how to rid himself of this damn emotion that wouldn't quit, no matter how much he tried to push it away.

So he took another sip. He'd numb the pain tonight, alone, and then tomorrow he would move on.

* * *

"ELIZABETH?" Her grandmother peeked inside the door of Elizabeth's bedchamber with a bit of trepidation on her face, and guilt coursed through Elizabeth at just how much she had disregarded her grandmother's own feelings over the past couple of days.

"Yes, Grandmother?" she asked.

"Tonight is a dance at Lady Featherstone's. I was wondering if you'd like to accompany me?"

"Oh." Elizabeth had no wish to go, to potentially see Gabriel, of course, but also some of the clients she had lost since becoming a partner in the bank. There had been, however, a few prospectively interested. Perhaps she should go, if for nothing else than to show that she was not afraid of what others may think of her. She wondered if Henry had done any additional damage since she had dismissed him. "I suppose for a short time," she said. "When would you like to leave?"

"Is a couple of hours enough time for you?"

"Of course," said Elizabeth, managing a weak smile.

Precisely two hours later, they were within the carriage when Elizabeth finally remembered what she had been meaning to ask her grandmother.

"Grandmother, some years ago, did Grandpapa say anything to you regarding a situation at the bank? Of a clerk and a partner he was concerned with?"

Justine looked out the window for a moment, concentration upon her face.

"I do recall him letting go of a clerk for fraudulent behavior. I know he was concerned about a partner, but for the life of me, I cannot recall who it might have been. I'm sorry, darling."

Elizabeth sighed inwardly but smiled for her grandmother. "No problem at all. I thought I would see if you knew of anything."

At least now she knew that she could trust the clerks. She would ask them of the situation first thing on Monday morning. She was already on a roll dismissing partners — why stop now? Elizabeth felt as though a reckless spirit had overtaken her. It was somewhat freeing, thrilling even. All of her life she had lived by the rules, had followed entirely what was expected of her. Now that she had lost Gabriel and seemed to be losing the bank, all despite her careful practices, what did anything matter anymore?

Thankfully, Elizabeth saw no sign of Gabriel as she entered the Featherstones' London home. She did, however, see Sarah, who reached out a hand in greeting when Elizabeth approached.

"Elizabeth," she said, her smile warm, though she squeezed Elizabeth's hand as though she was aware something was the matter. "How are you?"

Unlike the polite greetings of most people, Elizabeth always knew that Sarah's question was genuine. Sarah looked into Elizabeth's eyes as she asked the question, searching out the emotion within. Sarah's brown eyes were so warm, so compassionate, that Elizabeth nearly shed a tear herself, but she stayed strong.

"I am..." She honestly didn't know how to answer that question, and she looked around her before leading Sarah into a corner of the ballroom, where they could stand against the wall and view the room without any worry of who may be listening from over their shoulders. Before she could stop them, the words came tumbling out. "I am questioning who I am, if I am being honest with you. I am questioning my life to this point, and the decisions I have made. Did I make the right choice in assuming and keeping my active role in the bank, or am I only bringing about its downfall? Should I have left the home of my parents? Speaking of them, they just arrived. You can see the look my mother is already sending my way. And then there is my decision regarding Gabriel..."

Elizabeth looked down at her hands for a moment, her gloves reminding her of the night he had kept the others from her. Gloves that she never did get back, she realized. Why, oh why, no matter what she did or to what extent she tried to keep him from her life, did everything surrounding her remind her of him?

Sarah said nothing as she waited for Elizabeth to continue, aware that there was more to this story that Elizabeth needed to get out.

When she looked back up at Sarah, her friend placed a hand on her arm, as though she could see the pain emanating from Elizabeth's eyes.

"Did I make the right choice?" Elizabeth asked, hearing her voice soft and low, the ache within it apparent even to her. "Was I being too harsh, too proud, too stubborn? Oh, Sarah, I'm just so afraid of being hurt again that I'm scared to let him in."

Now that she had spoken the truth aloud, relief filled her. Gabriel had been right about one thing — sharing burdens could be more helpful than she had ever realized.

"If you truly feel that your life would be better without him, then so be it — you've made the right choice, and you can move on. If, however, you let him go simply because you are scared of the risk you would have to take, well... everyone is scared, Elizabeth. No one knows what the future holds, and if you don't take the risk, then you could miss out on the most wonderful aspects of life."

Elizabeth took a deep breath. "That is true. Frightening, but true."

"Perhaps you need to speak to Gabriel again."

"If he will even speak with me."

"He's here."

"What?"

Elizabeth looked around, not seeing him anywhere.

"I saw him enter into one of the back rooms with Phoebe's husband and another man — the one you say loves the ladies."

"Ah. David Redmond."

"That's the one. A handsome man."

"But not the faithful, nor the marrying type," Elizabeth said wryly.

"But Gabriel seems to now be, which is most important. So what are you waiting for?" Sarah asked, and Elizabeth nodded at her, gathered her strength, and began for the back, however she was soon intercepted by her parents.

"Elizabeth, how are you?" her mother asked, and Elizabeth managed a smile, despite the fact that she was now impatient to get on with her next conversation, despite the fact she had no idea exactly what she would say to Gabriel, besides the fact that she knew she had to apologize. He had been nothing but generous of his time and attention for the past few months, and she had been rather dismissive of it in her stubbornness. But that would have to wait.

"I am well, Mother. How are you?"

"As well as can be, despite the fact that you have injured us so," her mother said with a pained expression, and Elizabeth tried not to let her mother's words affect her.

"I am sorry you feel that way, Mother, but it was time for me to step out on my own, live my own life — just as Terrence did."

"Terrence is a gentleman, not an unwed lady," her mother said with a sniff, and Elizabeth decided that the best course of action was simply not to respond.

"I do hear that you were spending some time with the Duke of Clarence once more," her mother continued, assessing Elizabeth with a critical eye. "Of course I commend you on whatever you did to encourage him to come back to you. I warn you, however, do not make the same mistake that you did last time."

"Which was?"

"Allowing emotions to impede your progress. He's the Duke of Clarence, Elizabeth!" her mother hissed, looking around her furtively. "It doesn't matter if the man beds half of London, as long as you have his name and his children."

"I feel otherwise, Mother," Elizabeth said, glancing to her father, who didn't even seem to be listening to them, but instead was looking rather bored as he glanced around the room. "But as a matter of fact, I must be going. Shall we have dinner together soon?"

"Very well," her mother said with a sigh. "Brush me to the side once more. But fine. I shall see if Terrence is available one evening."

Her words caused another twinge of regret within Elizabeth — not for her mother's apparent pain, but for the fact that she hadn't seen Terrence in some time now. He was likely busy himself, but still, she should reach out to him. She had always been the one to encourage closeness between them and she had become preoccupied with other things.

"Very good. Thank you, Mother."

"Oh, and darling," her mother said, her lips curling into a smile now. "I don't suppose you have received any of your benefits yet from your partnership?"

Elizabeth stared at her coldly. "Is that truly all you care about, Mother?"

Her mother's lips turned down in a pout.

"I am only wishing for you to spare a thought for your dear mother."

"You will be compensated accordingly," was all Elizabeth said, as she rolled her eyes and continued on. Her grandfather had looked after the entirety of his family, and yet it seemed it wasn't enough for most of them.

"Lady Elizabeth?" she heard a voice behind her and turned to find David Redmond approaching, the wide, usual smile on his face.

"I know this isn't the place for it, but I was wondering if we might have a discussion at some point in time? I know my father isn't pleased with his current banking situation, and perhaps we might see what Clarke & Co. could have to offer?"

Elizabeth was caught off guard but pleasantly surprised. Finally, a spot of good news. "Of course," she said. "I'm sure we would be a wonderful home for your family. Can we arrange a time for this coming week?"

"That would be ideal," said the handsome man with a cheeky grin, displaying how he had won the hearts of so many women. "I look forward to seeing you then."

He winked at her before continuing on, and Elizabeth knew that she should be thrilled with his question — which she was. But first, there was something else she had to do. If Redmond was here, then where was Gabriel? She continued on to the back rooms, intent now on her mission.

CHAPTER 29

When Redmond and Berkley decided to return to the festivities, Gabriel told them he would remain for a moment alone in the library, as he wanted to finish his drink in silence before returning to the noise and the crush of the ballroom. He'd had enough of these people and the endless introductions to eligible young women, and could hardly wait to return home. Which was interesting, as he had never been particularly pleased to be alone. Everything seemed to be changing now.

He finished his drink, set it on the table before him, and looked around the library with a sigh. It was a comfortable room, which was to be expected in a library. Bookshelves. Portraits of ancestors. A merry fire burning in the hearth. A brooding gentleman on the chesterfield.

Then suddenly the creak of the door captured his attention, and he turned around to face it. His thoughts flew to Elizabeth, his heart pounding slightly faster, but from the first footstep, he knew it wasn't her.

"Gabriel." The woman drew out his name, the syllables long, her tone sultry and practiced. At one point in time it may have caused a reaction in him, but now it only made him weary. He hoped that she was meeting someone else here, having an assignation of another sort. But, of course, she was alone.

"Lady Pomfret," he said, standing. "I was just about to return to the party, so I will leave the room to you."

She stepped more fully into the library, closing the door behind her and leaning back against it to prevent his escape.

"If you'll excuse me," he said, motioning her away, but instead she stepped closer to him, invading his personal space.

"Oh, Gabriel, that's no way to treat an old friend. I thought perhaps we could… catch up."

"It will have to wait for another time, Lady Pomfret. Now, pardon me."

He hardened his gaze at her, dismissing her pout and brushing past her and out the door. His old self would have welcomed the distraction of such a woman, but it seemed neither his body nor his heart could move on from Elizabeth. Not yet, anyway.

Ignoring her protest, Gabriel strode down the corridor, found his cloak, and was out the door in minutes. He was done with this damn party, this social scene, this life. What he was going to do, however, he had no idea.

* * *

ELIZABETH STOOD, stunned, as Gabriel marched by her and down the hallway. When she had seen him emerge from the library, she had instinctively stepped back at the look of anger on his face, and she must have been hidden from his view by the longcase clock next to her. Either that or Gabriel was so intent and focused on where he was going and what he was doing, he chose not to see her. For as angry as he was with her, he wouldn't have purposefully ignored her — would he?

She took a step forward in order to follow him down the hallway, but at that moment the library door opened once again and out stepped Lady Pomfret. When she saw Elizabeth standing there, a wide smile broke out on her face, and she sauntered toward her.

"Lady Elizabeth," she crooned. "How are you this evening?"

"I am fine, thank you," said Elizabeth, holding her head high despite the fact that her stomach was in knots. It was as though the past was coming back to haunt her. For five years ago, Lady Pomfret was saying nearly the same words to her after Elizabeth had witnessed their tryst in the gardens. Elizabeth hadn't seen anything untoward this time, it was true, but still…

"And how are you?" she forced herself to ask, and the woman smiled at her smugly.

"Oh, quite well," she said. "You must tell me, Lady Elizabeth, are the rumors true? I have heard it said that you and the Duke have become… friendly once more, and for my own peace of mind I would like to know if such a relationship exists between the two of you."

"No," Elizabeth choked out. "We are acquaintances."

"Oh good," Lady Pomfret said, clapping her hands together. "What a relief."

Elizabeth sorely wanted to ask her just *why* it was such a relief, but that would provide Lady Pomfret with far too much satisfaction. So instead, Elizabeth just forced a smile onto her face, nodded, and returned the way she came.

"Are you all right?" Sarah asked when Elizabeth returned to the party, and she gave her head a quick shake.

"No," she said. "Not at all. In fact, I think I will—"

"Lady Elizabeth?"

ELLIE ST. CLAIR

She turned to find Mr. Cartwright standing there, and despite her inner turmoil, she took a deep breath. He was not only an old friend of her grandparents, but also a partner of the bank and she must keep up appearances, not allowing any of the emotion she was feeling to overcome her.

"Mr. Cartwright, how lovely to see you."

"It is a pleasure to see you as well, Lady Elizabeth; however, I felt I must come to speak with you directly as I have heard the most distressing news."

"Oh?" Had word of the removal of the partners traveled so quickly?

"It is just that..." he trailed off, his eyes flicking from one side to the other, as he nervously tapped his fingers on his legs. "Well, I'm not sure how to say this."

"It's fine," she said. "You can say anything to me, particularly if it is important to the bank."

"Your reputation has been called into question," he blurted out, and Elizabeth looked down in some shock at the man standing in front of her, tufts of hair standing out on end about his head.

"My reputation? In terms of my role as senior partner?"

"Somewhat," he said. "It is more your personal reputation that is being questioned, but of course we know how that can affect what others may think of you in your professional role as well."

Elizabeth stood still, refusing to show any sign of the effect his words had upon her until she knew exactly what it was he had to say.

Mr. Cartwright cleared his throat, apparently struggling with telling her just what it was he wanted her to know.

"Just tonight I was told of a... liaison you may have had a few years ago with the Duke of Clarence," he said, and suddenly Elizabeth's entire body seemed to be flooded with heat.

"The Duke and I were courting a few years ago, that is true," she said slowly. "However, I don't believe that a broken courtship is anything to be particularly concerned about. We remain friends."

"Yes, well…" he fidgeted once more. "I was told it was more than that, that there was an… incident, at the Holderness' party. That you were seen in the gardens."

Elizabeth had no idea what else to say, and lapsed into silence. She had no idea what to say. She could — and should — deny his words, though it would be a lie to do so. Why now, all of a sudden, should someone feel the need to spread this?

Henry. Elizabeth had no idea how he knew, but who else would care enough, would feel slighted enough, to say such a thing now?

"As I said, Mr. Cartwright," she said, willing calm into her voice, "The Duke and I courted at the time. I will speak with you, and the rest of the partners, of this. But please be aware that nothing occurred which would have any repercussions on the bank. You can be assured of that."

He nodded, but he didn't look reassured. No, he looked concerned. And, as Elizabeth looked around the room, she noted more than a few stares directed her way. So Henry had done his work quickly. If only he would put his efficiency to good use, he could have done much more good in the world. She sighed.

"Mr. Cartwright," she said as he still stood there, seeming somewhat perplexed. "We shall have another partners' meeting this week. It seems we have much to discuss. I hope that will satisfy you, as well as the other partners."

"Yes, Lady Elizabeth," he agreed. "I'm sure it will."

"Would you mind telling me just where you learned such information?" she asked, looking at him pointedly, and he nodded, which told her that, if nothing else, at least she retained his loyalty.

"Your aunt," he said. "Mrs. Betsy Clarke."

"Of course," Elizabeth murmured and, seeing her mother begin to head her way once more, decided now was a good time to leave the party. "Thank you for coming directly to me, Mr. Cartwright. I shall see you this week."

And with that, she turned on her heel and left, feeling as though all was coming crashing down upon her.

* * *

It didn't take long for Gabriel to hear of the rumors regarding him and Elizabeth. Interestingly, no one seemed to care about his role within the garden liaison, though all seemed very concerned that a lady such as Elizabeth might behave so scandalously. If only they knew, he thought with a rueful grin. He actually rather enjoyed her scandalous behavior.

He wasn't surprised when he received a summons for a partners' meeting that week. She would need to meet with them all to not only renounce his partnership along with that of Henry Clarke but now to deny their previous encounter.

Gabriel had been asked about it at White's. He had been asked about it after Parliament. And he had been asked about it by everyone he had encountered in between. Gabriel would simply smile and ask whoever it was whether or not he had ever found himself part of a liaison outside of the marriage bed. It was usually enough to convince his interrogator to move on in another direction.

Now he read the summons of the meeting with a sense of dread overcoming him. He had no wish to see Elizabeth again. No wish to return to the bank. To be met by the faces of the other partners, men who would look upon him and

Elizabeth with their knowing gazes of just why exactly she was choosing to renounce his partnership.

Gabriel hated failure above all else, and this could be described as nothing but that.

He should deny the invitation. Then he could avoid it all. He refused, however, to act with cowardice. So he sighed and resigned himself to one last meeting with Lady Elizabeth Moreland. And after that? Well, that was the problem. For he had no idea what direction to take from here, but he better decide quickly.

Before the meeting, he decided he would visit Elizabeth's office to speak to her just once, on his own. If he continued to refuse her invitation to do so, then he was no better than even Henry Clarke. It was part of his responsibility as a partner, despite what his heart was telling him. And so it was the next morning that he called Baxter to help him dress in his favorite breeches and waistcoat. If he was going to see Elizabeth alone one last time, then he would be at nothing but his best.

CHAPTER 30

*G*abriel was astounded at the sight in front of him when his carriage rolled up to the front entryway of Clarke & Co. The bank certainly did a great deal of business, but never had he seen such a clamoring at the door. The closer the carriage came, however, the more Gabriel's curiosity was replaced by a feeling of dread. For there could only be one reason for a sudden demand at an institution such as a bank.

The bank sold no goods that would come so suddenly in demand, nor was there any way for nearly every bloke in London to unexpectedly have such pressing business at its doors — except for one reason.

That they were all drawing their money out.

Gabriel felt a slight panic begin within his chest. There was the concern for his own wealth and property, true, for as a partner he was responsible for all interests of the bank. His personal wealth could be at stake, though no more than the percentage of his shares, which for him, was not nearly as substantial as for others.

But for Elizabeth, whose entire fortune rested on this

bank, who would feel responsible for everything that occurred within its doors… this could be her ruin, and the destruction of the bank as a whole.

Gabriel began to disembark from the carriage before it even came to a stop, as he leaped out the door and ran up the stairs, trying to push through the throng of people.

"Whatever is happening?" he finally asked a man when his forward progress was thwarted.

"It's been said that the bank is folding. The partners are in disagreement. One of the partners, a member of the family no less, is being asked to leave, and I'm told the bank has no funds available in which to provide anyone with their savings. Those here are the first to know, so we want to receive what we're owed before it's all gone."

Gabriel raised himself to his full height.

"I believe you are sorely mistaken," he said, raising an eyebrow. "For I am the Duke of Clarence, one of the partners in said bank. I can assure you that the partners are not in disagreement and, in fact, will be meeting later this week. The bank is in full health and retains all the funds necessary for its clients. Where did you hear such a tale?"

The man looked confused, as though he wasn't sure whether or not to believe what Gabriel told him.

"From a friend. Who heard from a friend. Who heard from one of the partners himself."

"Clarke," Gabriel muttered and pushed onward until he made it into the inner foyer of the bank. A place typically recognized as one of peace and order, it now seemed completely chaotic. Gabriel glanced around him as he saw the manager, Mr. Bates, attempting to maintain control, while the clerks looked panicked, as though they weren't sure whether to continue in their mission of helping all of the clients as quickly as possible or if they should be refusing any service.

Gabriel looked around at the lot of them, determining how best to act. He would have to make a speech of some sort, dispelling them of their beliefs. The best place would be from the staircase, where it began to spiral up to the top, he decided, and began to make his way there.

He was stalled, however, when another figure filled his destination, coming from above. This one, however, was much more beautiful, a vision in her long aquamarine gown.

"Gentlemen," she called out to the throng below her, and when no one turned, she cupped her hands around her mouth, and in a surprisingly still very ladylike manner, repeated her call. "Gentlemen!"

Heads near her began to turn, and soon murmurings through the crowd caused the lot of them to begin to look her way. One began to shout at her, but she held up her hand, and they fell into silence. Gabriel could understand why. It wasn't every day a beautiful woman — a lady no less — commanded a room with simply her presence. Despite what he knew must be turmoil roiling within her, she looked as calm and composed as she always did.

"Contrary to what some of you have heard, the bank remains as strong an institution as it has always been," she said serenely, her voice alone seeming to somewhat placate the crowd as she stood with her hands crossed in front of her. "We are not folding, and I can assure you that we have the ability to cover any and all debts that are required of us. Our partnership is changing, but the remaining partners will be meeting this week to discuss moving forward. We will continue in our current capacity. If, however, you still wish to remove your money from this bank, that is, of course, entirely within your right to do so. Please simply make a line so that our clerks can help you accordingly."

She looked to the bank's manager.

"Mr. Bates will help direct you to the clerk who is able to

handle your business. Please see him first to assist you. If anyone would like to question me directly, please tell Mr. Bates, and we will form a line for inquiries to me as well."

She turned and spoke to Mr. Brant, who had appeared behind her, and he nodded.

With that, she nodded to them all and then returned up the stairs. Gabriel heard mutterings of people around him. Some of them questioned Elizabeth, but many actually seemed mollified by her words and began filtering out of the building. About half remained, standing in line now to see Mr. Bates.

Gabriel could only stare after Elizabeth. She had handled the entire situation with more grace and dignity than any man ever could, that was for sure. If there was ever a man who questioned whether a woman belonged in business, if he had seen Elizabeth's performance today, he would certainly revise his thinking. Gabriel wished he could tell her how magnificent she was, but she had been clear that she didn't want his affections, and how could he continue to belittle himself before her?

Besides that, he couldn't forget her dismissal of him — as a man, and as a partner. But until he was officially removed, this bank was still partly his, and he would do all he could to protect it.

Gabriel walked over to Mr. Bates and tapped him on the shoulder.

"If you need anything, Mr. Bates," he said when the man turned to look at him, his own control returning after Elizabeth's speech, "I shall remain at the side of the room in the chairs against the wall."

Bates nodded, clearly appreciating the thought that someone else was available to back him if needed.

Gabriel sat in the corner, crossed his arms, and watched the proceedings.

* * *

ELIZABETH HAD NEVER BEEN SO exhausted in her whole life.

If she lost this bank, she would lose everything. As of this moment, it was just holding on. Thankfully her reassurance seemed to have held off some of the clients, and most of their significant clients had come to speak with her directly. While Elizabeth knew that no matter the each account was important no matter the size, when it came down to the bank's financial picture, the larger accounts were, of course, the most vital.

Once she explained the truth of the situation, most agreed to remain with Clarke & Co., though she could tell some were skeptical. Between the lies spread by Henry, and the rumor — though true — he had shared with, it seemed, the partners of the bank, she wasn't sure how long she could continue in her current capacity, or whether the bank could survive this.

She was letting her grandfather down, she thought, sinking her head into arms as she sat behind her desk. Elizabeth was nearly too tired to move, to find her way out of the bank and return home. Maybe she should just sleep here, she thought with some chagrin. She had the partner's meeting in a couple of days. She could just stay here until then. What did it matter, anyway?

Elizabeth nearly jumped when there was a knock at the door, and when she bid entry to her visitor, she was surprised.

"Mr. Cartwright," she greeted the elderly partner when he walked into the room. "Please, have a seat."

He nodded, making his way over to the small conversation nook, where they sat next to one another. Elizabeth knew him fairly well, as the man has been a friend of her grandfather's for so many years, yet she knew he had been as perplexed as many others when Thomas had named her his successor.

She opened her mouth but wasn't entirely sure what to say. He was likely here to question her, suggest she leave the bank in the hands of someone else, but deep within she knew she wasn't ready to let go. Despite the exhaustion upon her shoulders, she still had some fight let in her.

"Mr. Cartwright, I—"

He shook his head before she could say any more, and laid a hand upon hers in a fatherly way.

"Lady Elizabeth," he said gently. "It has been a difficult day, I am sure."

She nodded, blinking back tears at his kindness. "It has."

"Your grandfather was one of my greatest friends, and he is a man I admired all of my life," Mr. Cartwright said, the tufts of hair bobbing around his head as he spoke, and Elizabeth could see that his fingers moved in concert, and she knew he was likely longing for the pipe he typically smoked.

"Did you know," he continued, "That we grew up together?"

"I did," Elizabeth said, having heard the story from Thomas a few times. "He said that you had always been a close friend."

"Since the day he protected me from the other boys picking on someone much smaller than them," Mr. Cartwright said with a sentimental smile. "Thomas was always looking out for everyone else. He was the type of man who succeeded at everything to which he put his mind. Look what he did with this bank. He took a simple business and turned it into one of the most successful banks in London. A man who came from little was soon socializing with the nobility. Not many men can bridge that gap."

Elizabeth nodded, well aware of all that he said, and Mr. Cartwright leaned forward, looking into Elizabeth's eyes.

"Your grandfather believed in you. He put this bank in your hands. I was skeptical at first, I will admit that. A woman, the senior partner of a bank? I'd heard it done before, it was true, but at Clarke & Co., I wasn't sure."

Elizabeth nodded again, not trusting her voice. He was right. Perhaps she hadn't been the best choice.

"But Lady Elizabeth," he continued. "You have proven yourself as much as your grandfather ever did. You have handled everything with the decorum you were raised with as a lady, and still the strength that has been passed down from both your grandmother and grandfather. Your cousin has done much wrong by you, and still, you have maintained your poise, responding in a manner that most would be unable to manage. Needless to say, Lady Elizabeth, I am impressed."

"But all of the clients today—"

"They will come back," he reassured her. "No other bank in London offers the service of Clarke & Co., which they will soon realize for themselves. In addition, the fact that you allowed anyone who wished it to remove their money only proves that this bank is, by no means, failing. If your grandfather were here, Lady Elizabeth, he would be proud of you. I wanted you to know that."

Elizabeth nodded, unable to form any words due to the lump in her throat. She swallowed a few times, and Mr. Cartwright, clearly seeing her struggle, patted her hand and began to rise.

"I shall see you at the partners' meeting. Do not worry yourself," he said with a smile as he began to depart the room, and Elizabeth finally managed, "Thank you, Mr. Cartwright," as he gave a little wave and continued out the door.

CHAPTER 31

*F*or the second time in the same week, Gabriel was stunned by the scene in front of him as his carriage pulled up before the doors of Clarke & Co. Once again, a line of people protruded from the entryway. Today, however, they were calm and orderly, and even Anderson didn't look the slightest bit flustered.

This time, Gabriel didn't rush into the building, but rather maintained the composed manner of the crowd itself and followed them in the door. Mr. Bates was standing at attention at his station, looking rather pleased, while clients were stepping up to clerks, some with hands full of papers.

"What in the world is happening?" Gabriel asked Mr. Bates as he looked around him.

Mr. Bates looked at him with a wide smile.

"They are returning, Your Grace!"

"Returning?" he looked back to Bates in surprise.

"Yes!" The man confirmed. "Can you believe it? It seems that most of them, upon returning home, realized that no other bank would have offered such a service, nor treated them so courteously despite the fact they were doing a run

251

on it. They are now returning to re-hire the bank to store their savings, as it were, though many are somewhat shame-faced."

"Well, I'll be…"

Gabriel had never heard of such a thing before. It seemed that a bit of decorum and treating the customer with the utmost respect was actually the best action Elizabeth could have taken.

It was becoming clearer than ever before why Thomas Clarke had selected her as his successor. Not only did she have the temperament and the intellect, but the original senior partner had also trained her well.

"Mr. Bates?"

"Yes, Your Grace?"

"What are the thoughts of the staff over all that has occurred?"

"They stand behind Lady Elizabeth," Bates said staunchly. "Just as they stood behind her grandfather. She is a good woman, Your Grace. She treats the staff fairly, pays them well, and knows them each personally. That's not typical in most banks, Your Grace. No, they will not be seeking employment elsewhere, that is for certain."

"Thank you, Bates," Gabriel murmured as Bates turned back to the next client looking for his service.

A flash of royal blue caught his eye as he turned, and Gabriel looked up to see Elizabeth standing at the top of the staircase looking down on the lobby below. Even from afar, he could tell that her gaze was incredulous, as though she herself could hardly believe what was occurring. And then the slightest of smiles graced her lips, and she nodded to herself before turning and hurrying back the way she came — likely to prepare for the meeting at hand.

Gabriel would miss this. Would miss her. It had been a strange position to find himself in, as a duke, and yet an endeavor he enjoyed. He sighed as he made his way to the stairs to find the meeting room. He would likely be the first to arrive, but perhaps a moment alone with Elizabeth would not be the worst idea.

* * *

ELIZABETH TAPPED her quill pen nervously on the table. She ran her finger over the pen's inscription once more as she awaited the partners to join her around the table. She had no idea what the reaction would be to her pronouncements today, and it scared her to think of it. But this was her role, her duty, and one she would not shirk.

The door nudged open, and Elizabeth looked up, expecting to see Mr. Brant, whom she had sent on an errand to collect a copy of the partners' rules in case she had to explain any of her actions. He must have found them rather quickly, she surmised.

The frame filling the doorway, however, was not Mr. Brant's. It was a wide, broad frame, one more familiar than any other man's had ever been.

"Elizabeth."

His voice, his very presence, caused her heart to beat more rapidly than it had been even moments before, yet at the same token, it was somewhat… reassuring to have him here. Which was ridiculous. She knew, however, that some way, somehow, Gabriel would always make sure everything would be all right. She didn't have to worry when he was there with her.

Which was ridiculous, but a truth she could not deny.

And as she stared up at him, his hard gaze looking back down on her as he said nothing, all she wanted to do was jump from her chair and into his arms.

She loved him. Part of her had always loved him, she

knew that. This, however, was stronger, more palpable. She yearned to be able to rush back into his arms as she had before, to be able to both tell him and show him all that was in her heart. She wanted to apologize, to tell him that she had been a fool and that they could do anything as long as they were together. She also knew, with every instinct she had, that nothing had occurred between him and Lady Pomfret, that the woman was being the nuisance she had always been. Gabriel was no more the same man he had been five years ago than Elizabeth was the same woman. And yet she had doubted him, holding onto her past hurts in order to protect her heart.

Elizabeth stood — to do what, she had no idea, but suddenly she was overcome by the need to tell him… something, to ensure that he wouldn't leave again without knowing the depth of her feeling toward him.

He didn't move back, and as she took a step toward him, all he said was, "I'm sorry, Elizabeth, for everything."

Everything. For their time together in the gardens years ago? For their time together more recently? To the fact their intimate time together had been shared with the partners of this bank? She had no idea, but she was astounded. Gabriel hardly ever apologized. And this time, he really wasn't the one who had done anything wrong.

"No, Gabriel, I—" But she was cut off by Mr. Brant's return. He was closely followed by some of the partners, who looked between her and Gabriel questioningly as they filed in the room.

The connection was broken, and Gabriel took his customary seat in the corner as they both began to greet the arriving partners. She would talk to him later — she had no choice, really. Though there was something she had to do first. She had made a mistake and it was time to rectify that.

"Mr. Brant," she said, her voice just above a whisper. "Could I speak to you for a moment?"

When they returned to the room, it was full, and the six partners looked up at her with expectant faces. Elizabeth took a deep breath and was about to speak when Henry sauntered into the room, taking a seat across from her. Elizabeth simply nodded in greeting and then began.

"There are two items of business to discuss today," she said, hearing the slightest of tremble in her voice, and she cleared her throat, willing it away. "The first is regarding our partners. It has come to my attention that there are two partners who are working not for this bank, but against it."

Murmurs began around the table, and she held up a hand to silence them.

"As many of you know, my cousin, Mr. Henry Clarke, joined our bank a couple of months ago. I welcome family at this institution, of course, but Mr. Clarke has chosen to discredit both me and the bank in an attempt for me to step aside and provide him with the senior partnership."

Henry began to protest, but as he did, Elizabeth held up a piece of paper.

"I have a signed letter from Sir Hugo regarding the information provided to him by Mr. Clarke. He has decided, upon learning from Mr. Cartwright that much of Mr. Clarke's information was incorrect, to return to the bank."

The chatter around the table began to swirl once again, and Henry stood.

"This is outrageous!"

"It is not, as you are well aware, Henry," she said before addressing the rest of them. "As senior partner, I am choosing to remove Mr. Clarke as a partner in the bank. He has been informed of this already, so it is not a surprise. He will be replaced by Mr. Bates."

"Mr. Bates?" came a voice from around the table. "The manager Mr. Bates?"

"The very one," she confirmed. "He has been loyal to the bank, he knows the inner workings of the institution better than anyone, and he will be an asset to us, as previously discussed. Thank you for your service to the bank, Henry. Now, I will be removing one other partner."

She saw heads begin to swivel, as they all turned to look at one another, nervous who it might be — each worried if he was the one? Gabriel simply stared at her, his face impassive, though the slightest of smiles teased his lips as he waited for his own dismissal.

"Mr. Lang," she said to one of the partners, a man who had been with the bank for decades and was one of her grandfather's close friends. "Have you recently come into an inheritance?"

The man furrowed his eyebrows together. "No."

"You were, however, in a great deal of debt, were you not?"

"Lady Elizabeth, I hardly think—"

"Were you not?"

"I was," he admitted, though the look he sent her way made her feel as though he was drawing his sword upon her.

"And that debt has been cleared?"

"It has."

"Mr. Lang, I could, perhaps, forgive your initial deception, as my grandfather did. You have been a supporter of the bank for years, and I am aware that people become desperate when they fall into situations such as yours. If the theft of bank funds had ended there, I would have overlooked your betrayal. However, upon further review, your theft continued past the time in which my grandfather first spoke with you. You have continued to harm this bank, using money belonging to our clients in order to fund your betting at the horse track, which is unacceptable for a partner. You are dismissed as well."

As she spoke, the man had begun to rise, and now he was standing, shaking his finger over her as he looked down upon her.

"You are a nasty woman! Your grandfather—"

"My grandfather forgave you the first time, due to your long friendship and standing at the bank. However, when I looked into the history of what had occurred and reviewed the current books, I realized that the pattern had continued. Thank you for your service, Mr. Lang. She turned to Mr. Brant. "Please note that Mr. Brant will be replaced by Mr. Larkin, as previously discussed."

She paused for a moment.

"That concludes our business regarding partners." She caught Gabriel's eye for just a moment, and he looked dumbfounded. She smiled. Good. It was hard to stun a man like Gabriel.

"And now, to discuss the recent accusations made against my character."

CHAPTER 32

*G*abriel could only stare at Elizabeth. He had been awaiting her dismissal of him. In fact, he had already been contemplating what he would do following this shortened meeting. For once, Gabriel did not have a plan. No scheme in order to keep his role, nor to win back Elizabeth. For the first time in his life, he was simply going to accept his fate. Elizabeth could have what she wanted. A life without him as a partner, in any sense of the word.

Then she had completely surprised him by not saying a thing about him. Why? What had changed? He wondered what she was going to say to him when he walked into the room, had they not been interrupted by the arrival of the other partners. Had she changed her mind? But no... for clearly she would have told him before now, would she not have?

He awaited her words regarding her reputation. Gabriel felt as though he should stand up there with her, shoulder to shoulder, for it was his actions as much as her own that had been called into question. Yet he sensed that she needed to do this alone, to prove to herself if no one else that she could stand there, as a woman, to defend herself and show how strong she truly was. When she denied it, he would support her. While she may have turned him away, it wasn't fair that she be the only one to have to respond to such accusations.

"The rumor that you have all heard is true."

Gabriel's jaw dropped along with the rest of the partners as she said the words. He could hardly believe it. Why had she not denied it? Once he backed her — as she had to have known he would — she could then have moved on, putting all of this behind her. Why was she risking everything with the truth?

The partners around him began to mutter to themselves, shaking their heads as they looked at her with some chagrin, judging her, questioning her.

"Lady Elizabeth," began Mr. Cartwright, a man who Gabriel knew was quite friendly toward her, but surprised nonetheless. Elizabeth held up a finger, as though to signal she had more to say.

"As many of you know," she continued, her voice strong, though her right pinkie was tapping nervously on the table before her, "The Duke and I were engaged to be married some time ago. Unfortunately, the marriage did not transpire, but we remained close. However, I firmly believe that anything that has occurred between us in a personal sense is, just that, personal, and should have no reflection upon the bank or the business we do. In fact, I will provide no further details as to what transpired. As you are partners in the bank, I have chosen to share this with you, but to anyone else, I will not justify their questions with an answer. They can think what they decide is true in their eyes."

"But Lady Elizabeth…" said Sir Gray, the young baronet. "How could you…"

"How could I… enter into any type of relationship with a

man to whom I was not married? Let me ask you this, Sir Gray," she said, holding her head high. "If I were a man, would you judge me as you are now? Would you be questioning my competence, my leadership?"

"I…" The man clearly had nothing to say in answer than that. Of course, he wouldn't have thought anything of it, but he could hardly admit to that now, could he?

"No, you would not," she finished for him. "In fact, you would probably hardly even give it a passing thought. Therefore, I would ask you—" She looked up and passed her gaze around the table. "All of you — to not concern yourself with this matter any longer. I have been honest with you because I feel that is one of the values held of this bank, one that we should all aspire to uphold. I would also ask that you not share anything I have said here with others outside of this room. Yes, I am asking for my own sake, but also for that of the bank. I should not want additional question to come upon it, and I hope you can understand that."

The partners were now silent. Gabriel smiled. Elizabeth had proven herself once more to be a woman of great worth, outsmarting all of the men who now sat in front of her. As he looked up at her, tall and proud, her head held high despite all that had been put to her, he couldn't help but be proud of her. And stunned by her. And— by God, he was in love with her. Truly in love with her. She had run quite the game around him — more than he had ever done to anyone else — and yet, he couldn't help the way he felt. He would love her for the rest of his life, even if they were to never see one another again. No other woman matched her. *My Lady of Providence,* he thought, amazedly.

And he realized now what his previous proposal had lacked. He had said nothing of how he felt about her. Sure, he had told her that she was intelligent, beautiful, that he wanted her. But what did any of that mean if she didn't understand that he would love her for the rest of their lives, whether she wanted him to or not? She may not want to hear it anymore — but he would tell her anyway, once this all was finished.

"And you, Your Grace?" Sir Gray turned his gaze upon him, and, startled by the question, Gabriel found himself now holding the attention of the room, the expressions on the partners' faces nearly surprised, as though they had forgotten that he was just as much as part of this as was Elizabeth. "What do you have to say about this?"

Gabriel looked back toward Elizabeth. "Lady Elizabeth, our senior partner, has said it all," he said. "What more is there to say? Clearly, someone," he looked over to where Clarke had been sitting, "has been attempting to sully Lady Elizabeth's name. As a partner, not as a named party, I would like to suggest that the information you have all learned within this room *remains* within this room, to protect our partners as well as the bank itself. We must have a united front, for we are much stronger together."

He looked at Elizabeth as he said the words, hoping that she understood their meaning for her.

"Are we all agreed?"

The other partners studied him, many with question and certainly hesitancy, but slowly they nodded their heads and agreed.

"Very good," he said. "If I hear that this story has emerged, I will know where it came from."

Some of the others looked uncomfortable, but no one spoke out.

"Thank you all," Elizabeth said, retaking her seat. "Before you depart, I would like to provide you with one last piece of information. The Redmond family has decided to now bank with Clarke & Co. You may have also heard of the run on the bank just two days ago. The malicious rumors that had been spread about this bank caused great panic among our clients, and many came to remove their savings. We provided them the same service that Clarke & Co. has always been known for, and I am happy to say that a very large percentage of them returned just this morning to re-invest with us. It seems that no other bank in London can offer the same service as we do. I hope that many other major clients will soon follow us, as we remain strong as a partnership."

The partners looked impressed with her words, and Gabriel's heart swelled with pride.

What a woman.

* * *

GABRIEL WHISTLED a tune as he departed the bank and entered his carriage. He had begun this day with the knowledge he was going to be dismissed as a partner, the worry that the bank itself failing, and the disappointment at the fact that Elizabeth continued to reject him.

Now, just a few hours later, he remained a partner, the bank seemed to be in sound and strong practice after all, and as for Elizabeth... well, she hadn't come any closer to accepting him as far as he was aware, but he could have sworn there was something there when she looked at him, that she was, perhaps, warming to him once more.

Could he be imagining it? Perhaps. But it was enough, for now, a glimmer of hope.

Never in his life had Gabriel had to work so hard for something — but had anything been so worth it before? The only reason he even had to do so was because of his own actions. Perhaps her refusal of him had also partially set her apart from any other.

Gabriel tried to picture his life in the future. First, life with another woman. A woman who would seamlessly devote her attention to following his orders in running his multitude of households and estates, demurely greeting guests when he hosted parties, bearing and raising his children as was expected of her.

The only problem was, he couldn't see a face on the woman, and that vision brought him nothing but additional boredom and an ache in his chest.

When he replaced the woman's face with Elizabeth's, everything changed. The wife in this vision did not follow his orders when it came to the running of his household and estates but rather determined what she felt were the best decisions. She greeted his guests, but not demurely — no, she wasn't a woman to stand behind him, but beside him, for she needed to be present and visible due to her own business interests. And as for bearing and raising his children — well, this woman still did that. And the thought of the woman as Elizabeth caused warmth unlike anything he had ever felt before to flow through him. When he pictured a family — with Elizabeth — that hole that had been growing ever wider not only shrunk but completely closed, and Gabriel was filled with a serene peace that he nearly didn't recognize.

It was his love for her. Love that he hadn't wanted to name, but that had been growing ever stronger until it finally made its way through his thick skull.

The carriage pulled up at his London home — so large, he thought as his eyes followed the expansive wings stretching out east and west, but so empty. He knew what it was he was longing for now, to fill that space with children, and additional caregivers for his family, and — most of all — his wife.

Only one problem remained — the fact that Elizabeth was still not entirely convinced that she wanted him in return. When she looked at him today, in that moment before the meeting commenced, he had thought he could feel her soul reaching his, sharing a moment of connectedness.

He knew she still didn't completely trust him, and worried about what her life would look like were she a duchess. As Gabriel now entered his study and sat behind his desk, his chin upon his fist, he thought of the way Elizabeth's mind worked. She needed to be convinced on multiple levels — both emotionally and intellectually. She worked best when her heart and mind were as one.

Gabriel called out to his butler, who appeared momentarily.

"Your Grace?" The man asked.

"Can you please arrange a meeting with my solicitor, as quickly as possible?"

The butler nodded, confirming the appointment but an hour later.

His plans concluded, now all Gabriel had to do was follow through himself. If he didn't succeed... then all would be lost.

CHAPTER 33

*E*lizabeth returned home that evening feeling as though a great burden had been lifted from her shoulders. Were she being honest, she hadn't meant to tell the partners the truth of it all. But in that moment, the denial on the tip of her tongue, she knew that she couldn't be dishonest while expecting that the rest of them model the integrity of the bank.

"So I told the truth," she said to her grandmother, providing her the entire story from the beginning. Her grandmother was not shocked, as Elizabeth had expected her to be by her confession.

"Just because I am an old woman now, it does not mean that I forget what it was like to be in the young blush of love," she said with a smile, and Elizabeth began to shake her head.

"That's the thing, Grandmother," she said. "At the time, I think it was more infatuation than love. I cannot use that as an excuse. We were two young people who were caught up in a moment of passion, not thinking of the consequences."

"I have seen the two of you together many times now,"

Justine said, "And I have a hard time believing that the two of you do not love one another."

"Therein lies the problem," Elizabeth said, her voice soft as she looked around the drawing room. "I do love him. So much. Only I was too proud, too stubborn to admit it when I should have, and now it is too late."

Justine leaned across the table between them and placed a hand on Elizabeth's. "Darling, it is never too late," she said, her smile gentle. "You have an entire lifetime ahead of you. A lifetime that could be filled with love, or could be filled with regret for what could have been. Tell him how you feel. What's the worst he could say?"

Elizabeth nodded, though a few of her reservations remained.

"I am afraid."

"Of what?"

"My love for him... it could be my undoing," she said, her voice slightly breaking, but she allowed it, for once. This was her grandmother, a woman who knew and understood her likely better than any other. If Elizabeth could not share her emotions with her, then to whom could she open?

"What of my role in the bank? If the impossible happened and I became his duchess... could I still be the senior partner of Clarke & Co.?"

"What does he have to say about that?"

"That we would make it work."

"Then you already have your answer," Justine said, waving a hand in the air in front of her.

"Do you think he would take other women? I find myself doubting that he would, but if he became bored with me and ever did... I simply couldn't bear it," Elizabeth said, her voice soft now, and her grandmother shook her head slightly.

"If he loves you the way I think he loves you, then no," she said, then crossed her arms and placed them on her knees as she leaned forward toward Elizabeth. "A few years ago, he treated you wrongly. You know that, he knows that. What you need to ask yourself now is whether he is still that man today, or whether he has matured into a man who you know will love and respect you no matter what happens."

"What if you are wrong — what if he does not love me?"

"That, you can only determine for yourself," Justine said. "You will know, Elizabeth. You are an intelligent woman."

"Intelligence has nothing to do with matters of the heart."

"It is intelligence of another sort," her grandmother said. "Which you have always had, even if you just haven't wanted to acknowledge it."

Elizabeth nodded, understanding. She had to talk to Gabriel again. But how would she get through his stubborn, proud, ducal exterior to convince the man underneath of what she truly felt as she asked for his forgiveness?

* * *

WHEN THE BUTLER opened the door to greet him, Gabriel had to force himself to slow a step and maintain his manners instead of bursting through the door to find Elizabeth. The urgency that filled him astonished him, but at the moment, he could think of nothing but finding Elizabeth, and convincing her— no. That had been his mistake. Unlike most aspects of his life, he could not *tell* Elizabeth to marry him. He had to lay his heart out, and then it would be her decision whether or not to accept him.

He smiled now. Whoever thought that he — the Duke of Clarence — would be leaving his life in the hands of a woman?

"Good day, Hampton," he said to the butler, taking him aback, and Gabriel understood why. Never before had he taken the time to acknowledge servants, but he recalled Eliz-

ELLIE ST. CLAIR

abeth explaining once how the smallest gestures could make the largest impact, and the odd time he had tried to put it into practice, it had surprisingly caused quite a reaction. Who would have thought? "Is Lady Elizabeth home?"

"She is, Your Grace," the butler responded. "I will announce you."

Gabriel wanted to tell Hampton not to bother — that he would find her himself. But he forced himself to be patient and allowed the butler to do his job and show him into the drawing room.

When he stepped through the door, his eyes found her without any effort. She wore a pale yellow dress, one that made her look youthful and innocent. Which she was — a light in a world of darkness.

Her face wore an expression of uncertainty — whether due to his presence, or the unspoken words between them, he wasn't sure, but it was time for it all to come out into the open.

"Gabriel!" He hadn't even noticed Mrs. Clarke sitting across from her until now, but Elizabeth's grandmother rose from the sofa and came over to bestow a kiss upon his cheek. "How lovely to see you. You look splendid, as always."

"Thank you, Mrs. Clarke. You always know how to make a man feel special," he said with a smile for her.

"I will leave the two of you," she said graciously, and with a swish of her aquamarine skirts, she was out the door silently, closing it behind her and leaving the two of them alone together, clearly no longer concerned at all about propriety — if she ever had been. Gabriel thought with a wry smile that the time for that between the two of them had long passed.

He took a deep breath.

* * *

"GABRIEL," Elizabeth began, standing, but before she could say anything, he crossed the distance between them and took her hands within his.

"Before you say anything, Elizabeth, there is something I must first say to you." He led her over to the settee, sitting down next to her as he kept his hands upon hers. "I told you that I would not propose to you again. I will keep that promise."

Her eyes widened as she broke their gaze for a moment, looking down to her lap before back up at him as he squeezed her hands to re-capture her attention and continued to speak.

"I am not proposing a third time. But I do need to slightly amend my second proposal. The one from a few days ago. I told you that we were a suitable match for many reasons — the fact that our minds seem to be on the same plane, that you challenge me in a way that no other woman does. Which remains true. However, I forgot one aspect that is more important than anything else."

He slid back down to the floor, on his knees in front of her, and Elizabeth was astounded that he would allow himself to be so vulnerable with her once more.

"Elizabeth Moreland, I love you."

She gasped, shocked at his words, but before she could say anything, he continued.

"You are stubborn, you are proud, and you hold all of your emotion deep within you," he said, and she narrowed her gaze at him. *This* was why he loved her? These hardly seemed to be her most redeeming qualities. "You have been raised a lady, one who keeps her composure at all times. I love knowing, however, that there is fiery passion within you, one you keep hidden beneath the surface. I've seen it, Elizabeth, and I love the fact that you have shared that part of yourself with me. You have a passion for doing what is right, for seeing to all of your responsibilities. You take everything upon your own shoulders, and I respect that, I do, but I always want to help ease those burdens, and I beg of you to allow me to do so. You have a fire for chasing your dreams, for going beyond what is expected of a lady of your station, and I admire that so greatly about you. You look after those who are important to you, be they your friends, your relatives, or the clients and employees of the bank."

He looked down for a moment before tilting his head back up toward her. His strong jaw was set in determination, and Elizabeth knew she had to allow him to finish his thoughts before she told him all that was on her mind.

"Five years ago, I was a fool. You know that. I realize now that it wasn't the time for us. I was too immature, too full of myself, too selfish to love another. Since then, I have come to realize that there is so much more to life than my own interests. For all that this world has to offer, it means nothing without someone to share it with. For me, that person is you, Elizabeth. I need you in my life. Your intelligence, your wit, your heart, your love."

He reached over to the table, picking up a stack of papers, which she hadn't even realized he had brought with him, so intent had she been upon simply seeing him.

"This is a marriage contract," he said, and Elizabeth stared at the papers in shock. He came prepared with such a contract?

"Is this a game?" she asked, her voice a whisper, and he shook his head.

"No more games, Elizabeth, not with you," he responded intently, his blue eyes blazing. "I cannot promise not to involve myself in situations that may present themselves, where I see that perhaps I could help. But I will always be upfront with you. There will be no secrets, Elizabeth. No lies, no manipulations. This I promise you. You can have anyone you'd like review this contract. It specifically describes the terms of our marriage. You remain in complete possession of your shares, of your finances. I will have no holds or involvement beyond my own interests and my own partnership, and you can have complete access to whatever income you earn. All I want is you — no other woman, no other business. If you would like me to leave the bank, then so be it. As long as I have you with me, then I will be happy, and I will do all I can to ensure that you are as well. And so I ask you, Elizabeth, as part of my *amended* proposal, will you fill the hole in my soul? Will you be my wife, my partner?"

CHAPTER 34

Gabriel held his breath. He knew he hadn't given her the opportunity to say anything, and yet it was somewhat working against him as he longed to know what thoughts were running behind those violet eyes, which were now filling with tears. Were they tears of joy? Sadness? Regret?

"Gabriel," she said, her voice breaking. "I can hardly believe you are asking me once more, after everything I have said to you, all I have put you through. The threat of taking away your partnership, my repeated denials of your offers toward me — I have not been good to you, and I can hardly imagine what you must think of me."

"I told you what I think."

"You have."

She blushed, her high cheekbones turning a pretty, becoming pink. Could the woman be any more beautiful?

"Gabriel," she said, her voice slightly breaking, and she astonished him when tears began to run down her cheeks. He had never seen her cry before. Not when she had found him with another woman, when she had denied his proposal, nor when her grandfather had died. She had kept it all within her, and the fact that she was now allowing her emotion to show in front of him meant more than any words ever could. "I've been a fool. I've held onto the past, held onto my hurts and my fears. I have been scared. Of what being with you could mean for my role at the bank. Of what I would do if you took another woman once more. And, more than anything, what I would feel if you didn't love me as I do you. Of how I could ever handle my heart breaking once more."

She took a breath, and his own chest ached at the thought that this was his own doing, for ever making her feel that this could be a possibility.

"We have both done things, said things, to one another, that we regret," he acknowledged, and she nodded.

"I have many questions about my future. I enjoy knowing what is ahead, to plan out my life, and to be aware of what may be coming," she said with a bit of a rueful smile, and he nodded, acknowledging her words. "The past few months have been complete chaos, something that I believe I have to come to accept, at least more than I ever previously have. I need to embrace my fears, accept the challenges to come and, if nothing else, to take a risk now and then. While taking a chance on our love would be a risk, not doing so would be even worse, for then I would spend the rest of my life knowing that I had thrown away what could be the greatest part of my existence."

Gabriel couldn't help the smile from appearing on his face.

"Correct me if I'm wrong, but did I hear you say that you love me?"

She laughed at that, some of the tension within her dissipating.

"I do," she said, the tears beginning to fall in earnest, and Gabriel reached into his pockets to find a handkerchief. Instead of passing it to her, he gently wiped away her tears himself.

"And does that mean," he continued, "That you will marry me? Or would you like me to ask again? For I will — for you. I will ask a third time."

"No, no!" she exclaimed, holding a finger up against his lips. "I will not force you to lose all of your pride. I appreciate your amended proposal more than you know. I do love you, Gabriel. I love the fact that while you do enjoy your games, what I have been remiss about in the past is that you always play them with the best interests of those you love at heart. I love the fact that you challenge me, that you possess an intellect above any that I have ever known. And I love that you have never given up on me. That you see beyond what I present to the world, that you are perceptive enough to know there is more underneath and that you have worked hard to bring it out of me. I have a... difficult time trusting others. Perhaps it is because of the way my parents raised me, always looking for more from me. I'm not sure, and it's no excuse, but it's time I put that to rest."

"You will share your burdens then?"

"I will share mine if you will share yours."

Gabriel tilted his head further toward hers, bringing their foreheads together.

"You drive a hard bargain, my lady, but I think that is one to which I can agree."

"Good," she said, her voice a whisper, and then reached into the folds of her dress, pulling out a box that looked awfully familiar. His heart began to beat harder as she opened it, slipping the ring out of the box and onto her finger. "So, yes, Gabriel, I will marry you."

He fused his lips against hers, the softness of them turning his bones to liquid. This was no quick, stolen kiss, whether in the gardens or even in his own bedchambers. This as a kiss of promise. Promise that they would have a lifetime together, that they would be one another's partner in every way that mattered.

She broke the seal between their lips with her tongue before he did, and the corners of his lips turned into the slightest smile at her forwardness. There was one thing he could say about Elizabeth — she certainly wasn't shy.

Her tongue sought out his as her hands swept up and around his head, her fingers stroking the nape of his neck where his hair curled over the collar of his jacket. Finding their position rather uncomfortable, he lifted her up and placed her upon his lap, his fingers digging into her bottom, feeling the lushness awaiting him there.

One thing she certainly would never have to worry about was him ever wanting another. She was more woman than he could ever imagine, and he loved everything about her. He wanted nothing more than to lay her down on the sofa and make love to her, but he knew how foolhardy that would be. A servant, or even her grandmother, could walk in at any moment.

She was apparently feeling the same, for she broke their kiss, her breathing as ragged as his.

"Come," she said, hopping off his lap and holding her hand out to him.

"Anywhere," he said, meaning it. "But..."

"Do you trust me?" She looked up at him from beneath her lashes, and he nodded.

"Of course. With anything."

"Then follow me."

And so he went, feeling like a young man again as she

looked out the door one way and then the other, before rushing him down the hallway after seeing no one about. They ducked past the back sitting room, wherein Elizabeth whispered to him her grandmother would be. She giggled slightly after they passed before leading him up the stairs and down the corridor, pushing open the door in the back corner.

He looked around, astonished to find her own room within. It was finished in deep purple and accented in cream, reminding him of her in every way.

"My home will need some serious redecorating," he said, looking around him in awe as she locked the door behind her. "Are you up for the task? Though that may be a foolish question as I hardly think there is anything you cannot do."

"There are some things," she said, her hands coming to the buttons on the front of his jacket, "That I believe you can teach me."

"Ah," he said, grinning down at her. "If my lady commands it, then teach you I will."

With a growl, he picked her up and laid her down upon the bed, lifting a hand to trail a finger down her cheek, her neck, to the swell of her bosom now rising above her dress.

"What would you like to learn today?" he asked, then quickly kissed her lips.

"How to truly make love, with all of the emotion behind it," she said, her lashes dropping as though she were somewhat embarrassed, and he chuckled.

"That, Elizabeth, we shall have to learn together."

As she worked the buttons on his jacket, her fingers somewhat trembled, but she was determined all the same. He brought his hands behind her back to rid her of her dress. He expertly released the small buttons from their laces and then nudged the sleeves down her shoulders. He lifted himself up on his elbows, appreciating that in the waning light of day through the open windows, he could see the silky dew of her skin. Needing to taste her, he dropped his lips upon her shoulder, kissing his way along her collarbone to her neck, then down lower. She gasped, arching up against him when he nudged her dress down and found one nipple, sucking it through the light, transparent material of her chemise. Her hands found his hair once more, lacing her fingers through it, and for once he had not a care for how disheveled he would look following this encounter.

Somehow, as he divested her of her own gown, she had rid him of his jacket and was now working on his shirt. While she was determinately stubborn, his urge to feel his skin against hers overcame all else, and he ripped his shirt off before lifting her chemise over her head. When he lay back down, he didn't think anything had ever felt as good as her bare breasts against his chest. He couldn't be sure, but he thought she might even be rubbing against him, and his desire for her began to burn even hotter.

And then she brought her hands to the fall of his pants, and when she freed him, the simmer he had been feeling before burst into flames. He had meant to make love to her slowly, softly, with the promise of forever, but he would do that later. For at the moment, he could think of nothing but finding himself inside of her once more, loving her with all that he was, his body and his soul.

She seemed to be of the same mind, as together they rid him of his breeches and guided him toward her. He was sheathed within her in one swift motion as they moved together simultaneously, and he let out a shout at how right it felt, how he knew that this was where he was meant to be more than anywhere else in the entire world.

"Elizabeth," he managed, bringing his lips to her ear. "I love you."

"And I you."

They began to move, synchronized together in an experience unlike any he had ever had before. They may have already known one another in a bodily sense, but now that they knew their love for one another was more than a fleeting desire, but something that would last forever, the physical manifestation of it tore through his body as he gripped her hips, unable to hold on much longer.

His dipped his head, taking a nipple within his mouth as he reached between them and found the bud of her desire, stroking it in time to the motion of his hips. She gave out a scream which he captured with his mouth, taking the sound within him, as together they found their release while the world seemed to explode around him with the brightest of intensities.

It took him more than a moment to calm down from it. He held himself up from her body, keeping his entirety of weight from her, but he allowed his forehead to rest against hers as their choppy breath mingled together.

Finally, he rolled to his side, bringing her along with him.

"Elizabeth," he said. "I don't think I can ever let you go."

"You don't have to," she said with a smile. "I'm here with you now — forever."

"Except tonight I will have to sleep without you," he said with a sigh.

"You will," she said. "Though for how many more nights, that remains to be seen."

"I suppose we will have to wait an acceptable amount of time."

She shrugged. "You're a duke... can you not find a way to shorten that?"

He laughed then, pulling her against him. "What's this now? Is my proper Elizabeth looking to do something against what might be expected of her?"

"I think I am long past that point now," she said, laughing

with him. "Except for the fact that I am marrying the man every other woman in England seems to want, I believe it is best to now forge my own path ahead."

"Together," he said, looking down at her.

"Together."

CHAPTER 35

 *hree weeks later*

"OH, Elizabeth, that was the most beautiful wedding I have ever seen — besides yours, of course, Phoebe, which was equally as lovely."

Elizabeth smiled at Sarah's wistful words. She was right — the wedding but two days before had been lovely. Never had she thought she would be the type of woman to want a massive wedding, with excessive amounts of lace and flowers and a sumptuous wedding breakfast, but when one married a duke, there wasn't much choice.

Her parents had been more thrilled and prouder of her than ever before. While Elizabeth wished for their approval in other aspects of her life, of course, she had been pleased that, at the very least, the four of them, along with her brother, had the opportunity to find a moment of peace with one another. Until, of course, her mother began to ask Terrence just when he thought he was going to find a wife of his own, for Lord Moreland was not getting any younger, and it was quite important for Terrence to continue the family line. Terrence had not remained long in the conversation following that.

In the end, however, it had actually been rather lovely to have the well-wishes of so many people. There were quite a few jealous stares sent her way, of course, but Elizabeth hardly noticed them. It was difficult, actually, to see much of anything besides Gabriel, and the way he had looked in his immaculately cut black jacket, breeches, and shiny leather boots as he awaited her at the altar.

"More than anything," Elizabeth said now, looking around at her friends as they walked through the lush greenery of the park, a tradition that they repeated more seldom now, only whenever the four of them had the time, "I am happy to finally be married. To be able to go home to Gabriel every night..."

She trailed off, feeling heat rise within her cheeks, and her friends laughed.

"No more sneaking around?" Phoebe asked with a knowing grin, and Elizabeth shook her head at her friend, but they knew her far better than that.

"Elizabeth, I never would have thought you would be the one out of all of us to repeat such impropriety!" Phoebe continued to tease, and Elizabeth knew her face must be quite a bright pink. Phoebe had mercy on her, however, and laid a hand upon her arm. "I am very pleased. It actually makes you more perfect than ever before."

"I am not perfect!"

"No, but it always seems as though you are," Julia said with a sigh. "I am always blundering one thing after another, though it all seems to work out in the end."

"That's what matters, is it not?" Elizabeth asked, and Julia smiled ruefully.

"I suppose so."

"How fares the bank?" Phoebe asked, focusing on business for a moment, and her question brought another smile to Elizabeth's face.

"Very well, actually," she said. "Many of the clients who requested all of their funds to be withdrawn have returned. When it comes to a lifetime of savings, people can act rashly. It is actually reassuring to know that Clarke & Co. offers such excellent service that no other bank can compete."

"And then there's the fact that you handled it with such grace," Sarah pointed out, and Elizabeth simply shrugged.

"It seems it was the best tactic I could have taken, which is reassuring. In addition, the original partners have embraced the former employees as new partners, and both Mr. Bates and Mr. Larkin have brought a massive amount of knowledge to the table that has been key in managing the staff. In addition, they have kept my secret, though I suppose it matters naught now that Gabriel and I are married."

"Are you able to work well together as partners in the bank?" Sarah asked, and Elizabeth nodded.

"Gabriel does not see much to the daily operations, but he has a tremendous amount of contacts of course. Together, we have been fortunate to bring a fair number of new clients to the bank."

"I'm so happy for you," Sarah said, looking up at her, though she squinted in the sun.

"Thank you, Sarah," said Elizabeth. "Have you any wish to find a man for yourself?"

Sarah sighed and shook her head. "I have other worries at the moment. Before I concern myself with the rest of my life, I wish to find my father, just to know who he is and whether we might have any type of relationship."

"We will help you with that," Elizabeth declared, and when Sarah began to protest, she held up a hand. "No arguments, now. Besides, it will give Gabriel something to focus his energies on — something productive, that is."

"Very well," Sarah finally agreed. "I do appreciate it."

"Of course," said Elizabeth. "Now, as for where to begin..."

They moved on from the subject of her marriage as they began to concentrate on Sarah's dilemma. It wouldn't be easy, but between the four of them — along with a little help — there didn't seem to be much they couldn't accomplish.

* * *

THAT NIGHT, Elizabeth and Gabriel lay together upon his bed, the huge, massive mahogany monstrosity, at least to Elizabeth's way of thinking. They would compromise, he promised, and find a style that matched the two of them. Masculine, yet... aesthetically pleasing was how he had put it, if she remembered correctly.

"Do you miss your own home?" Gabriel asked as they lay together after making love, and Elizabeth shrugged. "I do appreciate the opportunity to change some of the decor here to my liking," she said. "The other home will always truly be my grandmother's, though I know she enjoyed the company when I was there. Terrence, however, has decided to make his home there now. I think he was becoming rather lonely at the boardinghouse."

"I'm pleased to hear it," said Gabriel. "He's a good man, your brother."

Elizabeth nodded.

In the glow of the candlelight, Elizabeth marveled at the sinewy delight of Gabriel's body. While she had not exactly seen many men in their naked form, she couldn't see how any other could possibly ever compare to Gabriel. Though he certainly worked at the way he looked, she thought with a smile.

"Whatever could be so funny?" he asked now at her expression as he leaned his head on his fist, his elbow on the bed beside her.

"You," she said, and he raised an eyebrow.

"I cannot say that I have often been one found to be humorous," he said. "Witty, sure. However, when one is a duke, people tend to laugh *with* him and not at him."

"I would not consider myself just anyone."

"That, you certainly are not," he said, tapping her on the nose with his finger. "Now, out with it. What has caused such mirth?"

Elizabeth tried to think of the best way to word what was currently running through her mind.

"Well," she began, beginning with a compliment. "You are a very attractive man."

He grinned, bringing one hand around her shoulder.

"Go on."

"However I suppose I never before realized just how much... effort goes into making you look so perfect."

Gabriel's eyes widened for a moment, and Elizabeth was worried that she had somehow insulted him. But then he began to laugh — more than his usual slight chuckle, but a long, loud laugh that made her heart sing. This was a side to Gabriel that she had not, in the past, seen very much of, and a side she very much enjoyed.

"Are you calling your husband a vain man?"

"Oh, I wouldn't say vain," she said, turning to position herself on her back and face the painted gods and goddesses who danced across the ceiling. "Particular, perhaps."

His chuckle continued somewhat as he stretched out beside her.

"I am lucky to have Baxter, a valet who will put up with my particularities," he said. "I hope my wife will also forgive such ways."

Elizabeth reached up and trailed a finger along his cheek, where the day's stubble was just about to emerge — stubble that would be shaved down to the skin once more in the morning.

"There is nothing to forgive," she said. "It is part of who you are. And who am I to argue with the methods that provide me with the most attractive man in all of England?"

Gabriel reached an arm around her, pulling her close to him once more, and Elizabeth's skin tingled as it touched his.

"I am the lucky one, love," he said, placing a kiss on her lips, one that was gentle, stirring, and felt like a caress more than anything else. How she had denied him for so long, she had no idea, though she knew that, in the end, their timing could not have been better.

"I do know one thing for certain," he said as he pulled back from her, a smile crossing his lips one more.

"Which is?"

"I will never be bored with a woman like you in my life."

"I am glad to hear it," she smiled. "There will be much to manage, between the bank, your estates, Parliament, children..."

His eyes gleamed at her last word as he nodded.

"I believe that if there were ever two people who were capable of accomplishing all, it would be the two of us, would it not?"

"I hope so."

"I know so."

They smiled at one another, but when she saw mischief begin to dance within his blue eyes, Elizabeth became suspicious.

"You don't have another scheme brewing, do you?"

"Who me?" He asked in mock outrage.

"Gabriel..."

"I have nothing planned. Although..."

"Out with it."

"You know my friend, Mr. Redmond?"

"David Redmond?" Elizabeth raised an eyebrow. "An affable gentleman, but quite the rake, I do believe."

"He's misunderstood."

"Has he, or has he not found his way into the beds of many of the available women of the *ton* — and some who are not so available?" she asked with an arched eyebrow.

"Perhaps you do understand some of his actions, though not his character in particular."

"Go on, tell me what you are thinking."

"Only that, perhaps, Redmond is trying to fill a void — an emptiness in his life. He doesn't know what he is missing — a good woman, like you."

"I don't believe this is a matter in which you should become involved."

"Well, there is your friend, Miss Jones—"

"No!" she exclaimed sitting up now. "Sarah is the gentlest, kindest soul that I have ever met. A man like Mr. Redmond would break her heart."

"But if he were only to find the right woman, as I did—"

Elizabeth continued to shake her head, and finally, Gabriel sighed.

"Very well. I will leave it be."

"It is, however, a lovely thought, Gabriel, to look out for your friend. In addition to the fact that you are attributing your happiness to us."

"Of course," he smiled. "Not long ago, it would have been hard to convince me that the purpose I was searching for was the right woman to love."

"I do love you, Gabriel."

"And I love you, Elizabeth. Only you. Forever."

EPILOGUE

A YEAR LATER

Gabriel smiled contentedly as Elizabeth walked through the door of the drawing room. He could tell she had rushed in, likely hearing the sounds of the baby, little Justine, chattering away in her own language, one that Gabriel couldn't help but laugh at himself. Before saying anything to him, Elizabeth descended upon the two of them, kissing the little girl on Gabriel's lap before picking up the baby boy who began clamoring for her attention in the bassinet beside them once he had sensed her presence.

"Hello, husband," she said with a smile and a kiss for Gabriel.

"Wife," he acknowledged. "How was your day?"

"Perfect," she said, sitting beside him on the sofa. "I spent most of it with the children and then visited the bank for but an hour or so."

Her time at the bank had considerably lessened since she had given birth a few months ago, but Gabriel admired the

ELLIE ST. CLAIR

fact that she was still keen on attending to her responsibilities there. As she had settled into her role, however, the work had somewhat lessened, especially as both employees and clients became aware of just how capable she was, and that nothing would change upon the passing of the bank from Thomas Clarke to his granddaughter.

Gabriel stared fondly at his wife now, appreciating the fact that motherhood had, in a way, softened her. Her desire for perfection had somewhat relaxed, though she maintained her calm control. In those moments when she needed someone to lean on, someone to help her, then he was pleased to be there for her to provide a word of advice — or not, as he had come to realize that sometimes she simply needed to talk through the situation before her own brilliant mind would find the solution.

He had been more fearful than any other time in his life when she gave birth, but if there was ever a woman who could do so in such a capable manner, it was his Elizabeth. That there were two babies had been something of a shock, but they were a blessing. The physician had been concerned at first, once the first baby arrived, why Elizabeth continued to be in such pain. Gabriel had been outside of the door, pacing, as one of the maids within had continued to provide him with updates as he had requested of her — every ten minutes, he had told her, and not a minute more between.

When she questioned how she would know the time, he told her to count the seconds if she had to, and that was the last she had protested.

When he had heard the baby cry, he had knocked on the door, but all was silent except for the baby and his wife's own cries of pain. When they continued, he had pounded on the door so hard, he had nearly knocked it down.

Then the maid opened the door a crack to tell him

another baby was beginning to come out, and he had nearly fainted in shock.

"I have some news," he said now, coming back to the present, and Elizabeth looked up from baby Thomas to Gabriel.

"Good news or bad news?"

"Good for us, I believe. Somewhat bad for those in America."

She waited for him to continue.

"It seems a Mr. Henry Clarke recently boarded a ship that will take him west, with the intention of eventually ending up in to New York. He is intent on opening a bank there and finding his way in a place where he is unknown."

"Oh dear," she said, raising a hand to her cheek. "Those poor people."

"Who knows?" Gabriel said with a shrug. "Perhaps away from everything here, he might find a place for himself. We can only hope. At the very least, he is no longer a part of our lives, and that is something for which to be grateful, is it not?"

"I suppose," said Elizabeth, though with some hesitation. "I can hardly believe how intent he was on removing me from the bank, destroying my life."

"More than that," said Gabriel. "But it only brought about his downfall, with his debt beginning to increase, and no friends to be found in all of London. Interestingly, Mr. Lang has accompanied him."

"Really?" Elizabeth said, surprised. "He is of a rather advanced age to do so, but then, he never married, and was no longer welcome at the horse track with no money in his pockets for a bet. It's interesting to think of — our two former partners, beginning a bank of their own. I do hope they do not pretend any connection to Clarke & Co."

"Their actions at Clarke & Co. would have been an

embarrassment more than anything," said Gabriel. "I am sure they will leave it all behind them."

"And we can move on," she said.

"We can."

They smiled at one another, at the babies on their laps, and Gabriel could hardly believe the contentment that filled him. He hadn't needed another scheme, another estate, another project. He had only needed a woman — this woman — to make his life complete.

THE END

* * *

Dear reader,

I hope you enjoyed Elizabeth and Gabriel's story!

While Elizabeth's story is, of course, one of fiction, it is based on the true stories of incredible women who were far ahead of their time. It may have been rare to find women in banking during the nineteenth century, but, in fact, between 1750 and 1905, at least seventy-five women were partners in banks across England. History, unfortunately, has not well documented female bankers, and I must thank Margaret Dawes and Nesta Selwyn for their work in telling their stories in *Women who made money*. Many of the experiences these women faced and confronted are woven into Elizabeth's story, and I wish to dedicate this work to them.

Next and finally is Sarah's story. She's a healer searching for answers, but her quest is interrupted when a very dashing rake shows up on her doorstep. You can read a sneak peek of her story in the pages after this one, or find Lady of Charade here.

If you haven't yet signed up for my newsletter, I would love

to have you join us! You will receive Unmasking a Duke for
free, as well as links to giveaways, sales, new releases, and
stories about my coffee addiction, my struggle to keep my
plants alive, and how much trouble one loveable wolf-
lookalike dog can get into.

www.elliestclair.com/ellies-newsletter

Or you can join my Facebook group, Ellie St. Clair's Ever
Afters, and stay in touch daily.

Until next time, happy reading!

With love,
Ellie

* * *

Lady of Charade
The Unconventional Ladies
Book 4

RAISED in a small American village after her mother passes
away, Sarah Jones is sent a cryptic letter about the true identity of her father, an English nobleman. She travels to
London in search of the man while she passes herself off as a
family member of the aristocracy. No one is aware — not
even her closest friends — that she spends her nights in a
boardinghouse, making money by treating people who come
to her for her healing abilities. But one night, a nobleman
appears on her doorstep, nearly dead, and her life will never
be the same again.

Lord David Redmond, second son of the Earl of Kilkenny,
loves his life of pleasure and in pursuit of fun. He has never

been able to understand the appeal of settling down with one woman, much to his parents' dismay. Until one night, he suffers the consequences of a liaison that should have never occurred, and he finds himself out-dueled in a brawl outside a gaming hell.

Left for dead in the streets, David wakes up to find himself in the hands of a beautiful woman who treats his injuries. But more than that, she sees inside his soul. Soon they each discover a connection they never asked for and are not sure they can live with. When she finally shares her story, he vows to repay her by finding her father.

What if the truth of who they are is more than either of them can take?

AN EXCERPT FROM LADY OF CHARADE

NEAR BALTIMORE, 1812

Sarah picked up her musket, hoisting it over her shoulder as she closed the door behind her and walked outside, inhaling deeply as the sounds of forest life filled her ears.

She smiled to herself as she began down the path toward the gathering of houses. She greeted the people she met within the small village as she continued on through it, her boots crunching over the leaves at her feet as she re-entered solitude — from the human variety of living creatures. The forests around her were full of animals of every type. The birds sang to her as she continued along, the rustle of trees around her telling her that there were squirrels or rabbits or something of the like following along beside her. She felt no fear, however — only appreciation for the company. She carried the musket as a precaution, if ever a bear, wolf, or human decided to attack, but she had rarely had to use it, and hoped to not require it anytime soon.

Sarah was well aware that she could have waited for a neighbor to accompany her for her weekly visit into the town, but today she had felt the need for a walk alone. Her mother, gone two years now, would have chastised her, but it was on days like today that Sarah felt her presence remaining with her the most.

She stopped suddenly, seeing long green stems with white fluffy flowers — black cohosh — emerging from the greenery just off the path, and she clipped a bit of it before placing it into her bag. One never knew when it might be required, for she had found it quite effective in treating a variety of women's ailments.

An hour later she emerged from the brush into the cleared land, where the slowly growing town awaited her. Sarah's mother had taken her east to the city enough times for Sarah to know that this town was still rather primitive despite the influx of new residents, but she enjoyed being away from the busyness of Baltimore or another such settlement. She appreciated knowing the names of all who lived near her and of being close to nature, which called to her. She could hardly imagine living in a place surrounded by tall stone buildings and strangers rushing by her, deep within their busy lives.

"Hello, George," she said as she entered the general store, which also doubled as the post office.

"Miss Jones!" he said, his lips beneath his great beard and mustache turning up into a smile. "I was wondering when you might come in. Here for supplies, are you?"

"I am," she said as she began to quickly peruse the shelves for her regular purchases, before more slowly searching the shop for a few additional items.

"Let me guess," George said, leaning over the counter on his thick arms. "You are looking for food stores for not only yourself but also for others in that little village of yours."

"Mabel just had her babe, and Landon has no wish to leave her at the moment," she said with a smile as she thought of the young married couple. "They do not need much, just a few things to get by."

"You're quite a woman, Miss Jones," George said, eyeing her. "My Lois and I worry about you, out there all alone."

"I'm not alone," she said, raising her eyes to his. "There are people settled all around me. I only need to shout and my protectors will come running."

"That may very well be," he agreed, "But are you not lonely?"

"I am far from lonely, George," she said with a smile. "In fact, there always seems to be someone at my door seeking my company."

"Company or treatment," he amended, and she nodded.

"True. But I am happy to help."

Sarah had learned from her mother, Mary, how to use the land to tend to the ailments of others. Her mother had learned from her own mother in England, where she was considered something of a witch. Here in America, Mary had added to her wisdom with knowledge assumed from both villagers and an Accohannock woman, who was married to a white man and had seen in her a shared spirit.

"Well, one of these days, I hope you accept a man who comes calling upon you," George continued, not moved from his mission. Sarah inwardly sighed. He meant well, but she did wish that for just one week she could come to see him without having to discuss the fact that she remained alone, unmarried. It was not as though she had not had any propositions — oh, no, there were plenty of them. But each man seemed to come from a place of wanting a woman to take care of him, rather than being interested in her, Sarah Jones.

"I appreciate your concern, George, truly I do, but I promise you that I am perfectly fine. If the right man comes along, well then, I would not turn him away. But I have yet to find him, and so I will remain alone with my potions and my nearby friends."

"Very well," he said, throwing his hands in the air as if he simply had to accept defeat. "Oh, before I forget — I have a letter for you."

"A letter?"

"Aye. Seems to be all the way from England."

"England?" Sarah raised her eyebrows. She had no ties to anyone in England, as far as she was aware. "You are jesting."

"I am not," he said, holding the envelope out to her. It was slightly torn in one corner, looking as though it truly had traveled all the way from her mother's country.

The moment she had the letter in her hands, every instinct within her was telling her to rip it open to determine just what the contents held, but she decided to wait until she was within the confines of her own home, where she could read and react accordingly. Sarah could tell George was nearly as curious as she was herself, but she simply thanked him, paid for her items, and slung her bag over her shoulder as she left the store, greeting others she knew before she made the return trip home.

She was halfway there when she could no longer resist the suspense. She could practically feel the letter calling out to her, begging to be read. Sarah walked over to a fallen log, and took a seat upon it as she rifled through her bag before finding what she was looking for. She pulled out the envelope, ripping the seal at the back, opening it to find a light scrawl atop a piece of flimsy paper. Crisp bills fluttered out with it, as well as a ticket.

Sarah,

You do not know me. I wonder at how you are — have you made a life for yourself there in America? I can hardly think of

*living in such a place, but then, your mother was always something
of a wild one. She could not be contained, certainly not by her
father, nor by any other man.*

*I have heard of her passing, and for that, I am sorry. I can
imagine what you must be feeling. Now that this has occurred, I
have found myself wrestling with the thought of whether or not to
share the following information with you.*

*I finally decided, however, that I would want to know, and so I
will tell you.*

*Your father remains in England. He is certainly alive and well,
and I am sure he would want to know his daughter. I urge you to
return, to make his acquaintance. He is a powerful lord, one who
could provide you with a fortune, I am sure.*

*I have included for you enough funds to help you find your way
to New York City, as well as a ticket aboard the* Hercules. *I booked
it long in advance as I am unsure how long this letter will take to
reach you. You have until June 1st to find your way on board.*

Good luck, Sarah. I hope you will consider my words.

Yours truly,

A friend.

Sarah allowed the letter to float to the floor of the forest
at her feet. Her father? She couldn't deny that she had
wondered about him from time to time. Her mother had
always been enough, but in the same breath, she longed to
know about the man who had sired her. Her mother had
always refused to speak of him, though whenever Sarah
mentioned his name, a sad, faraway look came into her eyes.

Sarah lifted her hand in front of her, staring at the ring
fitted around her thumb. She had found it after her mother's
passing, had known that it must have belonged to her father.
It was a man's ring, heavy and gold, an intricate symbol
inlaid into its black surface. It had fit perfectly on her thumb,
and she became inclined to wear it, despite the fact that it

was impractical for her way of life. Yet, somehow, it had never fallen off. She had known it was silly, for the ring should mean nothing to her. However, she had felt a strange tie to it, and to a past that she had never known but could now be there, waiting for her to learn it.

Her thoughts in turmoil, confusion and a strange yearning to know more swirling within her, Sarah carefully tucked the letter back into her bag. June 20th. The date was but a month away now. If she was going to follow the instructions of the letter and find herself on that ship, she would have to make arrangements quickly, for it would take nearly a week to travel to the port in New York City. Her heart began to beat wildly. Could she really do it? Leave all of this behind — her friends, the people who were near to family?

And yet... there was some truth to George's words. She was close to many here, true, but she was the only single woman in sight. Did the people truly appreciate her for who she was — Sarah Jones — or did they simply want her for her healing powers and what she could offer them? She had no idea, but she wouldn't like to leave her villagers without anyone to tend to their ailments. Abigail, the daughter of one of the original families, had been following her for a time now, but she was young, and not nearly experienced enough in the ways of healing. The town was nearby, however, and there was a healer there. Perhaps she could be enough.

"We'll be fine here," Abigail assured her, the girl's eyes bright and innocent when Sarah tentatively raised the idea of leaving the next week. She had been unable to think of anything else but the letter and the ticket since she had first received it. This morning they were foraging for supplies not far from the village and it seemed like the ideal time to raise her concerns.

"Of course you will be," Sarah said, not wanting Abigail to see her hesitation. "I just wish… that I had taught you more."

"You've taught me plenty. And not only that, but there are others nearby I can turn to for help, if needed," Abigail said before laying her hand on Sarah's arm and proving herself wise beyond her years. "And Sarah, if you do not go, will you not spend the rest of your life wondering about who your father is?"

Abigail's words resonated. For Sarah had no desire to continue to question half of who she was, from where she had come, and whether her father had ever or could ever care anything for her.

"We don't have much time," Sarah said slowly, turning to look at Abigail now, and the girl blinked her eyes a few times, clearing tears, but nodded with a smile. "I won't be able to share all with you, but over the next few days, we have to cover as much as we can."

And so they did. Sarah spent the next week full of nervous anticipation, continually questioning herself as to whether or not she was doing the right thing. This was the only home she had ever known, and how in the world would she go about finding a man she knew nothing about? She had to put her trust in this mysterious letter writer, and hope that when she arrived in England more information would be provided to her.

When she wasn't working with Abigail, she was speaking to all of the villagers who had spent part of their lives in England, attempting to learn all she could about her mother's country.

She didn't feel nearly as prepared as she would have liked, but soon, with nearly all of her few belongings tied in a satchel at her shoulder and the money clasped in her palm, she began the arduous trip to Baltimore. There, she could take a small ship to New York to meet with the ship on which this mysterious messenger had purchased her a ticket, for Sarah had not enough to purchase another passage from Baltimore. She supposed the ticket had been specifically purchased so she couldn't spend the money on anything else, and if she wanted to accept it, she had limited options.

As she finally stood on the deck of the *Hercules* following a quick but wearying journey, looking back at the land that had become her home, Sarah wondered whether she would ever see it again.

CHAPTER ONE

London, 1815

Lord David Redmond parried the blow from his opponent, quickly flipping his sword up and about until the man was disarmed and defenseless in front of him. He grinned in victory as he heard a slow clap from behind him.

"Well done, Monsieur," said the Frenchman, who had been David's fencing instructor over the past two years. "Once again, you have proven yourself as one of the best."

"Of course," David said, proud of himself. He only wished his father could see him here, where he wouldn't be able to help but find some sort of admiration for his second son. "All because of you, Monsieur Perrault."

"You are far too kind," the small man said, as David bent to pick up the fallen sword and pass it to Berkley, who stood with his hands on his hips, out of breath as he shook his head at his friend.

"One of these days, Redmond," he said, shaking a finger at him. "One of these days."

"A day I eagerly await," David said with a grin, though he vowed the day would never come as he removed his fencing helmet.

"Every time I come a little closer," Berkley protested.

"I would hardly agree."

"Perhaps we should ask Monsieur Perrault."

"No need. Evidence speaks for itself," David countered, and Berkley laughed at that, shrugging to show that on this, perhaps, he conceded.

He and Berkley continued to banter back and forth as they removed their fencing gear. David was well aware that the company he kept was somewhat above his station, as the second son of an earl. A duke and a marquess were lofty companions, but they seemed to enjoy his company, though he often wondered if they were simply living somewhat vicariously through him, both of them now married, though happily at that.

"Where are you off to now, Redmond?" Berkley asked as they walked out into the London sunshine. The weather was slowly drifting into spring. Before long, his family's country homes would be opened, though David was unsure when or for how long he would visit. He found a sense of peace in the country, though in the same breath, if his family was present, they would likely spend the majority of their visit discussing his lack of intentions to marry and their intentions that he do so.

"A return home for dinner, then I suppose I will find myself an engagement of some sort or another this evening."

Berkley eyed him. "And what type would that be?"

"I haven't yet decided," David said with a wink at him. "One of my favorite widows has been rather lonely lately, so perhaps I'll take her up on her offer for a nightcap after a game or two of faro at one of the clubs."

Berkley shook his head, though he seemed amused.

"I'm not sure how you do it," he said, and David shrugged.

"It's fairly simple — you just enjoy yourself."

"Do you never get tired of chasing after these women?"

"It doesn't take much, and they are chasing after me in equal measure."

"I used to think along some of the same lines as you," Berkley said. "But there is something to be said about coming home to the same woman each night — a woman who knows you, and not just the superficial. Who can tell if you need time to yourself, who knows how to comfort you, how to discuss certain aspects of your life."

David shook his head. "I'm glad you have found what you are looking for, Berkley, but that life doesn't suit me. I'm perfectly happy living as I am, and I don't need a woman involved to make things more difficult."

"Suit yourself," Berkley said, spreading his hands wide. "In my opinion, having multiple women would be much worse."

"It's just a matter of keeping them all separate," he explained, as they walked into White's for an afternoon drink before they would go their own ways. Within, they found the Duke of Clarence awaiting them, and as they took chairs near him at the table, Berkley continued the conversation, which David felt was hardly fair, for clearly the two other men would take the same side, the Duke newly married himself.

"What do you say, Clarence," Berkley said, "We are currently in a debate as to what is more difficult to manage — one woman or multiple."

The Duke's eyes sparkled somewhat at the question.

"Had you asked me a year ago, I likely would have agreed with Redmond here, as I believe I can ascertain which of you is taking which side of this argument. However… keeping one woman happy, gentlemen, is far more rewarding than what multiple women could ever provide. Especially if that woman satisfies you more than you could ever imagine."

"You've both gone soft on me," David said despondently

as they were served their drinks. "I hardly think that I shall ever feel that way. Though if I do, I know who to turn to for advice."

His two friends just laughed at him. Sometimes David wondered why they preferred his own company to that of his brother, who was far more straight-laced and responsible. He quickly shrugged aside the thought, however, not seeing the importance of it, as he began looking forward to this evening's festivities.

* * *

SARAH LET herself into her rooms on the first floor of the tall building. The door, though recessed down a back alley, was accessible to the street, which was both fortunate and not. It made it easy for anyone to find her if she was needed, but at the same time, it put her at additional risk. Not that she wasn't prepared to defend herself, she thought with a smile, as she patted the dependable dagger in the piece of fabric tied around her ankle, before ensuring that her shotgun was in its resting place in the corner of the room, her handgun where she had it hidden next to her bed.

Cheapside was not as dangerous as many neighborhoods, but despite its close proximity to some of London's better-renowned areas, there were certainly risks involved, particularly as a woman living alone on a back street. However, risks abounded no matter where the location for any young woman living alone, did they not?

Upon arriving in London three years ago, she had little knowledge of the city nor its neighborhoods. She had been advised to find a boardinghouse for young women, and in fact had stayed in one for a time. But after two weeks, she had found the rules and boundaries to be suffocating, and had sought other lodgings where she would have the freedom to do as she pleased.

Sarah had thought her stay would be temporary. She had assumed she would find her father fairly quickly, and would know within a month or two whether or not there was any reason to remain in London. But nearly three years later, she was still here — though for how much longer, she wasn't sure.

Without removing any of her clothing, she walked down the small corridor and tossed her bag on the hard wooden floor before throwing herself on the lumpy mattress that passed for a bed. She would have far preferred the furs she had slept upon in America, but then, this was what she could afford, and she should be grateful that she had somewhere to sleep.

Her eyes nearly closed the moment she lay her head back, but she jumped up to attention when she heard a knock at the door. Hurrying over, she opened it but a crack, shocked when she saw who stood on the other side. Her secret, apparently, was no longer that.

"What are you doing here?" she asked, as she opened the door wide to reveal three ladies standing there staring at her.

Soon upon her arrival three years ago, Sarah had the fortune to meet Lady Phoebe at one of the dances Lady Alexander had escorted her too. Soon she had been introduced to two of her friends, Lady Elizabeth and Lady Julia, and despite the fact that she had never quite felt herself worthy to call these women friends, she had bonded with them in a way she had never thought possible. In fact, if it hadn't been for the three of them, Sarah didn't think she would still be here in England. Despite their closeness, however, Sarah hadn't quite shared everything with them.

Elizabeth, Phoebe, and Julia walked the few feet until they stood in the center of her makeshift parlor room and bedroom, looking around them in shock. Sarah nearly laughed at how out of place the three ladies looked in all their finery in the middle of this run-down room. She had done the best she could to provide color to the dingy interior with a few blankets, but there was not much to it — two mismatched chairs stood around the grate, her bed was pushed against the wall, and a wooden screen separated the two.

"Is this where you live?" Phoebe asked, turning her direct gaze on Sarah, who shrugged. "It is — for the moment."

"How could you not tell us, after all this time?" Elizabeth demanded. "We had always assumed you lived with Lady Alexander!"

"I know," Sarah said with a sigh, sitting down upon the bed herself, as she bid the rest of them to take a seat next to her in a ratty chair across the room. "I allowed you to think it."

"But why here? Why don't you live with her? And why didn't you tell us? You could have stayed with one of us!" Julia said, and Sarah leaned back against the wall.

"It's a long story," she said. "But first, how did you find me here?"

"When you didn't attend Lady Nuffield's party this evening, Phoebe and I were worried,"

Elizabeth explained. "We asked Lady Alexander if you had taken ill, and she wasn't entirely sure. As Julia and Eddie were in London, we asked her to accompany us to come to visit you to assure all was well. Lady Alexander's butler was most confused when we asked for you at her home. It was her maid who followed us out and told us where we could find you. We didn't entirely believe her, but decided to follow her anyway."

"I'm sorry to have worried you," Sarah said. "One of my neighbors' boys took ill. I believe it was some bad meat, but we got it out right quickly enough and I think he should be fine. I couldn't leave them and it happened so quickly, I didn't have time to get word to Lady Alexander that I wouldn't be attending tonight."

She looked down at herself in chagrin. She hadn't changed from her evening wear when she had been summoned, and now her beautiful pink gown would have to be laundered or the nobility would smell her coming from far away.

Her friends nodded. They knew of her work as a medicine woman or healer — whatever one chose to call what she did — but they weren't aware of the entirety of it, that she used her skills to survive, although more often than not many of those who asked for her help could hardly afford to pay anything. She typically gratefully accepted whatever they had to offer, be it a loaf of bread or a bag of potatoes.

"You know that I left America to find my father," she said, attempting to determine the best way to complete the story, and they nodded. "Only I didn't come here with the intention of meeting Lady Alexander. It was once I was upon the ship to London that I met her. She was frightfully seasick, and I helped as best I could to ease her stomach pains. In return, she was kind to me, and we became friends. Near the end of the journey, she asked what I was doing in London. I provided a small portion of the story, and when no one met me in London as I assumed would happen, she offered to act as my chaperone. As the widow of a viscount, she has access to social events of which I could never dream of an invitation. I must admit, it has been immensely helpful in order to meet a wide variety of nobles who may be around the age of my father, to try to determine whether any of them resemble me or if they might have any connection to my mother. Not that my strategy is working overly well."

"But why didn't Lady Alexander offer for you to live with her?" Julia asked, and Sarah shrugged.

"She never mentioned it, and her help is incredibly generous as it is. Most people are under the assumption that I am an American relative of hers, and I have found that I do not have to lie about it much — most just accept the fact. Lady Alexander made the offer with the caveat that I ask for no money or further attachment to her, which is perfectly fine with me, for I have no wish for it. I believe she is a bit lonely but had no desire to disrupt her current lifestyle. It works for both of us. She wouldn't want all manner of people at her doorstep in search of a healer."

"That's how you are supporting yourself here," Elizabeth said, more in statement than question, and Sarah nodded.

"I am. Though I would do it anyway, for it seems I cannot help myself when it comes to attempting to heal what causes others pain."

"Well," Elizabeth said matter-of-factly. "I do wish you had told us sooner. Please tell me you have not been living here ever since you came from America."

"I have," Sarah said with a nod. "Nearly three years now, if you can believe it. Though... I have been thinking that it is time I give up on this quest and return home."

"Three years!" gasped Julia as Elizabeth shook her head in disbelief.

"Sarah, you cannot leave us!"

"I cannot believe you have kept this from us," Elizabeth said, as Phoebe sat in the corner watching them, patting her stomach, which had rounded once more with their second child.

"I am sorry to have deceived you," Sarah said, "That was certainly not my intention. It just seemed... easier, and I didn't want you to worry."

"I suppose I can somewhat understand that, though I feel

a fool," said Elizabeth. "But now that we know, you can come and stay with me. Gabriel is eager to help you find your father, though we have not much to go on. He has made inquiries, and thus far, there are no connections to a woman and child who left for America — though I'm sure there are more than a few who had some liaisons to which they would certainly not want to admit."

Elizabeth strode over to the wardrobe, opening it to reveal Sarah's dresses, the only items in the room upon which she had spent any money. She had used the additional funds the letter-writer had provided her, though each season she stayed was beginning to stretch what she could afford.

"Do you have a bag into which we can pack everything?" Elizabeth asked, taking charge as she usually did.

"Thank you for your generously kind offer, Elizabeth, but I am not leaving."

Elizabeth swirled around, looking at her incredulously. "Whyever not?"

"I'm comfortable here, and more than anything, those who need me know where to find me. They could never track me down if I were to move, particularly to one of the greatest manors in all of London."

"You do not need to worry about providing for yourself," Elizabeth affirmed. "We will support you in whatever you need, will we not Phoebe?"

Phoebe nodded, though she looked somewhat hesitant.

"Of course we would, Sarah, you know that. However... this has to be what you want," she said softly, and Sarah smiled at her.

"I appreciate that — I appreciate what all of you would like to do for me, I do," she said. "I know if I ever need somewhere else to stay, I can turn to any of you. But for now, I will remain where I am, content in what I am able to do. And at the moment, as much as I would love you all to stay, I very much need to sleep."

"Of course," Phoebe said, rising from the bed and walking to the door, the other two following her, Elizabeth quite reluctantly as she spun around, continuing to look at Sarah's accommodations. "We shall see you tomorrow."

After they left, Sarah locked the door tightly behind them and fell back on the bed, into a long, dream-filled sleep.

KEEP READING! Find Lady of Charade on Amazon and in Kindle Unlimited.

ALSO BY ELLIE ST. CLAIR

The Art of Stealing a Duke's Heart

A Jewel for the Taking

A Prize Worth Fighting For

Gambling for the Lost Lord's Love

Romance of a Robbery

Thieves of Desire Box Set

The Bluestocking Scandals

Designs on a Duke

Inventing the Viscount

Discovering the Baron

The Valet Experiment

Writing the Rake

Risking the Detective

A Noble Excavation

A Gentleman of Mystery

The Bluestocking Scandals Box Set: Books 1-4

The Bluestocking Scandals Box Set: Books 5-8

Blooming Brides

A Duke for Daisy

A Marquess for Marigold

An Earl for Iris

A Viscount for Violet

The Blooming Brides Box Set: Books 1-4

Happily Ever After

The Duke She Wished For

Someday Her Duke Will Come

Once Upon a Duke's Dream

He's a Duke, But I Love Him

Loved by the Viscount

Because the Earl Loved Me

Happily Ever After Box Set Books 1-3

Happily Ever After Box Set Books 4-6

The Victorian Highlanders

Duncan's Christmas - (prequel)

<u>Callum's Vow</u>

<u>Finlay's Duty</u>

<u>Adam's Call</u>

<u>Roderick's Purpose</u>

<u>Peggy's Love</u>

<u>The Victorian Highlanders Box Set Books 1-5</u>

Searching Hearts

Duke of Christmas (prequel)

Quest of Honor

Clue of Affection

Hearts of Trust

Hope of Romance

Promise of Redemption

Searching Hearts Box Set (Books 1-5)

Christmas

Christmastide with His Countess

Her Christmas Wish

Merry Misrule

A Match Made at Christmas

A Match Made in Winter

Standalones

Always Your Love

The Stormswept Stowaway

A Touch of Temptation

For a full list of all of Ellie's books, please see
www.elliestclair.com/books.

ABOUT THE AUTHOR

Ellie has always loved reading, writing, and history. For many years she has written short stories, non-fiction, and has worked on her true love and passion -- romance novels.

In every era there is the chance for romance, and Ellie enjoys exploring many different time periods, cultures, and geographic locations. No matter when or where, love can always prevail. She has a particular soft spot for the bad boys of history, and loves a strong heroine in her stories.

Ellie and her husband love nothing more than spending time at home with their children and Husky cross. Ellie can typically be found at the lake in the summer, pushing the stroller all year round, and, of course, with her computer in her lap or a book in hand.

She also loves corresponding with readers, so be sure to contact her!

www.elliestclair.com
ellie@elliestclair.com

Ellie St. Clair's Ever Afters Facebook Group

Printed in Great Britain
by Amazon